SHOTGUN LAW

Rhodes and Bonner threw their shotguns to their shoulders as the seven horsemen galloped toward them. Rhodes was just about to pull the trigger, when the riders pulled to a noisy stop ten yards away, breath clouding in the cold air.

Rhodes lowered his shotgun. "I'm Marshal Travis," he said calmly but loudly. "You boys are breaking the law. I'd be obliged if you put them weapons away and go about your business peaceably. 'Course, you want to start some trouble, I'll finish it for you."

"Hell, Marshal, we was just funnin' some," one of them said. "We don't want any trouble."

The riders put their pistols away. In silence they turned their horses and rode down the street. Rhodes and Bonner stood watching.

Suddenly the outlaws wheeled their horses and spurred the animals. Pistols in hand once again, they rode hell-bent for the two lawmen.

ZEBRA'S HEADING WEST!

with GILES, LEGG, PARKINSON, LAKE, KAMMEN, and MANNING

KANSAS TRAIL (3517, $3.50/$4.50)
by Hascal Giles

After the Civil War ruined his life, Bennett Kell threw in his lot with a gang of thievin' guntoughs who rode the Texas-Kansas border. But there was one thing he couldn't steal—fact was, Ada McKittridge had stolen his heart.

GUNFIGHT IN MESCALITO (3601, $3.50/$4.50)
by John Legg

Jubal Crockett was a young man with a bright future—until that Mescalito jury found him guilty of murder and sentenced him to hang. Jubal'd been railroaded good and the only writ of habeus corpus was a stolen key to the jailhouse door and a fast horse!

DRIFTER'S LUCK (3396, $3.95/$4.95)
by Dan Parkinson

Byron Stillwell was a drifter who never went lookin' for trouble, but trouble always had a way of findin' him. Like the time he set that little fire up near Kansas to head off a rogue herd owned by a cattle baron named Dawes. Now Dawes figures Stillwell owes him something . . . at the least, his life.

MOUNTAIN MAN'S VENGEANCE (3619, $3.50/$4.50)
by Robert Lake

The high, rugged mountain made John Henry Trapp happy. But then a pack of gunsels thundered across his land, burned his hut, and murdered his squaw woman. Trapp hit the vengeance trail and ended up in jail. Now he's back and how that mountain has changed!

BIG HORN HELLRIDERS (3449, $3.50/$4.50)
by Robert Kammen

Wyoming was a tough land and toughness was required to tame it. Reporter Jim Haskins knew the Wyoming tinderbox was about to explode but he didn't know he was about to be thrown smack-dab in the middle of one of the bloodiest range wars ever.

TEXAS BLOOD KILL (3577, $3.50/$4.50)
by Jason Manning

Ol' Ma Foley and her band of outlaw sons were cold killers and most folks in Shelby County, Texas knew it. But Federal Marshal Jim Gantry was no local lawman and he had his guns cocked and ready when he rode into town with one of the Foley boys as his prisoner.

BLOOD IN THE SNOW
John Legg

ZEBRA BOOKS
KENSINGTON PUBLISHING CORP.

ZEBRA BOOKS

are published by

Kensington Publishing Corp.
475 Park Avenue South
New York, NY 10016

First Printing: April, 1993

Printed in the United States of America

With love
for my cousin
Susan Taylor Corona.
Thanks for being there.

Chapter One

Travis Rhodes stepped out of Claver's Mercantile and right smack into the middle of trouble. He stopped just outside the two wood doors and closed them carefully. There was glass in the top half of each door, and he wanted to make sure he did not break them.

As he eased the doors closed behind him, he watched the tableau before him. Then he shook his head in annoyance. He knew he shouldn't step in, but he also knew he would.

"These boys botherin' you, miss?" he asked softly, touching the brim of his trim, wide-brimmed hat.

The woman turned toward Rhodes, worried eyes flashing. She took stock of Rhodes quickly. He looked much more presentable than the others, but she expected that he, too, was a ruffian, like the others. Still, there was something about him that made her think he just might be different.

Travis Rhodes was perhaps five-foot-eight, not very tall, really, but what he lacked in height he made up for in broadness. His shoulders, back, and chest stretched the striped, collarless shirt he wore almost to splitting. His waist, while not slim, could not compare in breadth to his shoulders. Stocky, powerful legs were encased in blue denim pants.

Light gray eyes peered out over a partly flattened

nose. His face was almost square, with a large, solid-looking jaw. *He's almost handsome,* Mercy Crawford thought, shocking herself more than a little. She was flustered for the moment as a touch of heat dashed across her insides. Then she sighed, a fatalism spreading over her. She was certain Rhodes would be just like the others. Still, he did look neat, and he had spoken politely to her. She decided to take a chance.

"Yes," she breathed, her voice caught up in anxiety.

Rhodes nodded. "Excuse me, then, miss," he said quietly as he stepped around her, facing the three men who had been rudely crowding her, making lecherous and crude comments. When Rhodes had stepped out of the store, one of the three was even trying to paw at the woman.

"Ain't you boys got something better to be doin' than takin' indecent liberties with this here woman?" he asked quietly, voice drawling lightly.

As he waited for a response, he sized up the three men. All had the look of recent army service about them, and Rhodes figured they were like so many others these days—they knew no trade but violence and death. Having just come through the War Between the States, they did not know what to do with themselves, so they turned to violence, often bullying the less fortunate, as if they thought that a birthright. They had haunted, troubled eyes, and the stench of trouble and decay about them.

Travis Rhodes was much the same—rootless, troubled by all that he had seen and done and been subjected to. Unlike these others, though, he kept his torment to himself. He did not take it out on others, especially the defenseless, like the woman standing behind him now. He wished that all men who had served—on either side—could try to put all that hatred and trouble behind them, as he had mostly done. Only once in a while, usually when the darkness of his past swept too strongly over him, did he let any of that

8

part of him out. That usually consisted of a solitary drunk for a day or a week, and the spilling of his hatred to some tart who was happy to sit there and let him rave on—as long as he was paying her for her time.

"Well, what've we got us here?" one of the three men said, as if making an aside to his two companions.

"Looks like one of them Johnny Rebs like those we just bested," a second said.

"That true there, boy?" the first one asked.

Rhodes turned cold gray eyes on the man. He was taller than Rhodes by several inches, but nowhere near as filled out. His face was covered with rough stubble, and his nose and eyes were laced with a latticework of red. He reeked of bad whiskey, sweat, and dirt. Tobacco and food stained his faded butternut shirt.

"What if it is?" Rhodes asked, still in that quiet, reasonable tone.

"Damn, boy, ain't it enough that we kicked your asses in the war?" the man asked, seeming incredulous at such a thought. "Lord, if he ain't a dumb ox, wouldn't you say, Phil?"

"You know, Carl, I think he's dumber'n any ox I ever saw," the second man said. Phil Thorndyke was a ratty, feral-looking man, seeming to be furtive even when he was standing stock-still and staring at someone. During the war, a rifle ball had torn away a fair-size chunk of his left cheekbone, and it had not healed well. It was a hideous mark that had turned an ugly man into a repulsive one.

"I'd advise you boys to move on before someone gets hurt."

Phil Thorndyke laughed, a high, quavering trill that reminded Rhodes of a barnyard of cackling hens.

His brother Carl smiled. "We're the Thorndyke brothers"—he pointed to each, in turn—"I'm Carl, that's Phil and back there's Frank." He smiled, but

9

there was no warmth of humanity in it. "And ain't a one of us don't mind you get hurt, Reb," he said evenly. "Especially when it's us doin' the hurtin'." He, too, broke into laughter.

The third brother, Frank—a morose, brooding cretin of large and lumpy proportions—had neither said anything nor moved, other than turning his dull, flat-featured head to look from either of his two brothers to Rhodes. His eyes—the windows of the soul, Rhodes remembered someone had told him once—were as empty as an unused attic.

Carl Thorndyke's face suddenly tightened and the laughter stopped. "You know what's good for you, Reb, you best get your ass out of the way." He sought a reasonable tone in his voice. "Why don't you just go on about your business, and no one'll get hurt. How's about that?"

Rhodes fixed an icy stare on the rumpled, leathery man. Rhodes noticed that Carl was missing the middle and ring fingers of his left hand. Over his shoulder, he asked, "You want the attentions of these men, miss?"

"Lordy, no," Mercy breathed. The very thought of the three men's crude attentions made her shudder with disgust.

"Looks like you boys got no more business here," Rhodes said, still quietly.

"Goddammit, Reb, I'm tired of you interfering in our business," Carl snapped. As the eldest of the Thorndyke boys, he usually set the rules and did the talking for his brothers, who were less well-versed in the social graces.

Rhodes shrugged.

Carl cursed quietly, then took a step forward and swung a big-knuckled fist at Rhodes's jaw.

Rhodes jerked his head to the side. As Carl's fist whistled past, Rhodes jerked up his right arm, crooked at the elbow, and then brought the back of the elbow down hard on the nape of Carl's neck. The blow added to Carl's momentum, and he crashed into several barrels and sacks piled up just to the side of the door.

A sound escaped Phil's lips when he saw his brother hit the mercantile goods. To Rhodes, the sound was suspiciously like that of a turkey's gobble. He had no more time for that, though, as Phil sprang toward him.

Rhodes managed to fend off most of Phil's wild punches and kicks. The few that got through had lost much of their intensity by the time they landed. Rhodes gave the scrawny man little time to continue the assault, before he grabbed Phil's shirt and threw him aside. Phil ended up in a pile of arms, legs, and farm implements a few feet from his brother.

Rhodes looked at the third Thorndyke brother. "You want to pick these idiots up and take them home?" he asked, voice still calm and reasoned. Relaxed, Rhodes watched Frank Thorndyke. The man was feebleminded, Rhodes figured, but despite that, Thorndyke appeared the neatest of the three brothers.

Frank looked like he wanted to say something but then decided he was incapable of it. He simply lowered his great, round head, grunted like a rutting buffalo, and then chugged forward.

Rhodes waited as long as he could. With Frank only a foot or so away, Rhodes threw up his left arm. His forearm caught Frank's outstretched right arm, straightening him a bit. Rhodes slammed a fist into Frank's gut. The thought flitted through Rhodes's head that it was like hitting a side of beef.

Thorndyke coughed out a bellyful of air, and a strange look grew in his already eerie eyes.

Rhodes didn't wait around for Thorndyke to regain his wind, he simply hammered the big man twice more, fairly certain that he had broken at least one of Thorndyke's ribs.

11

Rhodes was about to deliver the coup de grace, when he heard a maniacal screech. He spun just in time to catch Phil Thorndyke, who had flung himself wildly at Rhodes. The collision knocked Rhodes backward two steps, where his heel tottered off the edge of the boardwalk in front of the store.

They crashed to the ground, but the impact separated the two. Rhodes jumped up and kicked Thorndyke, who was struggling to rise, under the chin. The cracking of bones was audible even over the sounds of the bustling town of Clearwater, Iowa, to those nearby. Thorndyke slumped to the ground, groaning and mewling.

Rhodes calmly stepped up onto the boardwalk again, next to Frank Thorndyke. Frank was standing, bent over with his hands on his knees. He was trying to breathe, which was difficult with his damaged diaphragm and broken rib.

Rhodes grabbed Frank's hair in his left hand and jerked Thorndyke's head up. "You got yourself one hell of a family there, boy," Rhodes said quietly, just before he smashed the heel of his right hand against Thorndyke's forehead.

Thorndyke's eyes rolled up and he sank to his knees, but to Rhodes's surprise, he didn't go out. Granted, he was not going to be able to do anything for a while, but Rhodes had felt sure that the blow would knock Thorndyke unconscious. He shrugged. It didn't mean much right at the moment.

Suddenly, Mercy screamed, "Look out!"

Rhodes spun, crouched, his arms curled in front of him some to block an attack. Carl Thorndyke barreled into Rhodes, who more or less allowed Thorndyke to shove him against the store wall, almost hitting Mercy in the process. The two men grappled for some moments, but Rhodes's far greater strength quickly began to tell.

Finally Rhodes shoved Thorndyke down and to the side. Thorndyke fell.

"You get up, boy, and I'm going to pound you somethin' fierce," Rhodes warned. He showed few signs of exertion, other than a sheen of sweat across his brow.

Thorndyke stayed where he was. Rhodes turned and walked the few steps to where his hat lay. He bent and picked it up. He dusted it off, and restored the crease to it with a few deft hand movements on the supple felt. He set it on his head and looked over his shoulder.

Thorndyke was just getting to his feet.

"You apologize to the lady now, boy," Rhodes said. He still had shown no anger; he remained calm and reasonable.

"Like hell I will," Thorndyke growled.

"Where'd you learn your manners, boy?" Rhodes mused. "Your mother a sow or something?"

"Don't you talk about Ma like that, you bastard," Thorndyke snapped.

"You should've thought of that before you started acting like a barnyard animal," Rhodes said with a shrug. "Now, you apologize to the lady or I'm going to pound you into the ground like a tent stake."

"I'll do no such thing," Thorndyke said. He straightened, sliding up along the wall for support.

"That's a pity," Rhodes said. He moved slowly toward Thorndyke. "But if that's the way you want to be . . ."

Thorndyke shoved his hand into his pocket and jerked out a pistol. "I'll get you, you son of a bitch," he screeched. He shakily moved to cock the small pocket pistol.

As his hat flew off again, Rhodes grabbed the nearest thing he could—a pitchfork. He swung it and managed to hit Thorndyke's pepperbox pistol, but not enough to knock it loose.

Thorndyke began again to bring the weapon to bear on his foe. Rhodes acted without thinking, seeing

13

himself in war again. The butt of the pitchfork flashed out, blocking Thorndyke's arm some. Then Rhodes swung the pitchfork back, in both hands and lunged forward, as if he were in a bayonet charge.

Rhodes's powerful back and shoulder muscles drove the pitchfork's tines through Thorndyke, impaling him on the wood wall of Claver's store.

Chapter Two

Mercy Crawford stood, the back of one slim, pale hand pressed against her lips. She stared in horrified wonder at Carl Thorndyke's body, which was still pinned to the wall by the long, thin tines of the pitchfork.

Rhodes had turned, eyes sweeping the boardwalk and the area just off it. Frank Thorndyke lay on the boards as if dead, though his slow, heavy breathing showed that he was still alive. Phil Thorndyke remained in the dirt, emitting pitiable weeping sounds.

Rhodes straightened and turned to Mercy. She had dropped her hand, though her pert lips were still rounded in wonder at all that had happened.

She was looking at Rhodes now. She was confused. Rhodes had been as ruthless as the three Thorndykes had been, maybe even more so. Yet, Mercy was attracted to him. She thought that wrong, and she hoped it did not show in her face. It would not do for a genteel flower of the South to openly display affection for any man, let alone one she had met less than two minutes ago, even if he had saved both her life and her chastity.

Rhodes brushed off his shirt, though it did not really need it. He pulled a bandanna out of his pocket and wiped his sweating forehead with it. Then he

15

looked around for his hat. Spotting it, he started toward it. As he knelt and picked it up, someone said, "Stop where you are, son." The voice was a rich, deep baritone.

Rhodes rose and turned slowly, cautious but unworried.

A tall, thin, leathery-faced man stood at the edge of the boardwalk. In his hands was a 10-gauge shotgun, on his chest a German silver five-pointed star inside a circle. Iron-gray hair poked haphazardly from under his bowler, matching the thick mustache that sagged over both his lips. He wore a weathered brown suit, including vest and string tie, all brown, except for the white boiled shirt. He looked tough as rawhide.

"Looks like you had yourself quite a time here, son," the lawman said.

"Reckon so," Rhodes allowed.

"Name's Sam Crown, town marshal for Clearwater."

"Marshal," Rhodes said agreeably. He paused, trying to decide whether to give the marshal his own name. He shrugged mentally. There would be no harm in doing so, he figured. After all, Crown could have just shot him, yet he hadn't. "I'm Travis Rhodes."

"You mind tellin' me just what went on here, Mr. Rhodes?" Crown asked.

Rhodes shrugged. "Not much to tell, Marshal. I came out of the store there and found these things . . . gentlemen harassin' the young lady here."

Crown looked at Mercy and bobbed his head. "Miss Crawford," he said politely.

Mercy smiled wanly. "Marshal Crown."

The lawman looked back at Rhodes. "So they were harassin' Miss Crawford," he said. "Then what?"

16

Rhodes explained it short and fast, ending with "I expect Miss Crawford here'll back up what I've said." He had not showed it, but his interest in Mercy had risen considerably when Crown had addressed her as "Miss." He wondered what the possibilities of getting to know her well were.

"That right, Miss Crawford?"

"Oh yes, sir, Marshal," Mercy drawled. Though there was still fright in her voice, it still conjured visions of slow, warm days and cold mint juleps for Rhodes.

"All of it?"

"Yes, sir. If it wasn't for Mister Rhodes here, I'd of been . . ." She flushed prettily and hid her embarrassment behind her ghostly hands. She had known as soon as they had moved up here from Louisiana that there would be nothing but trouble in the hated North. But there wasn't much left of the old homestead and so here she was.

"No need to go on, Miss Crawford," Crown said. He had never taken his eyes off Rhodes. "You armed, Mr. Rhodes?"

"No," Rhodes said, voice unchanged. He sounded bored almost. "If I was carryin', there'd be three dead now, 'stead of just one."

"No arms at all?"

"Not unless you consider this a weapon." He turned slowly and patted the knife in the sheath at the small of his back.

"Ease it out, Mr. Rhodes, and drop it."

Rhodes did as he was told, then turned back around. He kicked it lightly toward Crown when told to do so. Crown picked it up, still not taking his eyes off Rhodes. He figured that if Rhodes was carrying a gun, it would be a pocket pistol or a belly gun, which meant it was hidden under his clothing somewhere. That would make it difficult for Rhodes

17

to get at it. He was not really worried about Rhodes, though he was a cautious man. Seeing how Rhodes had driven the pitchfork so easily through Carl Thorndyke did give the marshal pause, though.

Crown glanced down at the knife in his right hand. It was a no-nonsense piece of equipment. It had a blade Crown figured to be ten or eleven inches long. The tang was burned into a simple wood hilt. There was nothing fancy about it. He flipped it easily back to Rhodes.

Though he was a bit startled by the marshal's move, Rhodes caught the knife by the hilt and slipped it away. He knew now that Crown was not about to arrest him. That was a relief.

"What're you doing in Clearwater, Mr. Rhodes?" Crown asked. He was completely at ease, scattergun cradled in the crook of his left arm, right hand curled around the twin hammers and the triggers, ready.

"Lookin' for work."

Crown sized Rhodes up. He decided that Rhodes was basically a decent man, but one hardened by the recent troubles between North and South. Normally, Crown would not mind having a man like Travis Rhodes around town, but after this display of violence, that was not feasible. Not when it involved the Thorndykes. They were enough trouble at the best of times. Now the five living brothers—Frank and Phil here, as well as Lyle, Will, and Dick— would go on the rampage if Crown allowed Rhodes to linger.

"Best look for it elsewhere, Mr. Rhodes," Crown said quietly.

"You runnin' me out, Marshal?" Rhodes asked. He was sure of it, but wanted Crown to make it official.

18

"I am." There was no apology in Crown's voice. Nor was there any condemnation.

"After I helped Miss Crawford?" Rhodes wasn't all that worried about being run out of town, but he thought it only proper that he present at least some sort of protest.

"Yes, Marshal, what about that?" Mercy asked. She had considered not saying anything, thinking that perhaps she would be considered too forward, but then she decided it would not be improper. After all, Rhodes had saved her honor.

Crown shrugged. He was not afraid of the Thorndykes, or anyone else. He was just a man trying to do his job for the fifty bucks a month they paid him. If he could prevent a bloodbath by running one drifter out of town, the choice was not all that difficult for him.

"A shrug isn't much of an answer," Mercy said boldly, surprising herself a little.

"Be that as it may, Miss Crawford," Crown said, unfazed, "it's got to be."

"You damn Yankee," she snapped, hazel eyes blazing in anger. "Take the side of those animals"—she pointed from one Thorndyke to the other—"while you run a good Southern gentleman out of town."

"I don't much give a hoot, Miss Crawford," Crown said levelly, "what side anyone was on in that war. It's over now, and should be laid to rest. All I'm doin' is sendin' a troublemaker on his way."

"He wasn't the troublemaker, Marshal," Mercy said, still angry, as she aimed a thin finger at Rhodes. "It was those others."

"Don't matter none, miss," Crown said. He was not fond of explaining himself to people, especially those who disliked him from the start, but he figured that in this case, an explanation might prevent problems later. "There's some folks who just attract troubles. Maybe Mr. Rhodes here ain't such a man, but I don't aim to find out." He looked at Rhodes. "So I'd be obliged if you was to be on your way, son."

"I understand, Marshal," Rhodes said quietly. "I'd be obliged for a favor though."

"What's that?" Crown asked, looking at Rhodes.

"I just rode into Clearwater this mornin'. I ain't slept in a proper bed in a long time, and I got a few pieces of business to take care of." He smiled a little. "I'd be grateful if I was to be allowed to leave tomorrow mornin', instead of right now."

"I catch your drift, Mr. Rhodes," Crown said. He paused, thinking. He looked at Phil and Frank Thorndyke. The two were still lying in the dirt, but they were displaying some signs of life. Then Crown looked up at the sky. It would be dark in perhaps an hour and a quarter. He nodded. "I expect that'll be all right," he said, flatly. "But," he added, holding up his right hand, "you got to stay in your room — you do have a room, don't you?"

Rhodes nodded. "Over at Grelb's. But, like I said, I got business to see to."

Crown sighed. "Can you finish your business before dark?"

"I expect."

"As soon as it's dark, I want you back in your room and stay there till you pull out in the morning."

"Why're you so anxious to keep me out of sight, Marshal?" Rhodes asked. It did seem odd to him.

"Phil and Frank there have three brothers. Not a one of 'em is the kind to let go what you done to these boys today. Soon's these two get home and tell the other three, they're gonna be lookin' for blood. Your blood, Mr. Rhodes."

Rhodes nodded, then smiled. "Why don't you lock

those two up?" he asked.

Crown bit off his retort, and instead pondered the suggestion. The Thorndykes were a vicious, ill-mannered lot, a group that individually or collectively had little intelligence. But for some reason, they had taken to Marshal Sam Crown. They would not be too angry at him for locking up Frank and Phil, especially if he said he did it to protect them, or gave them some other story. It would, he decided, stave off a lot of trouble. He nodded.

"Very well, Mr. Rhodes," Crown said slowly. "But I still want you in your room after dark. The other brothers might be comin' into town for a whoop-up."

"Thanks, Marshal," Rhodes said quietly. He was glad the lawman had taken his suggestion, but he did not think it worth gloating over. "If there's anything I can do for you . . ."

"Be gone by first light," Crown said flatly. He spun and started mouthing orders. Within minutes, citizens of Clearwater were taking down Carl Thorndyke's body. Others were carting his two brothers off toward the jail.

Rhodes watched. When the body was gone, and one of Claver's boys was washing down the wall to remove the blood, Rhodes turned to Mercy. He smiled at her.

She returned it, the brightness and warmth dazzling. "I don't know how to show my gratitude for what you did for me today, Mr. Rhodes," she drawled, batting her eyelashes a little and favoring Rhodes with another sparkling, inviting smile.

Rhodes smiled back and twirled his hat in his hands. Mercy's allure was powerful, but, Rhodes knew, empty. He had met such women before, and it was always the same: their faces, eyes, bodies held out great promises that the women would not — could not — keep. It was, he thought, a pity. "It was nothing, Miss Crawford," Rhodes said. There was no need to chide her for the falsity of her warm persona.

"Nothing?" Mercy said, her eyes widening. "Why, those damn Yankees" — she did not even flinch at the oath, for it was not considered as such — "would've abused me something powerful if you hadn't of come along. I am deeply grateful, sir, for your timely appearance and your most thoughtful actions on my behalf. You are, sir, a true Southern gentleman, and I pray to God that there were more of you. Had there been, the glorious South would've never . . ." She stopped and smiled again. "My apologies, sir, for running off like that."

"No need to apologize, miss," Rhodes said. He paused. "Well, I must be on my way." He clapped his hat on. "Good day to you, miss."

"Good day, sir." Mercy opened her parasol and leaned it on one shoulder. She turned and began walking away.

Rhodes watched for a moment, then he called softly to her. When she stopped and looked at him, questioning him with her eyes, he said, "I'm a damn Yankee, miss." He paused a heartbeat. "And I'm damn proud of it, too." He smiled and walked off.

Chapter Three

Travis Rhodes stopped his sturdy palomino horse on a small ridge and turned it to face Clearwater, half a mile away. He wasn't sure where he would be going from here, but he had made the only night in Clearwater a memorable one for himself.

He actually had no business to complete in the town. He had just told the marshal that so he could have at least one night under a roof. He had gone to one of the saloons—he hadn't even bothered to find out the name of the place—and cut the dust in his throat. After a filling meal at the restaurant next to the saloon, he went to the line of cribs behind the saloon and hired one of the girls. She was the best looking one he could find there, out of a poor lot.

"Well, come on in here, then, sweetheart," the brassy brunette with too much face paint said, taking Rhodes's arm.

"That ain't my style, sweetheart," he responded.

The woman—who had given her name only as Annie—looked up at him in surprise. "Just what's that mean, sweetheart?" she asked suspiciously.

"It means, missy," Rhodes said quietly, "that I'm not fixing to spend five sweaty minutes in that damn shack of yours."

Annie swung in front of Rhodes and planted her feet wide, her arms akimbo. "And what've you got planned for us, sweetheart?" she asked, her interest piqued.

"My room for the night."

"Hoo, boy," Annie whistled, the possibilities bouncing around in her head, "that's gonna cost you a heap more'n two bucks."

"I figured." He held out a twenty-dollar gold piece. "That do you?" he asked.

"That it would, sweetheart," Annie said reaching for the glittering coin.

Rhodes yanked it out of her reach.

"Hey, what's the big idea?" Annie demanded. She was angry and bewildered.

"The big idea is that I don't favor the idea of consortin' with such a painted woman."

Annie broke into a coarse laugh. "Well, hell, sweetheart, that's what I am."

Rhodes nodded. "I know, but you don't have to go out of your way to prove it."

"I think I've been insulted." Annie was confused again.

"Just statin' a fact, ma'am," Rhodes said easily. "You want the twenty, I want you cleaned up. We should be able to deal."

"You mean, I should take a bath?" Annie asked incredulously.

"Precisely."

Annie looked askance at him, wondering if he was on the up and up. "How do I know you're just not gonna have me do somethin' so foolish as that and then sit there laughin' at me?" she asked, voice growing more raspy.

Rhodes reached out, took Annie's right hand in his left, and turned it palm upward. He dropped the gold eagle into her hand, and then closed her palm over it. He released her hand.

Annie opened her fist and looked down. She wanted to make sure he hadn't pulled some sleight of hand on her. But the coin shone dully in the late afternoon sun.

"I want you to get yourself cleaned up, and good. Then you come on over to Grelb's. Room 15."

"All right, sweetheart," she said, trying to fight down her excitement. This fool was going to let her go off and bathe when she had the money already in hand. She'd lay low for a couple hours, maybe a day, and he most likely would ride out of town, leaving her with the money while he got nothing in recompense.

"Oh, and Annie," Rhodes said evenly, "don't think of running off with my cash."

She looked into the flat gray eyes and felt a shudder of worry ripple up her spine. "You the one did in Carl with the pitchfork, ain't you?" she asked. Her fear was a pulsing knot in her intestines, trying to break free.

"News travels fast around here." He paused. "I'm not aimin' to hurt you, girl," he said, still in his quiet voice. That soft, pleasant voice had been considered more than once as a sign of weakness in Travis Rhodes. Most who made that mistake did not live long enough to regret the error.

Annie nodded, her fear not lessened any.

"Go on now," Rhodes said. "Be there in one hour." He grinned a little. "Hell, missy, you might even like it."

Annie smiled wanly before turning and shuffling off. Darkness was coming as Rhodes strolled away, heading for Claver's Mercantile again. Since he would be leaving so early in the morning, he needed some more supplies. As he headed for the hotel, Rhodes stopped at the livery. He paid the owner and told him to have his horse ready early. The livery man growled a surly assent and went back to his work.

Rhodes shrugged at the man's rudeness. Once, long ago, he would have taken offense at such a thing. But he had learned during the war that if he tried to take on every man he met who was rude or coarse or contrary, that he would go crazy in a very short time. Now, he tended to shrug such things off—unless the other grew too ornery.

In his room, Rhodes set his supplies down, broke out his straight razor, mug of shaving soap and a brush, and a small metal mirror. He filled the small basin with water and then proceeded to shave. When done, he tossed the dirty water out the window and then put his things away. He looked at his pocket watch and nodded.

Annie finally arrived, only four minutes late. Rhodes did not criticize her for her tardiness. Instead, he grinned, nodding his head. "My, but don't you look fine," he said enthusiastically.

Annie blushed, shocking herself. She hadn't done that in a dog's age. "Aw, you're just sayin' that, sweet—um, mister," she offered lamely.

Always gallant when he could be, Rhodes shook his head. "No, ma'am, I'm not. Gospel truth." He would never admit that he was exaggerating, but it was not completely untrue. With the mounds of face paint gone, her hair clean and brushed, wearing a simple, modest wool dress, she was not unattractive. He was not lying in that, just stretching things a tad.

Annie smiled, relaxing. Little did she realize that in doing so, she made herself even prettier in Rhodes's eyes. Once she lost that hard, tense cast on her face, she was more alluring.

"Whiskey?" Rhodes asked.

"Please." Annie bit her lower lip. She was still nervous, and more than a little afraid of this man. She had seen his handiwork at Claver's. Any man who could do what he had done was a man to be feared, and respected.

Rhodes walked to the small table, on which sat a lantern, flickering low, a bottle of whiskey, and two glasses. Rhodes pulled the cork from the bottle and filled both glasses about halfway. Picking them up, he walked to where Annie still stood. He handed her one glass.

"Here's to an interesting night," Rhodes said, raising his glass in a little salute.

Annie was still too frightened to really smile again, but she made a halfhearted effort at it. Then she drank a bit, grateful when the whiskey hit her insides. It seemed to strengthen her a little.

When they had emptied their whiskey glasses, Rhodes took them both and put them back on the table. He turned to face Annie, and he grinned widely. "C'mere, darlin', and let's start this fandango."

Feeling as if she were heading for her own execution, Annie walked slowly toward this short, bearish man. She learned fairly quickly that Travis Rhodes could be as gentle and considerate as he could be ruthless and vicious. She allowed herself to relax completely, and then she began enjoying herself.

Annie was still sleeping when Rhodes slipped out of the bed. He looked at the time on his pocket watch after he had inserted the little key in it and wound it. He figured he had maybe an hour before daylight. He dressed quietly and then picked up his pistols. He checked over the two .36-caliber, cap-and-ball Whitney revolvers, making sure they were loaded, then he slid them into his belt, butts facing forward. He checked to make sure the four extra cylinders he carried were loaded and ready. Then he dropped them back into a hard-leather pouch hooked to his belt. Last he checked the .31-caliber, five-shot Ells revolver. He stuck the small backup pistol into a shoulder holster under his shirt.

He picked up his sawed-off Darby 10-gauge shotgun and then his saddlebags, in which he had placed his supplies. He headed for the door. With his hand on the knob, he stopped and looked back, smiling a little. Annie had been much more warm and congenial than he had expected, especially once she lost her fear of him.

With a shrug, he walked back to the bed. Dipping into a pocket, he found a five-dollar coin. He set it on the small table next to the bed. With another smile into the darkness, he left the room.

He walked straight to the nearest restaurant — Wickham's — and took a table. He could see Marshal Sam Crown leaning against a building across the street. Rhodes ignored him as he wolfed down some bacon, eggs, and biscuits. He took the time for a last cup of coffee, before he hefted all his worldly goods and marched out. He touched the brim of his hat in Crown's direction. Crown returned the gesture.

Ten minutes later, as the sun crept over the horizon, Rhodes was riding out of town. He stopped at the ridge and looked back. There was nothing in Clearwater that he missed, but he didn't know where he would go.

Such a thing had never bothered him before, but then again, he had never been a restless veteran of a war before. He hadn't known what to expect when he was mustered out a few months ago, just before the peace was signed at Appomattox Courthouse.

He had tried going home again, but there was nothing left for him there. He had had no sweetheart, and his parents had passed on some time ago. True, his sister Edna was still living back in Vincennes, but Rhodes and Edna had never gotten along. Neither had Rhodes and his two brothers, Jason and Bert. For a long time, Rhodes thought it was his brothers who were in the wrong, but in the past year or so, he realized that he most likely was the problem. He did not fit in with his family, or just about anywhere else, for that matter.

Which led him back to his problem of the moment. He had thought that perhaps he could find a place like Clearwater and settle down, at least for a while. But now that possibility had gone by the wayside. He supposed he could head on to the next town like Clearwater and try it again, but he knew in his heart that he would not last there either.

With a sigh, he turned the horse west and rode off slowly. There was gold to be found out that way. That much he knew. Hell, even during the war he had heard the stories of the gold strikes in Colorado Territory and other places out that way. In those wild mining camps, he would find his home, he thought. He would not be out of place in such an area. He could lose himself in anonymity.

There was only one problem with that idea, though — getting there. This late in the summer, there were no wagon trains plying the Oregon Trail or the Smoky Hill Trail either. Had there been, he could've hooked on with one as a hunter or guide. That was out of the question now.

He figured he had no choice but to make a go of

it on his own, hoping he might meet some other people along the way. There was safety in numbers, and he was smart enough — and humble enough — to know that he might be good with a gun, but he could not beat a war party of battle-hardened Lakotas.

Well, he reasoned, he would be safe enough for a while. The Indians around here were little trouble these days. Travis Rhodes was not the type to worry much about things he could not change, so he just rode on. He would deal with whatever he found when he found it. Or when it found him.

Chapter Four

After three days of leisurely riding westward, Rhodes came to a small trading post. There was nothing else around besides a cockeyed sod building and a rickety corral of poles dragged in from God knew where. A few bony nags stood in the corral alongside a rotting prairie schooner.

As desolate as the place looked, it was an oasis because of its remoteness. It was the first — and only — place people could get supplies once they had left Independence or Saint Joe. At least until they got to the next forlorn place just like it.

Rhodes sat on a grassy knoll looking down at the dismal trading post. Such places had reputations of violence, which didn't concern Rhodes too much. Besides, he figured as he eased the horse down the little hill, he had no choice. He was low on his basic supplies, since he had no real way of carrying them. He would have to depend on isolated trading posts like this one, or on forts, for supplies every few days.

He stopped in front of the building, a few feet from the sagging door. A log had been dragged there, half hollowed out and was filled with water for the horses. Rhodes let his palomino drink. He looked around, but saw nothing untoward.

He patted the horse on the long, white mane and

then headed for the door. Rhodes hooked his right thumb in his belt, near the butt of one of the Whitneys. With his left, he pushed open the door, standing a little to the side of it. Then he stepped inside.

It was about what he had expected. The place was dank, dim, and rank. The only light was provided by several foul-smelling lanterns. Goods and supplies were heaped and piled haphazardly all over. A wizened old man stood behind the counter—two planks torn from the wrecked wagon out in the corral. They rested on a small cook stove at one end and two butter churns, sans stirrers, on the other.

"Welcome, friend," the old man said with obviously false cheer. "Name's Claude Fenniman. What can I do for you today?"

"Some flour, a side of bacon, beans, coffee," Rhodes said as he walked through the trading post, looking behind bales and boxes.

"Anything else?" Fenniman asked.

"I'll think on it while you get that stuff."

Rhodes had finished looking around—after all the place wasn't that big—and had found nothing disturbing. He relaxed a little as he strolled back to the counter.

Fenniman held up a can. "The best flour you can buy, mister," he said. "Elton's Stone Ground. Good coffee, too." He tapped another tin. "Franklin's."

"Fine," Rhodes said with a nod.

"Anything else?"

"Buffalo jerky, sugar, salt . . ." He stopped when the old door, which was hung by a few pieces of old boot leather, opened, letting in a blast of unwelcome light. Rhodes melted backward, against a pile of buffalo hides, and waited, right hand resting on a pistol.

Two men clumped inside. One was tall and husky;

the other short and scrawny. Both wore battered, holey buckskins, and Rhodes could smell them even over the foulness of this den. As they moved inside, Rhodes could see that both had not shaved in some days nor bathed in some months. Their hair was long and filthy. By the look and odor of them, Rhodes pegged them as buffalo hunters.

"Izzat your horse outside dere, mac?" the big one said, clomping up to right in front of Rhodes.

"Might be," Rhodes allowed. He sounded casual, unconcerned. "Why?"

"Why, hell, boy, I'ma buy'm."

"He ain't for sale," Rhodes said flatly.

"I dint ast was he for sale," the big man said. The statement was accompanied by various disgusting noises that grated on Rhodes's ears. "I just said I was gonna buy'm."

"Perhaps you didn't understand," Rhodes said calmly, though he was getting his dander up. "I said he ain't for sale."

"You speak mighty fancy, boy," the man said. He stuck a sausage-size finger into his right ear and rolled it around. When he popped it out, he wiped a large clot of wax on the front of his shirt. "Now, like I said, I ain't ast if you was sellin' your horse. I'ma buy it. Give you a fair price, too."

"No." Rhodes kept his gaze on the man's festering countenance.

"Don't rile me, boy, goddammit," the man snapped. "My pal Ralphie needs hisself a horse, and Claude dere ain't got a decent horse inna whole goddamn place."

Rhodes shrugged. Argument was useless. The man had neither the willingness nor the intelligence to hear what Rhodes was saying anyway.

"Hey, now, Ern, don't go causin' no trouble in my

33

place, dammit," Fenniman said. "You want to thump on that poor bastard, you go on and do it outside."

"Hell, Claude, that ain't gonna be needful. Since dis guy talks so fancy, I expect he'll come to his senses." He turned his rotting gaze back on Rhodes. "Ain't dat right, pal?"

While Ernest Biggers had looked at Fenniman, Rhodes had slipped one of his Whitneys out from his belt. With the big man blabbering, Rhodes had eased back the hammer.

Rhodes said nothing, he just continued staring at Biggers. The big man got angry, and it reminded Rhodes of a storm blowing up over the mountains. Biggers took a step closer to Rhodes.

"Jesus Christ, you are a foul smellin' bastard, ain't you," Rhodes said calmly. Then he brought the pistol up and fired twice.

Biggers did not fall, at least not at first. The balls punched all the way through him, surprising him with the shock. So close was Rhodes's gun when it was fired that Biggers's shirt almost ignited from the sparks. His eyes grew large, as he stared at Rhodes. Then he looked down at the two small, almost neat holes in his belly, and the blood draining out of each.

"Jesus," the smaller man said as he stared at the larger holes in Bigger's back.

Then Biggers began to topple. Rhodes saw it coming and slid easily to his right. As Biggers fell into the pile of buffalo hides, Rhodes raised the pistol and shot Ralphie Conway. It took only one ball to take care of Conway, who had pulled his own pistol even as he was marveling at the damage Rhodes had done to Biggers. He fell in a small pile.

Rhodes swung in a crouch toward Fenniman, his pistol up and ready.

"Hold there, mister," Fenniman said nervously, half raising his hands, showing that he had no weapon.

Rhodes stood, grinding his teeth together. He almost ached to pull the trigger again, ridding the world of one more piece of vermin. He fought back the feeling, though it took some effort. After a few moments, he sighed and eased the hammer down as he straightened. "Sorry about the mess," he said evenly as he jammed the pistol back into his belt and stepped back up to the counter.

"No problem, mister," Fenniman said hastily. He wanted no part of this short, broad man.

"You got all my stuff set up yet?"

"No, not quite. You was about to tell me a few more things you needed when you . . . we were . . . interrupted." He felt like he was going to wet his trousers.

Rhodes nodded. He looked at what was on the counter. "Buffalo jerky, sugar, salt, some mess beef, powder, lead, lucifers, chawin' tobacco, and a few cigars—if you got any."

"Got the best," Fenniman said, giving his speech by rote.

Rhodes nodded again. "Best be movin'," he said quietly. "I ain't aimin' to spend the rest of my life here."

Fenniman scurried about, getting what was needed. Finally everything Rhodes had requested was on the counter. "You got somethin' to carry all this in?" Fenniman asked.

"Just put it in burlap sacking." He considered taking one of the two dead men's horses, but for some reason, the thought bothered him. Besides, any horses that those two would ride would be poor beasts at best, Rhodes was sure.

"If I might make a suggestion," Fenniman said tentatively.

"What's that?"

"Ol' Ern there rode hisself a mule. A great ugly beast, but strong's an ox. I doubt much if Ern'd mind that you took it for carryin' supplies and such."

Rhodes might be reluctant to take a man's — even a dead man's — horse, but a mule was another story. "Let's go take a look at it," he said. He let Fenniman go out first. Next to the palomino was a dark, hulking mule. It looked strong though none too friendly. Rhodes nodded. "It'll do."

Back inside, Rhodes said, "Well, hell, since I got that damn mule now, I can get some more supplies. Unless, of course, your prices are usurious." The last was a question.

"Oh, no, no, sir," Fenniman said nervously. Usually he gouged people with all he thought he could get out of them. After all, there was no competition.

"Good," Rhodes said in friendly tones. "Now, let's see, I could use a bigger fry pan, more jerked buffalo, an extra pair of pants . . ."

Fenniman was busy for a few minutes getting everything together. "That be all now?" he asked, wiping sweat off his crinkled forehead.

Rhodes thought about it, then nodded. "Except for a pack saddle. You do have one layin' around here, don't you?"

"Yes," Fenniman said sourly. He was going to barely make a profit on all this, he figured, and that did not please him at all. No, it didn't. As he went to get a pack saddle, he soothed his greedy heart with the knowledge that Ralph Conway's horse was now his. A couple weeks of letting the horse fatten on rich prairie grass and hay, and he could sell the horse to a traveler for a goodly sum.

With something of a renewed enthusiasm, he carried the pack saddle out and began putting it on the mule. Rhodes followed right behind, with an armful of supplies. When those were loaded on the mule, the two went back inside and got the rest of the things.

Fenniman did not like the thought that Rhodes wouldn't leave him alone. Had Rhodes done that, for even a moment, Fenniman figured he could grab his scattergun from where it rested against the two butter churns supporting his counter. He settled for thinking that as soon as this man had ridden off, he would get a rifle instead. Then he could drop this son of a bitch. Then he would not only have Conway's old nag, but the beautiful palomino and the big, ugly mule. Those thoughts made him happy.

Finally he had everything packed on the mule, and covered with a waterproof tarpaulin. He finished tying down the tarp. "There you go, mister," he said, realizing that he did not even know this man's name. Not that it mattered, though, not when the nameless man would be dead in a few minutes. Fenniman had no plans to bury him once he had killed him. Let him rot out there, or feed the scavengers, Fenniman thought. It was all he deserved.

"Obliged," Rhodes said. "How much I owe you for all this?"

"Twenty-three dollars and eighteen cents," Fenniman said, suddenly nervous again. There was nothing to stop this man from shooting him and riding off. He was relieved when Rhodes counted out the money and handed it to him. It was in coins, too, not that worthless paper stuff everyone seemed to be carrying these days.

"You sure you got all you need now?" Fenniman asked, trying to sound friendly. He could drop this man at a fair distance with a rifle, but it would be a heap easier if he just had a few moments to get his shotgun and take care of this man here and now.

"Expect I do." Travis had stopped to cut off some tobacco and shove it in his mouth. He chewed slowly.

With relief and expectation, Fenniman turned to head back into his sod store. Now was the time, he figured. Just a few more minutes . . .

"Oh," Rhodes said, "just one more thing."

Fenniman turned just in time to get cracked in the forehead by the butt of one of Rhodes's Whitneys. He went down and out without uttering a sound.

"Thought you'd back shoot me, did you, you sneaky bastard," Rhodes growled low. He had seen it in Fenniman's eyes; knew all along what the trading post owner was thinking. He smiled a little as he pulled himself onto the palomino.

Chapter Five

Rhodes moved on, warily. Though he had plenty of supplies, he was still alone and heading into the heart of a land where Lakota, Pawnee, Arikara, and other Indians still held sway. As such, the next several nights he made cold camps or, at most, made a small fire of buffalo dung before real darkness set in, ate hurriedly and then covered over the fire.

It annoyed him that he had to do such things, but he did not let the annoyance get to him too much. He had faced much worse things during the war. God, that had been a horrible thing, that war, he often thought. Bodies shattered by cannon fire or grapeshot; limbs hacked off in a crude hospital one after another and then tossed away; the cloying odor of gun smoke; the stench of death and decay; the screams.

It had taught him some things, though. Things like how to persevere under incredible hardships; how to push on through exhaustion, fear, and deprivation; how to handle himself in a fight, either with firearms or hand to hand.

It also had taught him to keep his own counsel more often than not, and to disguise most of his feelings. He figured it would never do to let the enemy know what was going on in your mind. That kept them off balance, and at times would give a man a chance to get out of a dangerous situation. People saw his placid countenance and easygoing demeanor, and often mistook it for gullibility, tranquillity, or both.

Despite those thoughts, which he could never completely keep out of his mind all the time, he still kept an ear and eye out for danger. Four days out from Claude Fenniman's trading post, Rhodes stopped and stared at a thin wisp of smoke off in the distance. He pondered it as he sat watching. It could be Indians, he supposed, but if so, there probably were only a few, since there was not much smoke. On the other hand, it could not be a wagon train or army patrol.

He shrugged and touched his spurs to the palomino's sides. There was one sure way to find out, he figured.

He stopped again in a shallow dip in the interminable prairie and then moved up the hill in a squat, one of his pistols in hand. At the crest, he flattened on his stomach and slithered the last few yards and looked over. Across the prairie, less than a quarter of a mile away, sat two lonely-looking wagons. A group of people huddled around a small fire. From the wind drifting in his direction, Rhodes knew it was a buffalo chip fire. He also saw that there were only four mules, not nearly enough to pull the two wagons. Because of that, Rhodes figured they were in poor shape.

He shoved himself backward down the slope a little, then stood and turned to walk back to his horse, shoving his pistol back into his belt as he did. Once on the palomino, he headed south and rode a little way before heading west again. As he neared the small camp he stopped. He sat a moment, then nodded. He pulled his two Whitney revolvers and dropped them into his saddlebags, one to a side. Then he rode on again.

When he was still fifty yards from the camp, he shouted and waved. He rode forward slowly, figuring that the people might be edgy. They were, and Rhodes made no sudden moves as he stopped near one of the wagons. "I'm unarmed," he said, raising his arms.

Two men held muzzle-loading rifles toward him, though the weapons were not really aimed. They were not friendly faces. Three women and several children stood behind the men, looking frightened.

"Looks like you folks've had a spot of trouble, here," Rhodes said genially.

"That's none of your affair," the older of the men said harshly. He appeared to be in his early fifties. "We'd be obliged if you was to move on. Follow your friends."

"I have no friends out here, mister."

"We don't believe you, mister. Now ride on."

Rhodes shrugged. "Good day, then." He turned the palomino's head and rode on. He stopped half a mile away and loosened the saddle to let the horse breathe. The mule could do with a little rest, too. Rhodes took his pistols out of his saddlebags and stuffed them into his belt again. As he stood there, he gnawed on a piece of jerky and kept an eye out on the land around him.

A speck of dust off on the horizon caught his attention, and he watched it. For a while, it did not seem to progress any, and he figured it was just a dust devil, or perhaps a mirage. He shrugged and looked off.

Finishing the jerky, he tightened the saddle. As he began to pull himself up on the horse, he glanced at where he had seen the dust before. The small cloud had moved closer, and Rhodes could see three riders. A moment later, he realized the three were Indians. And they were heading toward where the two wagons were.

Rhodes stood there, reins in hand, hand on saddle horn, thinking. He owed those people nothing. Quite the opposite, in fact. But he figured there was a reason the people had run him off. There must be more to it than was seen in that thirty-second encounter. He spun and hammered a picket stake into the ground, then tied the mule to it. He swung into the saddle and galloped off.

As the camp came into sight, Rhodes slapped the reins on the horse's withers, urging a bit more speed out of the racing horse. He surveyed the camp with one glance. Two women were standing behind the men with powder horns, shot pouches, and ramrods in hand, ready to reload. The third woman was under a wagon, huddling all the children around her.

Rhodes could tell when the two men fired by the puffs of powder smoke, though he could not hear the reports of the weapons over the sound of the horse's hooves and the rushing wind.

One of the Indians fell off his horse and bounced a few times, but the other two Indians appeared to be untouched. Both were firing arrows, and one of the men with the wagons fell, an arrow protruding from his chest or arm. Rhodes could not be certain which at this range. The man squiggled under the other wagon.

Rhodes flew into the camp as the two Indians circled it. He noted that the third Indian was on his feet and limping toward the camp. The uninjured man in the camp spun and fired wildly at the two Indians. He missed, but Rhodes thought the stray ball had come suspiciously close to his own head.

One of the warriors broke off the attack on the camp and headed toward Rhodes, firing two arrows as he charged. Rhodes never flinched. Another thing he had learned during the war was that you could not duck a bullet. Either it would hit you or it wouldn't. He figured it could apply to arrows, too.

He grabbed the shotgun from the saddle scabbard holding the sawed-off barrels with his left hand, which also held the reins. With his right hand, he snapped back one of the hammers. When less than twenty-five yards separated him from the warrior, Rhodes jammed to a halt. He threw the scattergun up to his shoulder, and a second later, fired.

A full load of buckshot hitting the warrior in the chest from little more than ten yards away slammed him to the ground. Rhodes slapped his spurs against the horse and raced off. In the few ensuing seconds, the other mounted Indian had circled the camp several times, chasing the unwounded man and the two women under the other wagon.

The warrior stopped, laughing at the frightened whites hiding under the wagons, as if that would save them. Still laughing, he turned to look for his friend. And caught Rhodes's second load of buckshot mostly in the face. His countenance disintegrated and he fell.

Rhodes pulled to a squealing stop and grabbed the rope rein of the warrior's pony. He looked up and saw the wounded Indian running away. "Take this horse," Rhodes snapped. When the man slid out from under the wagon and took the rein, Rhodes slid the scattergun away. Then he walked his horse around the wagons, and gave the animal its head. In moments he had caught up with the third Indian.

He stopped almost alongside the Indian, who spun, snarling. He had a war club raised over his head. Rhodes, who had pulled one of his pistols as he rode, shot the Indian twice in the chest. It was one more thing he had learned in the war—be remorseless in battle, for the enemy would. Such a thing sat hard on a generally decent man like Travis Rhodes, but it had to be done nonetheless. He knew these Indians would never give him any quarter, so he would give them none.

Still, he felt no pride or satisfaction at having killed the three warriors. It was simply something that had to be done. He rode back to the wagons and dismounted. "You folks all right?" he asked as he dismounted.

The younger man—who was in his mid-thirties—nodded. "Brother Flake is wounded," he said quietly, "but it is not too bad, I shouldn't think."

Rhodes nodded. "The women and kids all right?"

"All are fine." There still was no friendliness in the man's voice.

"You folks want me to ride on, I will," Rhodes said agreeably. He figured something had happened to these people to turn them away from any and all strangers. He wondered what, but he didn't wonder too much.

"That'd suit us just fine, mister," the man said.

Erastus Flake had gotten out from under the wagon and stood. As Rhodes turned to get back on his horse, Flake called for him to stop. Rhodes did and turned, still holding his reins in hand.

"We are much in your debt, stranger, and you are welcome to sit at our table." He almost grinned. "Such as it is."

"What about him?" Rhodes asked, jerking a chin in the other man's direction.

44

"I believe Brother Hickman will accede to my request."

"That right, Mr. Hickman?" Rhodes asked.

Phineas Hickman nodded once, curtly.

"There, you see now," Flake said. He smiled a little at Rhodes. "But where is your mule, Mr. . . . ?"

"Travis Rhodes," Rhodes said, shaking hands with both men. "I left him back there a ways when I saw those Indians heading your way."

"Where did you leave him?"

"About a half-mile yonder." He pointed over his shoulder. "Now, if you'll excuse me, I'll go get him and bring him in." He paused. "You got some rope?"

Flake nodded. "Brother Hickman, some rope please."

Hickman scowled but got the rope and handed it to Rhodes, who took it while staring coolly at Hickman. He took the rope and tied it around the dead Indian's ankles. He mounted and walked the horse away, dragging the warrior behind. When he got to the first one he had slain, he stopped and tied the rope around that one, too. He dragged both out a little distance and then undid the rope, leaving them there.

When Rhodes returned to the camp, it was apparent that Flake, who obviously was the leader here, had spoken to Hickman, since the latter was rather more cordial. It seemed forced, but at least it was not outright hostility.

Flake was sitting on the ground, his back resting against a wagon wheel. The arrow shaft was still sticking out of his arm just above the biceps. Rhodes pointed to it. "You havin' trouble getting that out?" he asked.

"Some," Flake admitted. "Brother Hickman has

45

never done such a thing. Nor have the women." He paused. "Have you?"

Rhodes shrugged. "Never an arrow. I've pulled bullets out of folks, though. Want me to take a crack at it?"

"If you would be so kind," Flake said. "Though I am afraid we are so far in your debt as to never be able to pay you back."

"I ain't keeping count." Rhodes tied his horse and mule to the other wagon, then came back to where Flake was sitting. The man was ashen-faced but otherwise was not displaying any pain. "Get some whiskey out," he said. When there was no response, Rhodes looked at Flake, a question in his eyes.

"We do not partake of spirituous beverages, Mr. Rhodes," Flake said evenly.

"Not even for cleansing wounds?"

"There is no reason to bring temptation along in our own wagons, Mr. Rhodes. A dose of hot steel, the proper poultice, and faith in the Lord should be enough."

"My apologies, Mr. Flake, I didn't know." Rhodes was surprised.

"Most Gentiles don't."

"Gentiles?"

"Those not of the faith. You see, Mr. Rhodes, we are Saints."

Rhodes knew there was a chance he might regret asking, but he felt he had to. "Saints?"

"Latter-day Saints. Most know us as Mormons." He shrugged.

Rhodes shrugged. "Never heard of such folks," he said easily, not wanting to offend. "But if that's your way, then so be it."

"We appreciate your concern, Mr. Rhodes. Many—well, maybe most—are not so congenial." He paused. "And our church does not make Gentiles subscribe to our ways. We have no objection to using whiskey to cleanse a wound if it is held by someone else."

Rhodes nodded, and then grinned a little. "And if I need a snort?" he asked.

Flake also smiled, seeming none the worse for his wound. "We all have our weaknesses, Mr. Rhodes," Flake said, still smiling. Then his face hardened. "Of course, we cannot abide drunkenness."

Rhodes nodded. The threat did not concern him. He went to his horse and pulled a small bottle of whiskey from his saddlebags. Kneeling in front of Flake again, he asked, "You want to do this sitting? Or would you rather be lying down?"

"Sitting will suffice."

Chapter Six

Rhodes reached out and gave the arrow shaft an exploratory tug. Flake hissed but otherwise was silent. "Don't seem to be in there too strong," Rhodes said. He ripped open Flake's sleeve enough to give him some working room. Then Rhodes pulled his big knife and poured a little whiskey over the blade.

One of the women handed Flake a piece of twisted cloth. Flake nodded and shoved the thing into his mouth.

Rhodes flipped the excess whiskey off the blade. Grabbing the arrow shaft in his left hand, he brought the knife up with his right. Without hesitation, he quickly slit Flake's flesh in two quick, short cuts. He gave a yank with his left hand and the arrow came out with a minimum of rending flesh.

Rhodes glanced at Flake. The Mormon's eyes were closed and his face was coated with a sheen of sweat.

"You want me to stitch that?"

"No," Flake gasped, pulling the rag out of his mouth.

"Heat?"

"If it needs it."

Rhodes shrugged. "I've seen men come through bigger ordeals all right. A good poultice ought to take care of it, if you have anything to use."

"We do," the same woman who had spoken before said. "If you'll excuse me."

Rhodes nodded, stood, and stepped back. The woman — a middle-aged, matronly sort — took the spot where Rhodes had been squatting and slathered something over the wound in Flake's arm. Then she bandaged it.

While she was at work, Rhodes picked up the cork and stuck it back in the bottle of whiskey. He felt like having a jolt or two, but decided against it. He figured there was no need to flaunt it in front of these people. He stuffed the bottle into one of the saddlebags.

When the woman had finished and stood, Rhodes asked, "Anything I can contribute to the pot?"

"Mother Eliza?" Flake asked the woman who had just patched him.

"Flour, if you have any, Mr. Rhodes, would be a welcome thing. We have not tasted biscuit or bread for more than a week now."

Rhodes nodded. "Regular flour? Or cornmeal?"

"We would prefer regular, I think."

Rhodes got the tin of Elton's flour and handed it to the woman. "You folks got enough coffee?" he asked.

Eliza dropped her eyes. In question, Rhodes turned to Flake. "Another thing you folks don't partake of?" he asked.

Flake nodded. "However, if you have coffee and want some, we won't object."

Rhodes nodded. "Obliged, Mr. Flake. Now, I best see to my animals." Rhodes unloaded his mule nearby, stacking the goods as neatly as he could and covering them with the piece of canvas. He took a few minutes to put some water and coffee into his small coffeepot and put it on the fire, which, he noted, now had a few pieces of wagon planking in flames.

He unsaddled the palomino, storing the saddle, bridle, saddle blanket, bedroll, and saddlebags near his supplies. Then he curried the horse well.

"Would you like some oats for your horse, Mr. Rhodes?" Eliza asked quietly from behind him.

"I'd be obliged, ma'am," Rhodes said politely. He took the feedbag of oats and hooked it over the horse's head. Then he finished brushing the animal down and hobbled it and the mule. Finally he washed up a little, using water from one of his two canteens.

The others were sitting around the fire now, the women and two of the children with blankets or shawls over their shoulders. With the darkness had come a chill. Rhodes squatted down and self-consciously poured himself a mug of coffee.

"What brings you out here, Mr. Rhodes?" Flake asked. He had gained a little of his color and looked good considering the circumstances.

Rhodes shrugged. He was tired and hungry and did not want to answer questions. "Searchin'," he finally said.

"Searchin' for what?" Flake asked.

"I ain't sure," Rhodes said honestly. "I reckon I'll know what it is once I find it."

"A frustrating quest, I would think," Flake said.

"I suppose." Rhodes paused for a sip. "How'd you folks come to be out here with too few mules?"

Flake sighed. "A sad tale," he said, then laughed a little. "We were to join one of the caravans heading to Deseret, where our church is headquartered. I was unavoidably delayed in New York on business. By the time I reached Independence, the caravan had been gone almost a month. Brother Hickman and our families here decided to press on anyway, despite the lateness of the season."

"Where is this Deseret?" he asked.

"Beyond the Wasatch Mountains, on the shores of the Great Salt Lake."

Rhodes nodded. One of the men he had served with during the war was a veteran of the useless campaign against Brigham Young and his followers out in the vastness of the west. Rhodes had not put together Mormons and Deseret in his head until just now.

"That's a hell of a trip, Mr. Flake," Rhodes said. "Excuse my language."

"It is indeed."

"You ever been there?"

"No, sir. But we will be welcomed, have no fear."

"It ain't your reception there I'm wonderin' about. It's you gettin' there at all." He paused and sipped some coffee. "It's more than a mite late in the season for such a trek. I ain't ever been out there, but I know others who have. It's a man-killin' and animal-killin' trek, Mr. Flake, and one not to be taken lightly. Besides, you don't get out there in a hurry, winter'll catch you out here."

"We are well prepared," Flake said, a note of indignation in his voice.

"Like hell you are," Rhodes said roughly. "Pardonin' my language. Just two wagons," he said, shaking his head in amazement, "is no match for a good-size war party."

"You are out here alone, Mr. Rhodes," Flake pointed out.

"A-yup, I am. I'm also a heap scared of it, too. But things look bad for me, I can ditch the mule and hightail it to other parts in a hurry. But you, you have plodding old wagons, and more impor-

51

tantly, women and children to be considered."

"A point well made and well taken." Flake winced as a pinch of pain nipped at his arm.

"And if all you brought were them four mules, you're a damn fool, pardonin' my language again."

"That was one area in which we were quite prepared. We had two teams of six each."

"You lost eight mules this close to the settlements?" Rhodes asked incredulously.

"Not quite," Flake said, irritated. He sighed. "We were set upon by some men the day before yesterday, a few miles back."

"Set upon?"

"Yes," Flake said dryly. "Three men came along. As all good people would, we invited them to join us in our evening repast." He shrugged, annoyed at it having happened. "When Brother Hickman and I had our backs turned, they drew their pistols and . . . well, damn it all, we were caught flatfooted."

Food was ready, and the three women began doling it out on tin plates. Rhodes took his and went right to eating. The others looked at him with annoyance or surprise. Rhodes realized they were all looking at him. He stopped and swallowed the mouthful. "Sorry, folks, I ain't much a one for sayin' of grace and such."

Flake nodded, but he was clearly annoyed. Still, he said grace quickly, thanking God for the bountiful food they had, and for having sent Rhodes to save them from the Lammanites. Rhodes was glad he wasn't eating at the moment when Flake said that; he would have choked for sure.

Moments later, they were all eating. As they did, the elderly woman, Eliza, asked, "What church do you belong to, Mr. Rhodes?"

"Don't have a church," Rhodes said flatly, knowing

that would annoy his hosts even more. It couldn't be helped.

"You should, you know," Eliza said.

"So I've been told," Rhodes said dryly. "But I never had much use for a church." He almost smiled, knowing the consternation *that* would rise. "Don't get me wrong now," he added. "I believe in the Almighty. I just don't think God gives a hoot for how much time we spend in a church, or how much time we spend listening to speechifying and all. I think he'll look upon us all in His own good time and judge us by the way we've lived our lives."

"And you think you will gain entrance to Heaven this way, Mr. Rhodes?" Flake asked.

Rhodes shrugged. "That's up to the Almighty. I expect, though, that I've got more of a chance for it than some I've known." He smiled ruefully. "Reckon there's a heap of other folks out there that've got some advantage on me there, too."

Rhodes finished eating and set the plate aside. "A fine meal, ma'am," he said to Eliza. "I ain't ate so well in a long time." He wanted to change the topic, having learned a long time ago that arguing about religion was a dangerous thing.

Eliza nodded and smiled. "Minerva helped a considerable lot." She pointed to one of the two younger women.

"I'm obliged, ma'am," Rhodes said, looking briefly in her direction. She was a beautiful young woman, maybe twenty-two or so. Her skin was pale and flawless and she was quite shapely. Rhodes had started to remember some things that his army friend had told him about these Mormons, now that he recollected what they were. His friend had told him that these people were known to marry more than one woman. Rhodes wondered if that was the

53

case here, and if so, who was married to who. Then he figured it did not matter, and he let it drop.

"So," Rhodes said in the gap of silence that had formed, "what'd these three fellahs who got the drop on you do?"

"Stole some of our belongings," Hickman said sourly.

Rhodes was surprised that Hickman had been the one to respond. "That all?" he asked. There had to be more to this, he figured.

"They were about to take indecent liberties with the women, but apparently they wanted some of the devil's drink before they lingered a while," Flake said. "When they learned that we had none, they grew quite angry. I was sure they were about to kill us all. Indeed, they even gave Brother Hickman a good thump on the head."

Rhodes looked at Hickman. "No wonder you weren't fond of another stranger comin' into your camp, Mr. Hickman."

Hickman scowled and said nothing.

"Anyway, they headed off with eight of the mules and our one saddle horse."

"It doesn't make sense for them to ride off and leave you alive," Rhodes said bluntly.

"I am aware of that Mr. Rhodes," Flake said. "We, too, thought we would be killed. But then one of them—he seemed to be the leader—told his two cronies to leave us alone, that we wouldn't get far with only a brace of mules for each wagon. The Injuns would get us, he said. Or the weather."

"I reckon they were right about that."

Flake nodded. "All too true, Mister Rhodes." He sighed. "Yesterday morning, we hooked all four mules to Brother Hickman's wagon and brought it this far. I left Brother Hickman, Mrs. Hickman,

Aunt Minerva, and three of the children here. Mother Eliza and the other children were waiting with our wagon back at the other place. I walked the mules back there, hitched up my wagon, and brought us to here."

"That's a hell of a way to make your way west," Rhodes said. He was impressed at the group's determination.

"It is that," Flake said. "But we have no other choice. We must make what progress we can."

Rhodes was silent for a few moments, thinking. Then he said quietly, "Maybe I can help you folks a little."

"How?" Flake asked, surprised.

"There's got to be a way station or trading post or something not too far from here. It was four days' ride from the last one. You and me can ride on ahead to try to find it."

"And the others?"

"They can stay here with the wagons."

"That will be dangerous."

"You're not in danger now?" Rhodes asked rhetorically.

"Another telling point, Mr. Rhodes."

Rhodes nodded. "Mr. Hickman can hitch the mules daily while we're gone, two to each, and haul the wagons a little ways, maybe a couple miles, with plenty of rest."

Flake nodded again. "That would bring them a little closer to us."

"Yessir."

"But how will I get there?" Flake suddenly asked.

"You can ride that Indian pony we took."

Flake smiled. "What do you think, Phineas?" he asked.

"I'm not so sure I endorse such a thing. I'll have

55

my hands full with the wagons, and won't have time to look out for everyone else."

"That could be a problem," Flake agreed. He thought a little, then asked, "Could we also use your mule, Mr. Rhodes?"

"I expect. Why?"

"I'd be in your debt—again—if we could take Mother Eliza and maybe one or two of the smaller children."

"She'd have to ride astride," Rhodes said. "Unless you have a sidesaddle."

"We do."

Rhodes nodded.

Chapter Seven

They left just after first light, setting a fairly speedy pace. Rhodes did not want to wear out the animals. Slowing them a little was the fact that his mule carried the formidably sized Eliza Flake as well as five-year-old Heber Hickman. Six-year-old Hyrum Flake rode behind Rhodes. The Indian pony carrying Hyrum's father was acting up, not sure it wanted this fairly large, strange-smelling man on its back.

An hour out, Rhodes stopped and gave Flake his horse and he took the Indian pony. With his size and strength, Rhodes could better control the fractious animal.

Shortly after noon, they topped a rise and saw a small trading post half a mile or so off. As they neared it, Flake said, "There're our mules." He pointed to the corral.

Rhodes stopped. "I've dealt with these kind of people before, Mr. Flake," he said. "Most of 'em'd rob their mothers for a buck. There's no way in Heaven or Hell that man down there's going to give you those mules."

"I'll have to buy them?" Flake asked. It seemed almost a bigger injustice than having the animals stolen in the first place.

Rhodes nodded.

"All right," Flake agreed. He might be offended at the thought, but he was smart enough to know he would get nothing but trouble if he tried to tell the trading post owner that they were his mules. Even if the man was honest, he most likely would have given out cash or supplies to whoever had stolen them. It would be unfair to expect the trader to take the loss.

They stopped and loosened all the saddles and let the animals drink. Then they all went inside. The place was much like the other one Rhodes had stopped at. It was small, dank, and malodorous, though this one was a little brighter, since there were two windows in the sod building. The windows were covered with oiled paper.

"What can I do for you folks?" a middle-aged man asked. He was of medium height and bald, and he wore ill-fitting wool garments. A large bulbous nose blazed proudly above a scruffy mustache. A pace behind him and to each side stood a young man, evidently the owner's sons. They were taller than their father and considerably bulkier. They had their arms crossed over their chests and made quite a formidable pair.

"We need some mules, Mr. . . . ?" Flake said.

"Clem Waters at your service." He grinned vacuously. "You say you need mules, eh? Well, we got some. Big, strong ones they are, too. So good, they're going to cost a bit more than one might expect." Waters tried to sound apologetic, but it rang false.

Flake nodded. "While we're inside, Mr. Waters, we will need some other supplies."

"Sure, sure. We got anything you want."

While Flake was getting his supplies, Rhodes beckoned one of the sons. The young man strutted

58

over, trying to impress Rhodes, who thought it laughable.

"What chu want, boy?" the young man asked with a sneer.

"What's your name?" Rhodes asked politely.

"Billy."

Rhodes nodded. "I took an interest in one of your horses, there, Billy. I'd be obliged if you'd help me take a look at him."

"Sure." The sneer seemed to be permanently implanted on the young man's lips. He walked outside, with Rhodes right on his heels. Just after turning right, heading for the corral a few feet away, Rhodes slammed a strong punch into Billy's kidney.

Billy groaned and staggered forward a few paces, stopping against the log fence of the corral. Rhodes stepped up behind him, grabbed the back of Billy's neck. He lifted the young man's head back, and then slammed his face into the top of an upright fence post.

Billy sagged, and grasped the fence for support. He turned his head and looked at Rhodes with pain-dulled eyes. His pulpy, fat nose trickled blood, and he spit out two teeth. "Jesus, God Almighty," he said, the words whistling through the new gap in his teeth. "What in hell you go and do that fer?"

"To get your attention. Now that I've got it, you might be of a mood to listen."

"Wha—"

Rhodes shook his head. He yanked Billy around to face him. Then he pulled Billy's two pistols and dropped them in a water trough. "How much did your old man pay for those mules?" he asked roughly.

"Seventy-five apiece," Billy said. His brain was dizzied by the pain and shock.

"Who brought 'em?"

"Couple of fellers."

"Two?"

"Yeah," Billy said, nodding. "No, no, it was three."

"You know 'em?"

"Seen 'em before but don't know their names. Mitch knows 'em."

"Mitch?"

"My brother."

"You know where they were headin'?"

Billy shook his head. Suddenly he spun. Leaning over the fence, he vomited.

"Shit," Rhodes breathed. He shrugged and went back inside. Flake and Clem Waters were still dickering over things, while Eliza tried to ride herd on the two children. "Hey, Mitch," Rhodes said in his friendly voice. "Billy says he needs your help."

Mitch strutted to the door, looking like a slightly older version of his brother. He stepped outside, spotted his brother and began to turn back, a curse on his lips.

Rhodes had seen a barrel of ax handles just inside the door. As he walked out behind Mitch, he grabbed one. When Mitch began to turn, Rhodes waited until he was just about all the way around before he slapped Mitch a good shot in the forehead with the piece of hickory.

Mitch fell sideways, and managed to stab out an arm and brace himself on the sod wall of the store.

Rhodes brought the ax handle back and then two-handed it across Mitch's side, staving in five, maybe six ribs.

Mitch bit his lip and a few tears of pain seeped out of his eyes. He turned and let his back slam against the wall and whimpered as the slight impact jarred all the cracked ribs.

"I have no time for foolin' around with you, boy," Rhodes said calmly. "Who'd your old man buy those mules from?"

"Clyde Laver," Mitch gasped, hands wrapped around his middle, trying to prevent his ribs from moving any more.

"Who else?"

"Um, I . . . Damn, this hurts, mister. Why in hell'd you have to do that?"

"Felt like it," Rhodes lied. "Who else?"

"Floyd Decker and Orson Mackey."

"How much you pay them?"

"Sixty bucks each."

"Damn," Rhodes muttered. One of the Waterses was lying. He shrugged. It didn't matter. He grabbed Mitch's two pistols—ones that matched his brother's, and tossed them in the trough, too. He glanced at Billy, who was still hanging half over the fence.

Rhodes walked inside, still with the ax handle in hand. He stomped up to the makeshift counter and slammed the ax handle down on it. Clem Waters leaped almost a foot in the air. When he landed again, his eyes were wide, and Rhodes could see the man's carotid pulsing wildly.

"What the hell was that all about?" Waters asked. He was regaining control of himself and began to relax. He had had troublemakers in the trading post before. Billy and Mitch would straighten it out. They always did.

Rhodes never took his eyes off Waters. "You have two hundred forty bucks, Mr. Flake?" he asked.

"I don't think that . . ."

"Answer me," Rhodes ordered.

"Yes," Flake said. He wondered just what was going on here.

61

"Hand it to Mr. Waters. Toss in another ten for the grub and such."

"Like hell," Waters protested. "Those mules cost me damn good money."

Rhodes reached out, grabbed a handful of Water's shirt, and dragged him halfway across the counter. "Listen to me, you thievin' pig. You'll sell Mr. Flake here those mules for two hundred forty bucks and throw in these supplies here for nothing — to compensate for all the troubles you've caused him and his companions."

"Hey, you've got no right to . . ."

"You have no right to bleed people dry, you toad-faced son of a bitch. I know where you got those mules, I know who you got 'em from and how much you paid for 'em."

"Billy! Mitch!" Waters bellowed. His eyes grew worried when there was no response.

"They're taking it easy for a while." Rhodes said. His face and voice hardened. "Now, you either take the two hundred for all this stuff or —"

"Hey, you said two forty. No, two fifty," a nervous Clem Waters bleated.

"That was before you started being a pain in my ass. Now, you either take the two hundred, or I'll mash you to a pulp and we'll just take 'em."

"That'd be robbery!"

"It ain't such a wonderful thing being on the other side of it is it, you maggot. Make up your mind. Now!"

"I'll take the money!" Waters screeched.

"Pay him, Mr. Flake." He paused. "Give him another twenty. We'll be taking that bay mare out there, too." Rhodes released Waters's shirt.

Flake had been watching with some interest all the while, He smiled when he pulled out his money and paid Waters. "Eliza, children, the packages," he said. As his wife and the two boys gathered up the supplies, Flake looked at Rhodes and asked, "Can we trust him not to shoot us in the back as we leave?"

Rhodes laughed. "I'd trust him about as far as I could toss your wagon." He looked back at Waters. "Did those three thieves try to sell you anything else didn't belong to 'em?"

Waters shook his head. "Nope. They had a pretty locket, with gold filagreein' all around, but they said it wasn't for sale."

At the mention of the locket, Eliza had stopped and stared.

"That yours, ma'am?" Rhodes asked.

"Yessir."

"Maybe one day you'll get it back. Now, Mr. Waters, if you'd be so kind to tell me what those scoundrels looked like."

Waters considered another protest, but he immediately ruled that out. He didn't know where Mitch and Billy were, and he was deathly afraid that this man had killed them. That set a chill up his spine. He figured he'd better answer. He could try to kill him later.

"Clyde Laver's a short, skinny fellow. He's got a face like a weasel, kind of thin and pointy. Orson Mackey's more close to your height and size, but he's got a lot of gut, and snowy white hair, though he's only thirty. Floyd Decker's a dandy when he's got the wherewithal. The scar on his face kind of sets him apart, though."

"Scar?" Rhodes asked.

"Yeah, a big, nasty one. Starts near the center of his forehead. Goes down the right side of his nose, just missin' the inside of his right eye and curls around the lip to his chin." As he spoke, he traced the scar on his face.

Rhodes nodded. "You about ready, Mr. Flake?"

"I suppose I am."

"Mr. Waters, if you'd be so kind to escort us outside."

"I don't think . . ."

"That's a good policy. Don't think; just do."

Trembling, Waters climbed over the counter and walked toward the door. It seemed as if he were walking to his doom. As soon as he stepped outside, he heard a moan, and looked to his right. "Mitch!" he shouted. Then he saw his other son. "Billy!" He started to go to his boys, but Rhodes warned him off.

"Saddle the bay, Mr. Flake. Mr. Waters will round up your mules, won't you, Mr. Waters?"

Waters glowered, but nodded.

Chapter Eight

Rhodes tied Clem Waters to a fence post, knotting the rope enough to keep him there for a while but not so tight as to leave him dead. Then Rhodes and the others pushed on, herding Flake's mules. They moved as swiftly as they dared, hoping to get back before nightfall.

At their first stop—an hour after leaving—Rhodes called Flake aside. "This might be immodest, Mr. Flake, but I'd suggest have the missus ride astraddle," he said in low tones.

Flake did not seem as horrified as Rhodes had thought he would be. Still, he was contemplative for a few moments. "Your reasoning, Mr. Rhodes?" he finally asked.

"Call me Travis," Rhodes said. "Ridin' that side-saddle is slowing us down quite a bit. She rides astraddle, we can make better time."

Flake stared at Rhodes a moment, as if looking to see a lecherous grin on the man's face. He saw nothing of the kind. He looked up at the sky. "How much time before dark?" Flake asked quietly.

"Two, three hours, as best I can figure it."

"And it took us, what six hours, seven to get to that trading post?"

Rhodes nodded. "About that."

Flake thought about that for a bit. The idea

65

bothered him, since it was an indecent way for a woman to travel. On the other hand, he knew they must get back to the others as quickly as possible. He did not like the idea of leaving Hickman and the women and children on their own too long. Phineas Hickman was a competent, hard-working man, if a little hotheaded at times. Still, he was only one man, and after the Indian attack yesterday, Flake had turned much more wary. He had heard about Indian attacks, of course, but had discounted a good many of those accounts as the ramblings of frightened nonbelievers. Now, however, he could no longer dispute those stories.

"What will we do for a saddle?" Flake asked, still working the problem over in his mind.

"She can use mine. Or yours, if that will make you both feel more comfortable with this distasteful idea."

"What about you?"

"I'll ride bareback. It's nothing new." He regretted now not having grabbed an extra saddle at Water's trading post, and he berated himself for not having the foresight to figure on this problem.

Flake needed to think no longer. True, this was an immodest thing, but sometimes sacrifices were forced on people. Such was the case now. "So it shall be, Travis," Flake said firmly. "It'll take some arranging, though, if you don't mind. I believe Eliza will be much more comfortable using my saddle." He paused and grinned weakly. "Or at least as comfortable as she can be under the circumstances."

Rhodes nodded. "You go break the news to her. I'll start moving saddles."

It did not take long, and soon they were all back on the move again. A red-faced, embarrassed Eliza

Flake rode astraddle on the Mormons' horse. The two boys—six-year-old Hyrum Flake and five-year-old Heber Hickman—rode on one of the mules, looking a little worried, but excited at the same time. Flake rode Rhodes's palomino, and Rhodes rode bareback on the Indian pinto.

They stopped only twice more, for less than ten minutes each time to give the animals a short breather, before all were riding again. Rhodes kept them all at a good, steady pace.

They found Hickman and the others a half hour after dark had come. Rhodes's keen eyesight had picked out a flicker of flame against the spreading shadows of the night. Flake called out as the small group eased up on the horses, walking them into camp.

It was something of a joyous reunion. Hickman and the others had been certain that Rhodes was going to kill Eliza, Flake, and the youngsters. Hickman still believed that Rhodes was one of the ruffians who had brought them all this trouble. So it was with great surprise that he helped his son and Flake's son off the mule. Though it was dark, and no one could see his face, he avoided looking at Eliza as her husband helped her down from the horse.

"Come," he said, much relieved, "we have food ready." He felt ashamed, and it sounded in his voice when he said, "We even took the liberty of making some of your coffee for you, Mr. Rhodes."

"Obliged," Rhodes said flatly. In the short time he had been with the Mormons, he had come to like Flake. The man might be a stiff, strict patriarch, but he had no give-up in him. Flake had shown little sign of the wound he had received just yesterday, nor had he let that slow him any. Flake also had the intelligence and common sense to know that sometimes one had to adapt to things that were strange or repugnant to them. He figured he would never have convinced Hickman to let his wife ride astraddle. Hickman was, as far as Rhodes could see, an unbending, holier-than-thou prig.

"If it's not too much trouble, Mister Hickman, I'd be obliged if you were to bring me a mug of that coffee."

"Where will you be?" Hickman asked, surprised and a little annoyed that Rhodes would consider him a delivery boy.

"Tending the animals. They've been hard used and need care."

Hickman suddenly felt like a fool. "I'll help you, sir," he said contritely. "Have a seat at the fire, Erastus. You have been through much of late and need to rest yourself."

"Thank you, Phineas," Flake said gratefully.

Rhodes moved off toward the small herd of animals and began unsaddling his palomino. A few moments later, Hickman arrived, a cup of coffee in his hand. He handed it to Rhodes, who nodded his thanks and took a sip. "Obliged, Mr. Hickman," he said as the hot coffee seeped from his stomach into his veins.

"Please, call me Phineas—or Fin," Hickman said. He regretted having treated Rhodes so poorly. "And there's no need for thanks. As Erastus has said more than once, we are so deep in debt to you that we'll never be able to repay it."

"Hell, anyone would've done the same," Rhodes said lamely. Even to him it sounded false.

"Hardly." He paused, looking at the dim blob of Rhodes's face, which had only one side faintly lit from the fire. He did not know what he saw in Rhodes's strong, hard face, but he knew it was not depravity. "I must apologize," he finally said very softly, "for the way I've treated you, Mr. Rhodes." He was embarrassed and sounded it. "There was no call for it."

"Sure there was," Rhodes said agreeably. "I would've acted the same to a stranger had I just been molested by some punks who I offered my hospitality to."

"All well and good, Mr. Rhodes—Travis. But I didn't need to continue my ill feelings toward you after you had saved us from those Injuns. We would've been dead for sure if you hadn't come back."

Rhodes shrugged and took another sip of coffee. He wanted to get off the topic of how wonderful he was. Such talk always made him uncomfortable. "It's too bad," he offered after a bit of silence, "that you don't partake of coffee, Phineas. It's right pleasurable at times like these."

Hickman smiled weakly. "I have enjoyed it, Travis. Back before . . . until I became a Saint."

Rhodes nodded. "How long ago was that?"

"Five, no, six years ago."

"I admire the strength of your faith, Mr. Hickman," Rhodes said honestly. "I couldn't have done it."

Hickman was surprised. Rhodes seemed to be a man who could do anything he set his mind to. It was strange hearing him disparaging himself like that.

Rhodes took another drink of coffee and then turned and set the mug on a rock nearby. "Well, I'd best get back to work or I'll never get over there to eat before the others chaw it all down."

Hickman was horrified at Rhodes's lack of tact—until Rhodes chuckled a little. Then the Mormon joined in the light laughter. With renewed spirits, Hickman threw himself into the work. He did not want to be outdone by Rhodes again.

It took a while to get all the horses and mules taken care of, but finally the work was done. Rhodes and Hickman headed to the fire. There was plenty of food left, and the two men dug in—after Flake said grace for the two—enjoying the fare.

Just after starting, though, Rhodes looked over at Flake. "This is delicious, and mighty filling. I'm obliged for it after such a long day."

Flake nodded, then a question arose in his eyes. "But?" he asked, knowing that more was to be said.

"But I'd recommend you did without fires. If that's not possible, then make the fire small, preferably in the light, and put it out quickly."

"Why?" Hickman asked.

"Because," Flake said, answering for Rhodes, "we found your camp by the light of the fire. If we could do that, certainly more Injuns could, too." He looked at Rhodes. "Isn't that right, Travis?"

"Sure is. I've never been out this way before, but others've told me about it. Since many of those tales are stretched a mite, I didn't know whether to believe them or not. This particular one was true enough, I found out today."

Flake nodded. "Should we douse these flames right away, Travis?" he asked.

Rhodes shook his head. "I reckon once in a while won't hurt." When he finished eating, Rhodes pulled out a cigar. He did not smoke them often, but enjoyed one now and again. He held it up.

"This against your religion, too, Erastus?" he asked.

"Alas, yes," Flake said. He sighed. "There was a time, though, when I would have joined you."

Rhodes nodded. "Phineas said he once drank coffee."

Flake smiled. "As did I. And I drank to excess of spirituous liquors. But that was before we found the path of the Lord. Before we saw the light of truth. I regret those and other low amusements in which I had taken part." He paused. "You know, Mr. Rhodes, you, too, could find the path of enlightenment. We would be happy to show you the way."

Rhodes looked over the cigar he was lighting with a match, cupping it against the wind. The breezes whipped up the light smoke of the fire and swirled it around some before carrying it off. "As I told you before Mr. Flake, I don't hold to any one religion."

"But that should change. You'll need to see the light in this life, it there's to be a proper life for you after death."

"I don't subscribe to that, Mr. Flake. God'll judge me when I get to the Pearly Gates. And I doubt he'll be lookin' to see how many times I sat inside a church, or how much preachifying I've done. No, sir, I figure he'll take a look at what I've done here and judge me accordingly. I hope Saint Peter will recommend my entry into Heaven, but I don't see that there's a lot I can do about that decision now."

"Yes, but . . ."

Rhodes held up his hand, indicating he wanted Flake to stop. Flake did, and Rhodes said, "I'm not going to convert to your way, Mr. Flake. And since I don't want harsh words to come between us, I'd be obliged if you wasn't to harp on it anymore."

Flake suddenly looked like he was fighting a major battle within himself, but finally a serene look crossed his face. "My apologies, Mr. Rhodes." He smiled a little. "Part of our way includes spreading the word of God to the unenlightened. Sometimes, though, I forget that not all the unenlightened want to be enlightened." He paused. "Under normal circumstances, I might be a little put out by your obstinance," he added, pausing to smile again to take any sting out of the words. "But seeing as how much you've done for us, I can't with clear conscience keep proselytizing to you."

Rhodes nodded, accepting.

Silence grew as the womenfolk put the children to bed in the wagons. While they were gone, Flake asked, "What'll you do now, Travis?"

Rhodes shrugged. "Go back to what I was doing before, I suppose."

"Searching for something you won't know until you find it, eh?"

Rhodes smiled just a little and blew out a smoke ring. "I've been footloose since the war," he explained. "Maybe one day I'll find whatever it is I'm lookin' for."

Flake battled down the urge to preach again, and finally managed to succeed. Instead he said, "You're free to travel with us, if you've a mind to." He grinned. "And I promise not to preach to you anymore."

Rhodes laughed. "That might be a mighty big promise to keep, Mister Flake," he said, "considerin' how big a sinner I am."

"I'll try to refrain then," Flake said as he and

Hickman joined in the laughter. "So," Flake asked when the three had quieted again, "will you join us?"

The decision was not hard to make. He was alone in Indian country. The two Mormon men might not be Indian fighters, but at least it would be three guns against the Indians instead of one. He could put up with an occasional sermon for the comfort of a little safety. "I will," he said with a firm nod.

Chapter Nine

The three men talked about their plans a while, but then Flake rose unsteadily to his feet. "If you'll excuse me, friends," he said, voice distant. "I'm afraid my wound has left me in a weakened state, considering the exertions of the day. I feel a night of good rest will be beneficial."

"By all means, rest, Erastus," Hickman said, jumping up to help Flake get to the wagon.

"Goodnight, Mr. Flake," Rhodes said quietly.

Hickman returned in a few minutes, after helping Flake. He sat by the fire. He cut a sliver off a small piece of board in the fire and picked at his teeth with it. "You think we'll make it, Travis?" he finally asked.

"Make it where?"

"Deseret."

Rhodes stared at the cherry-red tip of his cigar a moment. "Oh, I expect you'll make it eventually — if the Indians or desperadoes or the weather don't get you first."

"Those are all too real possibilities, aren't they?" Hickman asked. He did not seem worried, merely concerned, which was sensible.

"Yes, Mr. Hickman, they are."

"Well, I don't think we can do much about the first two of those possibilities, short of praying for

God's intervention, which we will do fervently, I can assure you, Travis. But what about the third? Can we do anything about that?"

Rhodes smiled. "I ain't ever known a man who could change the weather," he said with a chuckle.

Hickman, who had been serious, looked at him in shock, before the humor of it caught him. He laughed a little. "Indeed, sir, that has never happened to my knowledge." He sighed. "Can we do anything to beat the weather, then," he asked.

"You askin' my advice?"

Hickman nodded. "I am."

"Was I you, I'd stop at the first town or fort I came to and plant myself for the winter."

"But it's not yet September," Hickman said in a mild protest. "I know we were late in leaving, but there should be ample time to reach Deseret. Shouldn't there?"

"How long did it take you to get here?" Rhodes countered.

"Two weeks, perhaps a day or two more."

"Even you have to realize that this is the easy part. There's enough grass for the animals, even game to keep you in meat. Most important, this land is, for most purposes, flat, and most of the rivers you needed to ford to get here were either narrow, shallow or both."

"That has been the case, yes."

"What're you going to do when you hit the mountains? I've never seen them, but reliable friends have told me they're unlike anything you've ever seen. Hell, half of them have to be gone around, or you'll have to winch your wagons up and down. The rivers out there are killers, too, from all that's been told me. They are deep, have large waterfalls and are fast-running. If it took you two weeks to get here, it might take you two weeks to make a few miles once you hit the mountains. Besides, winter sets in early in many places, particularly high mountains. I doubt if you'd like to get caught in a blizzard on the side of some mountain."

"I should think not." Hickman sat in thought, nodding. All that Rhodes had said made plenty of sense, though it would go against the grain to not push onward with all dispatch. However, as the elder here, Erastus Flake must make the decision.

They covered the same ground with Flake in the morning as they broke their fast around a small fire. Flake listened, nodding from time to time. Finally, he said, "I think such a decision is wise. But I'll wait until we're in the mountains, if possible, before making my final decision." He nodded at Rhodes. "Thank you for your observations, Travis. They're most helpful."

Rhodes nodded and shrugged. "No thanks needed." He pitched the last of his coffee on the fire. "We best get a move on if we're to make any progress."

Rhodes saddled his horse and loaded his supplies on his mule. Then he helped out where he could. As he worked, he sidled up to Flake. "A suggestion?" he said.

"By all means, Travis. All your advice has been top-notch so far."

"You and Fin should ride. Your wife, too, maybe. Let Minerva and Sarah drive the wagons. Put the kids in back."

"But there are no seats on the wagons."

Rhodes shrugged. "Either nail a chair in place, or tie it in place, if you can. If not, just pile up blankets and such and let 'em kneel there."

Flake pondered that. "It would make for faster

times, wouldn't it?" he asked, almost as if talking to himself.

"It would," Rhodes agreed.

Flake nodded. "Yes, by God, we'll do it."

Rhodes grinned ruefully. "Wish I'd thought of it earlier, though," he said.

"Such are the trials of life, Mr. Rhodes. We'll make adjustments easily enough." He paused. "If you would be so kind as to unload your mule while we take care of the other things, I'll have Eliza ride, too."

"All right. Dig out the sidesaddle and I'll put it on the mule soon as it's unloaded. I'll have to store my things in one of the wagons, though."

"Such a small amount will be no trouble."

Flake went to tell Hickman about the change in plans, while Rhodes headed back to his mule. It didn't really take all that long, but the sun — and the heat — was well up by the time they finally pulled out.

Rhodes was riding bareback again, with Flake borrowing his saddle. Rhodes did have the sawed-off shotgun and some extra ammunition with him, though, just in case. He ranged out ahead, stopping on every small knoll he encountered to sweep the countryside, alert. He turned the small caravan a little northwestward, so they could avoid going anywhere near Waters's trading post. Rhodes wasn't afraid of Waters and his sons, but he could see no reason for trying to start more trouble.

In late afternoon, he spotted four Indians off in the distance. He figured they had spotted him, too, since they veered off the course they had been taking in order to head toward him.

Rhodes turned and loped back to the wagons, and explained what he saw. The two Mormon men were

77

concerned but not afraid. "What do we do?" Flake asked.

"Best be ready for them." He began issuing directions. By the time the warriors appeared on the horizon, they had positioned the wagons parallel to each other, each facing in the opposite direction. Ropes ran from the lead mules of each wagon to the back of the other, so the animals could not run off. The enclosure was wide enough to get the three horses and one mule inside. Eliza held the reins to those animals, while Minerva and Sarah took care of the children inside one of the wagons.

It seemed terribly hot as the small group waited to see what the warriors would do. As the Indians neared, it did not seem to the people inside the wagon fort that they were a war party.

The Indians stopped twenty yards or so from the wagons. One of them shouted in his language, which none of the whites could understand.

"I wish we knew what he was saying," Flake mused.

"One way to find out, I guess," Rhodes said. He walked the Indian pony out as Flake and Hickman held up the ropes. Rhodes leaped onto the pony's back and rode slowly toward the Indians. His scattergun lay crossways on the horse, directly in front of Rhodes.

He stopped not far from the Indians. The one who had spoken before held up his right hand, palm outward. Tentatively, Rhodes did the same. Then the Indian rattled off a bunch of words in his own language.

Rhodes shrugged and lifted his hands, palms up.

"Where'd you get the damn pony?" the Indian asked in English. His accent was thick, making it a little hard for Rhodes to understand.

"Who wants to know?" Rhodes asked quietly.

"Me," the warrior said. He jabbed his chest with his thumb. "I am Yellow Horse, big medicine among the Lakota."

"Pleased to meet you, Chief," Rhodes said sarcastically. "I'm Travis Rhodes, big medicine among my people."

"Where'd you get the damn pony?" Yellow Horse asked again.

"Bought him," Rhodes said blandly.

"Where?"

Rhodes pointed over his shoulder. "Tradin' post back thataway."

The Indian nodded. "No Hair lives there."

"That's the one I bought the horse from. He had some others, too, looked a lot like this."

"It belongs to Bad Arm."

"His arm all broke up, like it doesn't work right?" Rhodes asked. He remembered that one of the Indians he had killed had a deformed arm.

Yellow Horse nodded.

"I seen him back on the trail a ways." He pointed again. "He was killed. Shot up somethin' fierce. There wasn't much left of him after the wolves and buzzards got done with him, though enough was left that I could tell he had a bad arm."

Yellow Horse looked grim and angry. "You kill him?" he demanded.

"Nope. Didn't kill him nor the other two we found." Rhodes was concerned. These Indians just might kill him for the hell of it. Especially if they did not believe what he was saying.

"You kill 'em," Yellow Horse said. This time it wasn't a question.

"No I didn't," Rhodes said evenly. "I think it was No Hair and his men who did it," he lied blithely.

"That's probably why they had some other Lakota ponies in the corral."

Yellow Horse stared hard at Rhodes, who kept the gaze. Finally Yellow Horse turned his pony's head. The four Lakotas trotted off, heading in the direction of Waters's trading post.

Rhodes breathed a sigh of relief. That had been a mite too close for him. He turned and rode back to the others. Flake and Hickman were already untying the ropes that held the two wagons in place.

"That was some pack of lies you told those Injuns," Flake said as he worked.

"You don't approve?" Rhodes asked, not sure if Flake was chiding him or lauding him.

Flake grinned. It was a worried grin, but a real one just the same. "It goes against God's wishes," he intoned. The grin widened a little. "However, God doth move in mysterious ways at times."

"That he does. But we'd better move in fast ways unless we want another visit with those Injuns."

"We can beat them," Hickman said cockily.

"Don't be a damn fool," Rhodes snapped, looking down on Hickman from his perch on the Indian horse.

"Well, you took care of those other three easy enough," Hickman said defensively. "We would've done the same, too, though possibly at greater risk."

"Only reason I was able to send those three devils over the divide was because of surprise," Rhodes said harshly. "I ain't prideful enough to figure I'm good enough to kill three hardened warriors in a battle, let alone four of them. Those boys decide to come back here and cause us some devilment, we are going to be in deep trouble."

"But they are just Lammanites—Indians."

"You keep thinking that way, and we'll find your

80

bones bleaching under the sun out here one day. I don't know much about Indians, Mr. Hickman, but I know they fight well."

"We have God on our side, Mr. Rhodes," Hickman said piously.

"That may be so, Phineas, but those Injuns don't know that."

"Enough arguing, gentlemen," Flake said harshly. "We have enough to do and enough troubles without you two having such dissension."

Hickman and Rhodes nodded. Within minutes, they were moving.

Chapter Ten

Everyone in the small group worked silently so they could get an early start the next morning, when Erastus Flake glanced up. "Look," he said, pointing.

The others turned to look southeast. They watched for some moments as strings of black smoke spiraled toward the sun.

"I reckon the Lakota have taken care of Mr. Clem Waters and his two damned offspring," Rhodes said.

The others nodded. "And a well-deserved death it was, too," Flake said quietly.

Rhodes turned toward the bearded Mormon. "I would've thought you'd be horrified at such a thing, seeing as how you're a God-fearing Christian and all."

Flake remained deadly serious. "We Saints have been persecuted since Joseph Smith had his revelation, Mr. Rhodes. We know the might of the unholy, and Waters and his sons were among the unholy."

"Am I?" Rhodes asked. He didn't care one way or the other; he just wanted to know where he stood.

Flake shook his head and stroked his beard. "No, sir, you are not. You may not be of the faith, but your actions show that you are not of the unholy either. Your morals might be questionable at times, but your heart seems correct, despite that all."

"Gee, thanks," Rhodes said dryly.

"You shouldn't make fun, Mr. Rhodes," Flake said solemnly. "While we are taught to turn the other cheek, we feel there is a time when one must visit vengeance on our persecutors. Clem Waters was an evil man, and got only what he deserved."

Flake paused, thinking, his eyes watching the lazy spiral of smoke, though he was no longer really seeing it. "I had thought at first, when I saw what you had done to Waters's two sons that you had overstepped propriety, Travis. But then I realized what kind of man Waters really was. It was evident in the way he treated us, with the disdain he held for us. He was about to rob us. He was not going to use a gun, of course, but it was robbery all the same. I also believe he would've killed us had he been given a chance." Flake sighed. "Ah, well," he said. "These are nothing more than the ramblings of an old man."

"Don't say such things, husband," Eliza said quietly, as she moved alongside him and took his arm in her hands and patted it some. Sarah had moved up on the other side of Flake.

Rhodes watched, wondering about things. Sarah had been introduced as "Aunt Sarah," but Rhodes had never been able to find out just whose aunt. He wondered if perhaps she was also one of Flake's wives and was addressed as aunt to hide that fact from outsiders. It mattered to Rhodes only that he wanted to see if she were unencumbered by a hus-

83

band. If so, he might seek her out to spend time with her. If she had a husband, Rhodes wanted no part of her.

He shrugged and looked away. The smoke was still floating upward. Rhodes went back to saddling his horse. "We best hurry some, folks," he said. "Those Lakota just might come back looking for us."

They pulled out as quickly as possible, though not before they were ready. Being unprepared would slow them more in the long run than cutting a few minutes off their departure time in the morning.

They continued along the north bank of the Platte, staying as near to the water as they could, but moving cross country when the bends in the river were too much to follow. They made good time, but often had to wait to stop for the night until it was after dark. Though they were traveling on the north side of the Platte, which was not held in as much favor by those traveling the Oregon Trail, it got enough use that forage for the horses at the better campsites was hard to find, making the small group push on into the darkness at times. In addition, the better campsites known to travelers also would be known to Indians. They hoped they would not see any more Indians. The ones they had met thus far were more than enough.

Hunting was somewhat easier, though, with large herds of buffalo seen almost every day, and though the Platte was mighty muddy, it still provided more than enough water.

Rhodes continued to ride out a little ways from the two wagons to keep a lookout for trouble. He rarely got out of sight of the wagons, though to the

Mormons, he was generally a small speck on the horizon. He also did the hunting, and it was a rare day when he returned empty-handed. Even that was not bad, as the travelers made do with stores they had brought from back in the States.

A week and a half past Waters's trading post, they saw another. This one was in a little better shape, having been a Pony Express station not too long ago, and so had seen almost constant use. The group did not stop, though. All of them had had enough of isolated trading posts for this journey, and saw no reason to place themselves at the mercy of those often heartless men.

They stopped for a day at Fort McPherson, where the Platte split into north and south branches. The wagons were in good shape and did not need repairs, which was a relief. The animals also were still in good shape, but they, and the humans, needed to rest a bit.

It did them all some good to spend a full day there, and they were in better spirits the morning after, as they all sat to breakfast. When they were finished, Rhodes said, "I believe I'll be going my own way from here."

"What?" Flake asked surprised. "Why?"

While he had been riding these past several weeks, Rhodes decided that he would try the gold fields in the forbidding Rocky Mountains. He had little other training, except handling a gun. Before the war he had been a farmer, and he had vowed long ago never to go back to such work. A man could make his fortune just picking up gold from the ground or from where it was clearly visible in fast-rushing, frigid streams. Or so he had heard. He discounted a fair portion of such talk as being dreams, but it was a fact that some men had gotten rich with some hard work—and luck—out there. There was no reason, he figured, that he could not join those ranks.

"I aim to see if Lady Luck will favor me with a kiss in the gold fields," he said without apology.

"The Good Lord would be more likely to show favor for you if you would but believe," Flake said. "Rather than depending on luck—which is more the devil's work, if you ask me."

"I didn't," Rhodes said flatly.

Flake glowered. "There is salvation in hard toil, of building things, of growing things. Good, honest, true work."

"I've done my share of farming, and I ain't going to do any more of it. And I don't know how to make things." He shrugged.

"But we can show you the way, Mr. Rhodes. We . . ."

"Leave him alone, Brother Flake," Hickman said. When Flake turned his scowl toward his companions, Hickman said, "Mr. Rhodes is not of our faith, and has indicated no willingness to join it."

"I know, Brother Hickman, but now is the time to reach him."

"No, it's not," Hickman said flatly. "Mr. Rhodes has given us service far beyond what we'd expect even from Saints. He's not beholden to us; rather the opposite, and if he wishes to not be preached at, we should respect that. Maybe some day he'll see the light, but for now . . . well, I wish we could offer him salvation. But we can't, so we should let him live as he wishes. We have no right to demand that he follow our ways."

"Sad, but true, Phineas," Flake said with a large sigh. "My apologies, Travis. I've overstepped my bounds."

Rhodes shrugged. "We all have our faults, Erastus," Rhodes said with a small grin.

Flake nodded. "I wish you'd reconsider leaving us, Travis," he said. "We are still deep in Indian country and as you once told us, there is safety in numbers." He smiled a little, abashed. "We have enjoyed your company, Mr. Rhodes. Alas, probably more so than you have enjoyed ours."

"I've enjoyed your companionship, Erastus." He laughed. "It's your preachin' I find tedious."

Flake laughed, too. "Then I must prepare my sermons better if I am to reach the wanderers." He paused. "So, what do you say, Travis. Will you keep on the trail with us?"

"I'm obliged for your offer, Erastus, but I really think I should be movin' on."

Flake smiled. "In a hurry to get nowhere?"

Rhodes chuckled. "Does sound kind of foolish when it's put like that." He sipped some coffee as he thought about it.

"How about you go with us as far as Fort Laramie?" Hickman said. "You can head south into the Colorado Territory from there, if that's your wish."

Rhodes nodded. "Reckon that'd be all right." Despite the piousness, which was sometimes a little overwhelming, Rhodes had come to like the Mormons. Or at least this small group of them. They were interesting, well-educated, full of chatter. That a good dose of the chatter was based on their Book of Mormon, lessened their appeal only a little. Besides, it would be safer riding along with them than going by himself.

"Good," Flake said with a great grin. "Very good." They all stood and headed to their chores.

A week and a half of fairly easy traveling later, they pulled to a stop at Fort Laramie. They were allowed to make a small camp down near the Laramie River not far from the commissary.

While they were setting it up, an old man, dressed in buckskins and carrying an old muzzle-loading rifle in hand, wandered up. "I'm Joe Bonner," the man said, spitting a stream of brown tobacco juice into the grass.

Flake introduced Hickman and Rhodes. "What can I do for you, Mr. Bonner?" Flake asked.

"You folks heading on?" he asked.

Flake nodded. "Yes, we're expected in Deseret."

"Nice place," he commented. "But you'd be wise to sit out the winter here."

"So we've been told. What's your interest in this?" Flake asked, a little irritated.

"My interest is in findin' work. I'm available for guidin'. Best damn mountain guide in all the goddamn Rockies."

"We might be able to talk business then," Flake said. "Will you be available in the next few days?"

"Hell," Bonner said, spitting again. He swiped the back of his left hand across his mouth. "I ain't goin' nowhere in the next few days. Nor in the next few months either. No, this ol' chil's fixin' to set out the winter right here." He shrugged. "Actually, I'll be spending the winter a few miles from here. I got me a Cheyenne wife. Helps me keep warm of a winter."

"You're afraid of heading west?" Flake asked gruffly.

"Hell, such things don't shine with this ol' hoss," Bonner grumbled. "There was a time I'd cut your goddamn heart out and then eat the damn thing for sayin' that to me." He paused to spit. "But I'm not so spunky anymore."

"Good thing, too," Rhodes said quietly. When

Bonner looked at him, Rhodes added, "I'd hate like hell to have to drop an old fart like you."

"Cocky little bastard, ain't you?" Bonner said.

Rhodes shrugged. "You got any more business here?" he asked.

Bonner spit again and glanced from one man to the other. "Reckon not," he said. He turned and shuffled away.

"You were mighty hard on him, Travis," Flake said. "He's just an old man who needs a job."

"I expect," someone interjected.

The three men turned to face the newcomer, who stuck out his hand. "Lieutenant George Hale. Bonner's a pest, but we let him hang around 'cause we feel sorry for him. He was one of the best of the mountain men, but that was thirty, forty years ago. Same with being a guide. He can still do it—when he isn't drunk. These days, about all he does is hang around here, looking for a handout."

"Is that what he wanted from us?" Flake asked. He was not adverse to giving money for a good cause.

Hale nodded. "Yeah, he'd promise to come back in the spring to guide you, but ask for some money to tide him over. Then he'd buy some whiskey and head back to the Cheyenne village. It's a sad case, but he can really try a man's patience."

Flake nodded, glad that he had not given Bonner anything.

"He was right about one thing, though," Hale added. "You folks'd be a lot better off if you would stick out the winter here, or some other place."

"It's that bad?" Flake asked.

Hale nodded. "Haven't you heard of the Donners?" When the others shook their heads, Hale went on. "A group left Independence late, just like

89

you folks. They got stuck high in the Sierra Nevada in snow. Wound up eating each other."

The small party was shocked.

"Heed Bonner's advice—or mine if you feel more comfortable—but heed it." He tipped his cap, turned, and walked off.

Chapter Eleven

Bonner appeared again the next day. He just came up, squatted at the fire, set his rifle down, and reached for the coffeepot. He grabbed the nearest tin mug with his left hand and poured himself a cup. Then he eased himself into a sit, legs crossed.

"It's usual for a guest to ask if he'd be welcome before he starts helping himself to other folks' victuals," Rhodes said. He sat on a stool a few feet back from the fire.

"It's just coffee, boy."

"Don't matter."

"Hell, sonny, them folks ain't gonna give a shit I take a cup of goddamn coffee."

"It ain't theirs, you old coot. It's mine."

Bonner shrugged. "It's still only one goddamn cup of coffee."

"You go around takin' other people's things and you're liable to get knocked on your ass," Rhodes commented.

Bonner shrugged again. "Damn, you are one tight-ass chil', ain't you?"

"Might be," Rhodes agreed. "But then again, I don't go robbin' folks."

"You callin' me a thief, you snotty little bastard?"

Rhodes grinned a little. "I am."

91

"Was a time I'd've knocked your ass clear over the river there, sonny boy," Bonner snarled.

"That time's long past."

"I could still do it," Bonner insisted.

"You couldn't whip your way out of a lodge full of dead rabbits, old man." Rhodes was trying to remain civil, though it was growing more difficult in the face of Bonner's obstinacy.

"I'll show ye, ye goddamn buffler pecker." Bonner set his coffee down and began pushing himself up.

"Sit down, old man," Rhodes ordered.

"Like hell," Bonner puffed.

"You get up, old man, and the next step you take'll be into your grave."

Halfway to his feet, Bonner looked at Rhodes. Hate was in the old man's eyes, but there was a fair measure of pain. It was not a physical pain, just the pain of a once-vigorous man who was suffering too many ailments of age. Where once he was full of energy and the juices of life, now he was simply a dried-out old shell of what he was.

Bonner sat back down, fighting back the tears of frustration and self-disgust. He shakily picked up the coffee.

Rhodes, who had gotten partly up to go help the old mountain man, sat back down. He could see in Bonner's face that he wanted no help. He still had a lot of pride, and Rhodes figured he could probably still hold his own in many a fight.

"There anyplace near this damn fort where a couple of fellahs like us could get us somethin' a tad stronger'n coffee?" Rhodes asked.

Bonner looked sharply at Rhodes, trying to see if the young man was making fun of him. Rhodes stared back calmly. "There's an enlisted man's saloon down yonder," Bonner said, aiming a thumb over his shoulder. "They usually don't mind much if a couple civilians have a snort or two."

"Let's go on there, then, Mr. Bonner," Rhodes said, standing.

"You don't have to go takin' no pity on me just 'cause I'm an ol' hoss now, goddammit," Bonner snapped.

"I'm not pitying you, Mr. Bonner," Rhodes said evenly.

"Buffler shit," Bonner snarled, rage engulfing him. It was bad enough, he figured that he couldn't do much anymore, but to have to sit here and be treated like some old, useless cripple was too much for him. "One minute you was ready to try knockin' the shit out of me. Now you're here callin' me 'Mister Bonner.' It ain't right, goddammit. No, it ain't."

"Damn, old man, you always yack this much when a fellah says he'd like to buy you a drink?" Rhodes said. His expression of calm earnestness had not changed.

Bonner grinned. His mouth was toothless on the top, and his upper lip fluttered in and out, his mustache looking like a hard-used broom. "Well, hell, boy, ye didn't say nothin' about buyin'."

"Well, I wouldn't expect an experienced fellah like you to do the buyin'."

A cloud passed across Bonner's face. "Why're you doin' this, boy?" he asked, voice trembling a little.

"I want to pump you for information."

"What kind of information?" Bonner asked warily.

"About the land to the southwest of here. About the best way to get there and to stay alive."

"I been all over that goddamn land, boy," Bonner said almost dreamily.

"I expected you had." Rhodes paused. "So, how about it, old man?" Rhodes grinned. "It ain't every day you're going to get an offer like this—somebody buying you all the rotgut you can drink in a couple hours, plus letting you run off at the mouth." Rhodes stepped around the fire, hand out.

"Come to think on it," Bonner said with another flapping grin, "it does seem like my idea of paradise." He held out his hand tentatively. To him, it was asking for help, but he realized there was no insult in it.

When Bonner was standing, Rhodes bent and picked up the old man's rifle and looked at it. "This here's a real Hawken gun, ain't it?" Rhodes asked.

"Sure as goddamn hell it is, boy," Bonner said proudly, taking the gun back. "Made personal by ol' Jake Hawken in Saint Louis, back in '35, I believe it was. Ol' Blackfoot Killer here's stood me in good stead over a good many years."

"I bet it has, Mr. Bonner." He grinned. "Now let's get on over there and cut the dry, unless you were planning to just sit here and tell me tales?"

Bonner laughed. "I can do both with the best of 'em, sonny boy, but I always tell better tales when I got a cup in hand."

They strolled off, Rhodes slowing his pace to match that of the shuffling Joe Bonner. In minutes, they were bellying up to the small bar in the enlisted men's saloon in one of the stone buildings.

Bonner was full of details about the mountains, and he never slowed down in his talking. Rhodes was content to listen, letting the information filter in, where it was sifted. Rhodes figured a fair portion of the talk was either exaggeration or outright lies, but he knew there was some valuable data like gold nuggets scattered throughout the ore of the stories.

Rhodes had no idea really of how much time had passed, but he was still enjoying himself when a soldier said loudly from somewhere behind him and Bonner, "Ain't that old fart ever gonna shut the hell up. Jesus, Mary, and Joseph, but he's a goddamn windbag."

"He stinks like hell, too," someone else offered.

Bonner began to turn, and Rhodes asked in a whisper, "You all right, Joe? You ain't had too much tanglefoot?"

"I'm fine, sonny boy." He turned. "Who's the chicken-humpin' son of a bitch who's so goddamn mouthy?" he demanded.

"I am, you dried-up old bag of shit," one soldier said. He stood, pushing the wood chair away. It landed on its back with a clack. "You fixin' to do anything about it?" he sneered.

The soldier was maybe six-foot-two and went close to two hundred pounds, Rhodes figured. He was certain Bonner would have no chance against the man. He wanted to step in and fight the soldier himself, but he knew that would enrage Bonner.

"Damn right I am, Murphy," Bonner said. He took a step forward, leaving his rifle leaning against the bar.

The soldier rubbed his hands in delight, as others hurriedly stood and shoved tables and chairs out of the way. Murphy rolled up his sleeves, making a great show of it. Then he spit into one palm and rubbed his two palms together.

"Hell, boy, if I knowed you was gonna primp for so long, I'd of had me another snort," Bonner said.

"Just hold your horses, old man," Murphy said. "Unless you're in a hurry to be pounded into the ground."

"I'll be dead of old age before you get around to comin' agin me. Now either shit or get off the pot, sonny."

Murphy hitched up his pants and made a little circle, his hands in the air, as most of the other soldiers clapped and cheered. He had just completed the circuit when Bonner slammed into him. "Damn!" Murphy exclaimed as he went down in a tangle of arms, legs, and table parts.

Rhodes rested both elbows on the bar and watched. He was ready — as were his pistols — if Murphy seemed to be getting the upper hand. Rhodes vowed he would not interfere before that point.

It seemed like it was going to be unnecessary, though. Bonner was savaging Murphy, pummeling the soldier, biting, kicking, and roaring as they rolled around on the sawdust-covered floor.

Rhodes winced a couple of times when he heard Bonner connect with a particularly good lick. He had not thought the old man would still be so hard and tough.

The two were still rolling around on the floor, and Bonner still had the advantage, when several other troopers darted toward the combatants. Rhodes thought for a few moments that they were just going to separate the two fighters, but it became apparent within a moment that they were interested only in helping their companion.

Rhodes figured that if Murphy had help, then Joe Bonner should have some help, too. Rhodes strode up and grabbed two soldiers — one in each hand — by the back of their uniform blouses and jerked them up and away, flinging them to the ground.

Bonner kicked another under the chin and whooped when he heard the man's jaw crack. At the same time, Rhodes grabbed one man in a bear hug and squeezed. He let the man drop after he heard ribs snapping. He wasn't out to kill anyone; he just wanted to keep it a fair fight between Bonner and Murphy.

Things got a little blurry then for Rhodes, as soldiers slammed into him from all sides. He fought like a wounded grizzly, kicking, punching, elbowing. He head-butted at least two men, broke another's arm, and smashed one soldier's nose flat. Someone grabbed him in a bear hug, and Rhodes lurched backward, slamming the man's back against the edge of the bar.

Then it seemed as if an entire company of bluecoats swamped over him. He went down, but not out—until someone hammered the back of his head with something hard and blunt.

Rhodes woke up in a dark cell. He eased up into a sitting position, taking his time at it to keep his head from pounding some. When he made it, he felt the back of his head. There was a fair-size lump on the back of his head, and his thick hair was matted with blood.

"Waugh!" he heard someone say. "Goddamn if you didn't make those bastards come now. Goddamn!"

Rhodes realized it was Bonner when he heard the old man's cackling laugh. "Jesus, Joe," Rhodes complained softly, "can't you shut up for a few goddamn minutes."

"Headache?" Bonner asked with another raucous laugh.

"I don't know as if that describes it properly, but in place of another term, yes, I have a goddamn headache." He paused and leaned back against the outside wall. "How long was I out?"

"Half an hour or so, best I can figure," Bonner said. He smiled. "It took six of 'em to take you

97

down, boy," he added, respect for Rhodes in his voice for the first time.

Rhodes grinned, too. It did no good to worry about the pain now. It was there, and he would have to live with it. He pushed gingerly to his feet and paced the cell some.

From the cell right next to him, Bonner said, "Best set, boy. You don't want to make yourself too dizzy."

Rhodes looked at the old man for a moment, then nodded. That set his head to hurting all the more. He lay down on the hard bunk in the cell. He was drifting back into the calmness of sleep when he heard Bonner say, "You would've made a hell of a mountain man, boy. A hell of one, I tell you. Waugh!"

Chapter Twelve

It was the next morning before Rhodes and Bonner saw daylight again. A small contingent of armed soldiers came to the cells just after the two inmates had eaten breakfast, and marched Rhodes and Bonner outside, across the parade ground to the commanding officer's office. The soldiers went in and smartly snapped to attention. The two prisoners strode in proudly, some might even say arrogantly.

Colonel Wesley Balfour stood behind his desk, arms folded across his chest. He was tall and had a fiery mane of wavy hair. Long, thick sideburns of the same hue cascaded off the corners of his square chin.

"Dammit, Joe," Balfour said harshly, "how many goddamn times do I have to tell you to keep your nose out of trouble?"

Bonner shrugged and grinned. "It's got a habit of findin' me."

"Yeah, bullshit. You cause more goddamn trouble than a whole goddamn company causes. Dammit all." He turned his square, angry face toward Rhodes. "And, you, whoever the hell you are, have no place helping that goddamn idiot"—he pointed at Bonner—"start a ruckus with my men."

"Your boys were the ones started it," Rhodes said easily.

"Oh, really?" Balfour asked sarcastically.

"Yessir. Joe and I were in the saloon mindin' our own business when that big, tall bag of shit Murphy started sassin' Joe."

"You watch your tone and your language around me, boy," Balfour warned.

"Beggin' your leave, Colonel, but go to hell," Rhodes said, still calmly.

Balfour's eyes bugged out as choler swept across his face. "Why you impertinent—"

"Christ, Colonel, back off before you bust a gut." Rhodes paused to allow Balfour to calm himself a little. "Joe and I are civilians, and there's not much you can do to us, short of shootin' us. Now, I know that's a distinct possibility, but on the other hand, would it be worth the trouble?"

"You're digging your grave a little deeper with each word, son," Balfour said. He had regained his composure. "And before we proceed, what's your name?"

"Travis Rhodes."

Balfour looked puzzled. "That name sounds familiar. You ever been stationed here?" He had a suspicion that this man might be a deserter.

"No, sir, but I was a member of the Fourth Pennsylvania for most of three years during the war."

"One of my men?" Balfour asked, surprised.

"Yessir, though I never had call to meet you personally."

"What rank were you, son?"

"First Sergeant."

"You still have a sergeant's carriage."

Rhodes shrugged. "It ain't been that long since hostilities stopped, sir."

Balfour nodded. "Too true." He paused, still suspicious. "Who was your commander?"

"Cap'n Carstairs and above him, Major Langtry."

"Good men, both of them. I was in West Point with Wesley. How is the major?"

"He was killed at Five Forks, sir," Rhodes said sadly. He had liked his commanding officer.

Balfour nodded, and was silent. The sounds of drilling men punctuated by sharp commands broke the silence in the room. Finally Balfour nodded. "Much as I hate to do it to an old comrade in arms, I'm going to have to ask you to leave Fort Laramie, Mr. Rhodes." He paused. "You, too, Joe. I can't have you two hanging around causing trouble."

"What about Murphy and the seven, eight sons of bitches it took to bring me'n ol' Travis down?" Bonner asked.

"I'll deal with Private Murphy. That big, ugly son of a bitch has been a thorn in my side long enough. But things'll go easier with you two gone."

Rhodes nodded. He had no plans to stay here long anyway. Still, he needed a little time to prepare. "When you want me gone, Colonel?"

"Soon as possible, son. Think it'll take you long to get ready?"

"No, sir. I'm travelin' light these days." Rhodes grinned a little.

"As are many of the boys who fought so well." He sighed. "On both sides." He looked at Bonner. "You need more time, Joe?"

"Nah. I'll be gone by mornin'. Maybe before."

Balfour nodded. "Sergeant Weems," he said to the man standing next to the desk. The man wore the three chevrons of a first sergeant. "Return these men's belongings, and then leave them to do what they need. Just keep Murphy and whoever else was involved in that fracas away from these two. If Murphy had any goddamn brains he'd stay away from them on his own account, since from what I heard, old man Joe here was whaling the shit out of him."

"Yessir," Weems said smartly.

A quarter of an hour later, the two men were sitting at the Mormons' fire, recounting their adventures. A considerable amount of chuckling accompanied the narration, until the end. Rhodes sighed and said flatly, "The commanding officer is throwing us out of the fort. We need to be gone by morning."

"Where will you go?" Flake asked.

Rhodes shrugged. "I still plan to head for the gold fields down in Colorado Territory. I expect Joe here'll go back to his Indian friends."

"This chil's gettin' a mite weary of livin' with savages."

"Don't you have an Indian wife?" Flake asked.

Bonner shrugged. "Don't mean much most times. It ain't like a preacher hooked us up, ya know. It's about time this ol' chil' settled down where there was some white folks." He looked over at Rhodes, leathery skin crinkling as he grinned and peered through shuttered eyes. "You mind some company, son?"

Rhodes had begun to like the old man. Sure, he had his faults, but so did everyone, when it came right down to it. Bonner had few habits Rhodes could really argue about. "Don't mind at all," he said. Then he laughed. "Just bring your own bedroll and grub. I ain't sharing no blankets with the likes of you."

"I'm gonna have to teach you some manners along the trail, sonny boy," Bonner said, not meaning a word of it.

"I'd learn better manners from a hog."

They all laughed, then Bonner looked at Flake. "What're you folks plannin'?" he asked.

"We hope to continue on to Deseret," Flake said

flatly. He paused. "Though I suspect you're right in suggesting that we wait out the winter here. I hate to lose that much time, though, not to mention the sloth that we will acquire with a winter of idleness."

Bonner nodded, absentmindedly. Rhodes stared at him. He had known Bonner only one day, but he was already able to pick up signs from the old man. Like now. Rhodes knew Bonner was cogitating on something. He wondered just what the old man had on his mind.

"You folks look like folks who like to turn a buck," Bonner said, squinting at Flake.

"We are," Flake responded. He was curious but wary.

"I know how you folks can make some pretty good cash."

"How?"

"First answer me this: You got money to make an investment?"

"Some," Flake said cautiously. He was not a rich man, but he was comfortable. "How much'll be needed?"

Bonner shrugged. "The more you put in the more you can make."

"I don't like this, Erastus," Hickman said in a low voice.

"We'll wait for Mr. Bonner to explain more fully," Flake said in a little irritation. He was intrigued, but he still remained cautious and skeptical. Bonner had shown no signs that he was any kind of businessman. Flake more than half suspected that the old mountain man was just trying to find out how much money he and his friends were carrying so that he could rob them. "Tell me about this plan, Mr. Bonner."

"Well, folks, it's like this." He stopped there to

pour a cup of the fresh coffee Rhodes had just made. Then he filled his pipe and lit it. Blowing out clouds of noxious fumes, he decided to continue his talk. "Them minin' camps and towns down there are half froze to get fresh goods."

"What does that mean?" Flake asked. He wanted no confusion in any business deal. He had to be sure he knew everything about it.

"They need supplies, badly," Bonner said. He was not offended by the request to explain himself. Flatlanders were always that way, as far as he had been able to ascertain. Never understood plain talk. "Goods is hard to get to many of them places."

Flake was fully interested now, the possibilities beginning to run through his mind. He thought he could see the plan. But he did not want to seem too eager. Better to let Bonner lay it all out. Then Flake could add his own thoughts to it, if that appeared necessary.

"Erastus," Hickman said nervously.

"Enough, Phineas," Flake snapped. "I'm the elder here, and I'll make the decisions that affect us all. If I want your counsel I'll request it."

Hickman stood and walked off in a huff.

"My apologies, Mr. Bonner," Flake said. "Now, where were we?"

"Well, if you can put up some cash and buy yourself a heap of goods here, we can all get it down to some of those minin' towns and sell it for four, five times what you paid."

Flake sat thinking. It had been what he had figured, and it seemed a solid plan. Still, the cautious Mormon needed more information before he would commit himself to the plan. "You're certain the goods could be sold for many times their cost?" he

104

asked.

"Hell, yes," Bonner said. His head could barely be seen behind the thick cloud from his pipe. "I was down there a while back and folks who was fortunate enough to have some flour were sellin' it for twenty, thirty bucks a sack, in some places a hundred a barrel. Eggs was goin' for a dollar or two — each. Sugar was five, sometimes ten dollars a pound."

Flake could hardly control his excitement. If this was true, he and his companions could make up the cost of their trip and still have plenty to tithe to the church once they got to Salt Lake City.

"That sounds workable," Flake said, trying to keep the excitement from his voice.

"I thought you'd see it that way," Bonner said from behind his screen of smoke.

"I think it'd be a worthwhile investment," Flake said slowly. "But let me warn you, Mr. Bonner, that if you are found to be misleading us or out only for your own personal enrichment, I'll personally see that you are brought to justice."

Bonner cackled. "Hell, boy, you don't scare me none. Shit, I've faced Crow and Blackfoot, Ute and Pawnee and come out with my hair intact. There ain't a goddamn thing you can do to me."

"Be that as it may, Mr. Bonner," Flake said flatly. "But take it as a warning." He paused. "What's your interest in all this?"

"I expect you ain't gonna believe me, boy, but I'm just of a mood to move on, and I'd like some company."

"That's a bald-face lie, and I'm insulted that you thought I'd fall for it," Flake said stiffly.

Bonner waved a hand in front of his face, dispersing enough of the smoke so that his face could be seen. He was grinning. "Hell, I just had to try it." He cackled a moment. "Tellin' true now, I'm a bit short of funds these days, and I'd be obliged if you was to see your way clear to givin' me a few pesos for guiding you down there."

Flake didn't know how he knew, but he was sure Bonner was telling the truth. "And how much of a fee are you expecting?"

"A hundred," Bonner said without embarrassment.

Flake thought it a fair figure. "Agreed." He paused. "But you'll be paid when we arrive at wherever it is we're going."

"Sounds like you don't trust me."

"I don't," Flake said flatly.

Bonner laughed so hard he almost fell over. "You are some, boy." He waited out another gale of his own laughter. When he had recovered, he said, "But you'll have to buy me some supplies for the trip."

Flake nodded. "That's only fair." He stood. "Well, if we're to leave in the morning, there is much to be done first."

Chapter Thirteen

They rolled out of the fort an hour after sunup, under the watchful eyes of Colonel Wesley Balfour. No one else paid them any heed that they could tell, though the two companies of soldiers drilling already on the dusty parade ground might have cast them an envious look or two.

Out front was old Joe Bonner. He had wheedled enough out of Flake to get himself a new outfit. He wore a new pair of fringed buckskin pants, a bright red calico shirt, and a floppy hat sporting an eagle feather sticking proudly up on one side. His long, greasy, gray hair was brushed into a sleek stream down over his shoulders. He rode a large, sturdy mule, and carried his plains rifle across his saddle in front of him.

Erastus Flake came next, sitting high and proud on a seat rigged up on a large freight wagon. The wagon was packed solid and full with whatever goods he had been able to round up from the fort sutler and anyone else who would give the time of day. By the time he had finished his buying spree the day before, it was nearabout dark. But that did not stop Flake. He just set to work loading everything he had purchased into the wagon he had bought. The others helped him, of course, though they made no bones about how they felt about it. Bonner snuck off as soon as he could. The wagon now was pulled by eight big mules.

Pulling out next was Phineas Hickman on his own wagon, and then came Eliza Flake who worked the reins to her wagon. The two wagons also had had seats added in the interest of saving time. The other women and the children rode inside the two wagons, while the extra saddle horses were tied behind the two wagons.

Travis Rhodes brought up the rear, riding his palomino. He didn't like the idea of eating dust like this, but someone reliable had to bring up the rear while Bonner was out front doing the scouting.

They didn't make it far the first day. Bonner was no longer used to so much traveling, plus the animals needed time to get accustomed to the large loads they were hauling. It was deemed wise to make an early camp that day.

But beginning the next morning, they began going a little longer each day, until they were putting in a twelve- to eighteen-hour day each day a week after they had left Fort Laramie.

The first obstacle they faced was almost right outside the door of the fort—crossing the Platte. As a river, it wasn't much. It seemed to spread all over creation, but couldn't fill itself up any. It was, in many spots, little more than a glorified mud puddle. But it was a treacherous piece of shallow river, with quicksand and a shifting bottom nearabout anywhere a man wanted to cross it. It was another reason why their first day out was a short one.

They worked southwest, making it through Morton Pass and almost all the way back to the Laramie River the second day. Things went smoothly if not quickly most times, and they progressed steadily, working their way westward then, around the northern edge of the Medicine Bow Mountains.

Once past those mountains, they turned almost due south, winding through a grand valley. Across Muddy Pass, they followed the Muddy River south and a little west, then cut due east along the Colorado River. Several days of hard labor later, they turned southeast along the Fraser River, getting ever higher into the mountains.

Finally, more than a month after leaving Fort Laramie, some of it with snowfall, they found a town. City was more like it, they thought as they wound their way down a muddy, wide, boisterous street in an intolerable place aptly called Intolerance.

"Jesus, I ain't ever seen the like," Rhodes mused, as he pulled up alongside Bonner.

"I have, boy. Goddamn if I ain't," the old man cackled.

All hell seemed to be breaking loose. Gunfire popped regularly, men raced up and down the street, on foot and on horseback, wagons clattered along, men whooped and hollered. But overpowering it all was the thunder of the two stamp mills, smashing ore by the ton, one mill on the southwestern outskirts of Intolerance, the other on the southeastern flank.

They finally pulled to a stop in front of what claimed to be a hotel. The travelers weren't so sure, but they had seen nothing other than this place that might be a hotel. They also were aware that some people were staring at them, and Flake figured it was because of the wagonload of goods.

"You go on inside, Erastus, and see if you can find rooms," Rhodes said. "Best take the women with you, too. Joe and I'll stay out here and watch things. Phineas, too, if he's of a mind."

"I am," Hickman said firmly as he wrapped the reins around the brake handle.

"Good," Flake said. He climbed down from the big

freight wagon, and walked back to help Eliza, Sarah, and Minerva Hickman down. Sometime during their travels, it had come out that "Aunt" Sarah was in reality Erastus Flake's second wife. Bonner had cackled at it, and said that such a thing was common among most of the Plains Indians.

"Hell, I even done it more'n onct myself," the old man had finished, his wobbling chuckle floating up to the night sky on the thick plume of smoke from the fire.

Rhodes had said nothing, surprised that he was not scandalized about it. He wasn't, though he was bothered a little. It took him several days to realize that he was put out because of jealousy. He couldn't understand why any woman would agree to be someone's second or third or whatever wife. Moreover, he felt that the young and attractive Sarah Flake was being taken advantage of. He thought she was wasting her life away with an old codger like Erastus Flake. He had gotten over that, though, partly because he saw that Sarah would never be his even if something happened to Flake. That was a good thing, too, because Rhodes was not about to put up with her cloying piety. The same applied to the even more beautiful Minerva.

Flake and the three women entered the hotel. Rhodes, Bonner, and Hickman waited, the first two patiently, the latter quite nervously. Bonner filled his small clay pipe with some foul-smelling tobacco and fired it up.

A few minutes later, Flake came outside, alone. "All is taken care of," he said. "Now I have to secure the wagon until I can begin selling things."

"Any idea of where you're going to do that?" Rhodes asked.

"Mr. Whipplemeyer, who owns the hotel, told me of a place." Flake climbed onto the freight wagon.

"One of you'll have to drive our other wagon."

"Well, I ain't no goddamn wagon driver, that's for goddamn certain," Bonner said joyfully. He figured that as he was aged and had survived all that life had thrown at him, he was entitled to be a mite crotchety.

Rhodes had known right off that Bonner was not about to do it, and had already dismounted. He walked to the wagon and tied the palomino to it. He climbed up and said, "Let's get it done."

They did not ride too far before turning down a side street. At the end of the street was a large barn made of stone and mortar. They rolled right inside and with the help of several men who worked at the livery unhitched the teams. It took the better part of a half hour, but finally the horses and mules were stabled, groomed, and were hungrily working over the hay and oats tossed into their stalls. The wagons were moved out of the way, too.

Flake, being new to this town, was not sure he could trust the livery workers. The owner tried to reassure him, but he was still uncertain. "No," he finally said, "I will stay with the wagons."

"You'll need to eat and make plans, Erastus," Hickman said.

"You can relieve me for a spell to do all that," Flake said firmly.

"But I—"

"Quiet! You're as much a part of this venture as I am, Phineas. You'll do your part." He looked from Rhodes to Bonner. "I don't suppose you two'd like to stay here a while?" he said, making a question of it.

"Not this ol' chil'," Bonner said with a laugh.

"Me neither," Rhodes said fervently. He had plans for the night. "I aim to go and sin some more," he said with a laugh.

"Bah," Flake growled, but he grinned, too. "Very

111

well," he said, once more the solemn businessman. "Fin, you'll stay here while I eat and make some plans. I'll relieve you so you can eat and get some sleep." Once more he looked at Rhodes and Bonner. "I'm obliged to you both for seeing us here. I'd be even more in your debt if you two were to stand guard whenever and wherever I set up shop."

Both nodded. Then Bonner clapped Rhodes on the shoulder. "Come on, boy, let's go fandango!"

"I'm ready," Rhodes said enthusiastically. During the long trip from Fort Laramie to Intolerance, he had come to know old Joe Bonner pretty well, and he had decided he liked the old man.

Bonner was high-smelling, opinionated, independent, crusty, crotchety, and sometimes downright ornery. Despite all that, Rhodes liked him. Bonner had seen more country than a dozen other men. He was old but had not given up on life. He had what seemed to be an endless supply of stories to tell. Half—hell, maybe even all—of them were pure, unadulterated lies, but that didn't lessen Rhodes's interest in them. He figured at least some of them—or parts of them—were true.

Even if the stories were all tall tales meant to confound flatlanders, it didn't mean much. That Bonner had been through all these places before was evident on the journey from Fort Laramie. Not once had Bonner lost the trail. Riding way at the back of the small caravan, Rhodes could watch Bonner's wispy figure up ahead. Rhodes could see just by watching that Bonner knew what he was about up in these high, bitter mountains.

It was also apparent that Bonner loved being up here. He could see that even more at night around the fire. Bonner's eyes had come alive almost as soon as the group had left the fort. Rhodes wondered if he would ever feel that way about anyplace or anything. He felt with some melancholy that he never would.

But this was not the time for gloomy thoughts. He grinned as he strode along next to old Joe Bonner. "How in the hell're we supposed to pick us out a saloon, old man?" In just two blocks, they had passed more than half a dozen saloons.

Bonner cackled. "Hell if I know, sonny boy. Maybe we might have to sample each and every goddamn one of 'em."

"I suppose that wouldn't put me out none," Rhodes said with a laugh.

"Hell, you'd be flat on your ass afore we hit even a dozen of 'em."

"I'll outdrink you any time, you old degenerate." They kept walking. "I expect I'd settle for a saloon that has whiskey that ain't watered down too much, has some gambling, and most of all, a place that's got some fancy women."

Bonner cackled some more. "The hell with the gamblin', boy. I might even say to hell with the goddamn whiskey, too, if'n there be women about."

"Shit, you old coot, you're gonna need that whiskey. One of the fancy gals latch on to you, boy, and you'll be pushing up daisies before you get time to drop your drawers."

Bonner cackled. Suddenly he grabbed Rhodes's left arm and gave Rhodes a little shove. "This place looks about right for this chil'."

Rhodes shrugged. The place looked no different from the dozen or so they had passed already. Still, Rhodes was ready to cut the dry in his throat, and this saloon would do as well as another.

The place had a false front, giving it a respectable look. The inside, though, was pure mining town saloon. The main part of the building was made with logs cut on the hillsides around the town. Some of

113

those walls had been replaced, or partly replaced with stone. Tables were jammed everywhere. The place sported numerous faro tables, and several poker games were in progress.

The place — Rhodes hadn't seen a name on it — was roaring at full steam, so much so that Rhodes and Bonner almost had to fight their way through to reach the bar.

When the bartender noticed them he came over with a bottle of whiskey in his hand. "Twenty bucks," he bellowed.

"That's goddamn robbery," Rhodes shouted back.

The bartender shrugged and started to walk away. Bonner leaned over the bar, stopping the bartender with his plains rifle. The man turned back a sour look on his face. Rhodes flipped a twenty-dollar gold piece on the bar. The bartender grabbed the money with one hand and put the bottle down with the other.

"Women?" Rhodes roared, trying to be heard over the din. "You got women here?"

"Cribs. Out back." Then he was gone, swallowed by the cacophony and the press of business.

Rhodes grabbed the bottle in his right hand, since his left was occupied with the cut-down Darby shotgun. "Let's get the hell out of here," he bellowed into Bonner's ear.

The old man nodded, and they battled their way across the room and into the street again.

Chapter Fourteen

The two men stopped just outside of the saloon, a little to the left of the door. They were out of the way of most of the saloon's business, and not many other people seemed to be using this patch of mud under the sagging overhang of the saloon's false front.

Bonner stuck the butt of his rifle into the mud and leaned it back against the saloon wall. Rhodes held the bottle out, and Bonner pulled the cork. Bonner grabbed the bottle. "Age comes afore beauty, boy," he growled. Then he tilted it up to his lips. When he finished the healthy slug, he held it out for Rhodes.

" 'Bout goddamn time, you blowhard old fart," Rhodes said with a grin. He, too, had a healthy snort. "Phew," he said after pulling the bottle away, "that goes down good." He grinned. "Even if it does taste like it just came out of a sick mule."

Bonner cackled gleefully. "Sure as hell." He grabbed the bottle and sipped. Done, he said, "Now, boy, let's go see what kind of man you really are." He grabbed his rifle in his right hand, keeping the bottle in his left.

As the two headed up the small alley toward the line of cribs out behind the saloon, Bonner looked surreptitiously at Rhodes. The younger man walked with straight back, head held high, as if daring the world to just try something with him. There were far too few men who had that much pride and self-esteem these days, Bonner figured. To him, most men nowadays were all boiled shirts — suited-up, lime-smelling, pale city folks.

Not Travis Rhodes, though, Bonner knew. He had taken to his young companion the moment Rhodes had flung himself into the brawl back at Fort Laramie. Old Joe Bonner was a tough old coot, set in his ways. He didn't take to people easily, but he plumb admired a man who gave little thought to himself while trying to help a friend. Like that night in the saloon. And with the Mormons. It had surprised Bonner when he found out somewhere along in their trip from the fort that Rhodes was not a Mormon. Not that Bonner cared one way or another what religion any man had — or didn't have. What surprised him was that it seemed for all intents and purposes that Rhodes was one of the Mormons. Why else would someone give others so much help?

For a little while, Bonner could pretend this was back in the old days, when he was young and hard, wild and fearless. Them had been shinin' times, and he missed those days. He was tired much of the time now, and he could no longer carry a hundred-pound bale of furs so easily. Old wounds and old bones ached with each change in the weather, and the rheumatism sapped him at times. He wouldn't admit it to anyone, but he knew his eyesight was failing. He had gone back East a few years ago and stopped by a place in St. Louis where the young doctor had tested him and given him a pair of spectacles. He carried the specs in a small brass case and wore them only when necessary — which usually meant when he was alone.

All these things wore on him, dragging him down, making him realize his mortality. He could not live forever. Hell, he didn't *want* to live forever. But he sure as hell would rather go out fighting or fornicating or raising hair on some painted goddamn Blackfoot. Travis Rhodes made him think that he was back in those days, like his blood was running free and singing in his veins, rather than moving like molasses. It was another reason old Joe Bonner liked Rhodes.

They stopped and surveyed the double lines of small, mostly decrepit shacks. Five women stood leaning against a wall, drinking and smoking, talking and laughing. They quieted, though, and looked toward the newcomers. The five headed toward the two men. All of them gravitated toward Rhodes, and he laughed. "See, you old coot, you ain't got anything these ladies want."

"Bah," Bonner growled. "There's life in this ol' chil' yet!" He grabbed one of the women, who was easily young enough to be his granddaughter, and pulled her close. Then he planted a big kiss on her plump lips. When he pulled back a little, he said, "Come on, darlin'. This old hoss's got somethin' to show you." The two shuffled off, the woman warming to the old man. Then they disappeared into one of the shacks.

"How about you, bucko?" a woman said to Rhodes. "You gonna let that old buzzard do better'n you?" Her brogue was muted but evident.

"Oh, I reckon I can keep up with him," Rhodes said dryly. He looked at her and smiled. She was a big woman, as tall as he and square-shouldered. Her face also was square, but not unpleasant. She looked better than the other three. He waved a hand. "After you, ma'am."

"Ma'am now he's callin' me," she said, standing with arms akimbo two feet in front of him. "Hoo, probably thinks I'm his mum."

Rhodes bit back the retort that fought to get past

the gate of his teeth and clamped lips. When it was defeated, he said, "Well, now, I suppose you might not be able to keep up with me, missie. You can't, I'm sure one of these other lovely belles'd be happy to . . ."

"The hell with them other girlies," the woman said, latching on to his arm protectively.

As they moved off, Rhodes asked, "There something I can call you?"

"You really want a name?" she asked with a grin.

Rhodes shrugged. "It'd sap our passion was I to call out the wrong name in the heat of things," he said smoothly.

"That'd never do, now would it, bucko," she agreed. "Call me Myrtle."

"You plannin' to stay awhile, bucko?" Myrtle asked half an hour later.

"I am. Unless you'd rather I didn't." His eyes questioned her.

"Oh, I don't mind, bucko," she said with more enthusiasm then she really felt. He was better than most, she acknowledged to herself, mainly in that he was polite, well-mannered, and didn't smell too bad. Left to her own devices, though, she would be alone for the rest of the night. The role-playing was tedious work for her, harder sometimes than the actual job. Still, if he stayed the night, he'd be paying her pretty well, and she would not have to spend the whole damn night on her back.

"Suits me," he said, pillowing his head on folded arms. "I could use a bottle, though, and it wouldn't put me out none to have a bite."

Myrtle was thinking the same thing. "Right, me bucko." She climbed out of the small, rickety bed and opened the thin door to the shack. Standing there without a stitch on, she shouted, "Hey, Fannie.

Get one of them darkies to bring us a bottle and some grub."

"You got you an all-nighter?" a voice called, floating in to Rhodes. He smiled. He had been called worse things in his life.

"Sure do." It sounded to Rhodes like Myrtle figured she had hit the mother lode or something. He shrugged. That did not bother him either.

The whiskey and food—in the form of boiled hen's eggs, jerked buffalo, cold roasted chicken and turkey and two kinds of cheese—arrived soon. Rhodes, still lying on the bed, quickly and quietly grabbed one of his revolvers from where they lay on the dirt floor of the shack, and he held it ready until he was sure there was no danger.

"Hell," Rhodes said when he saw the food, "I ain't eaten this good since I left home." Even though the portions were small, it still looked good to him.

After eating, and sharing some whiskey, they coupled again. Shortly after, Rhodes fell asleep, to Myrtle's relief.

Rhodes figured it was near midnight when he woke. He sat up in the dark, wondering what had woken him. He reached for a pistol. In the flickering light of a coal-oil lantern that burned low on a table, he could see Myrtle sleeping next to him.

Then he heard a sound, and he wasn't quite sure of it for a few moments. Then it came again, his wonder increasing. He grinned and as the sound continued, his smile widened considerably. Old Joe Bonner was singing—in one of the most beautiful tenors Rhodes had ever heard—*Old Rosin the Beau*. The pure, fresh notes and the mildly lascivious words were as clear as the night air.

"He's really somethin', ain't he, bucko?" Myrtle said in a whisper, not wanting to break the moment.

Rhodes nodded. "That he is," he answered in kind.

Ten minutes or so later, Bonner's wonderful voice wound down. No one had said another word that whole time. But as the final notes drifted up into the cool night sky, Rhodes turned to Myrtle. "Seeing as how we're both awake now . . ."

"I'd be delighted," Myrtle said huskily, surprising herself. She didn't realize until later that it was that old man's soft, sweet voice that had made her so willing, indeed, eager for a man's embrace.

Myrtle pleasantly suffered another go-round in the morning, before Rhodes rose and dressed. Outside, he went to the crib Bonner was using. He pounded on the door, almost breaking the fragile thing down.

"Get up, you lecherous old reprobate," he roared. "Come on, now, get up, before I come in there and drag your scrawny old ass out."

Rhodes moved back a step, hooking his thumbs in his belt. He had roused several people, who were watching from other cribs or from the back porches of the few nearby buildings.

The door was flung open suddenly and a bleary-eyed, disheveled scarecrow glared out.

"Jesus, Joe, if you ain't the ugliest looking son of a bitch I've ever set eyes on."

"Goddammit, boy," Bonner growled low in his throat, "you don't leave me alone I'll be usin' your ass for a goddamn target."

"You ain't going to do no such thing. Now get yourself together and let's go get us some grub."

"Goddamn young son of a bitch," he mumbled. "Ain't got no goddamn consideration for their elders . . ." He turned, still muttering.

Five minutes later, Bonner came out, squinting against the fierce glare of the sun. It was warm already, and they expected another barn-burner of a hot day, but the chill of last night was a reminder that Indian summer wasn't going to be around long.

The two walked off, Rhodes at a good pace, which

he had to slow considerably, since Bonner was barely shuffling. "You really are a sorry bastard, ain't you, gramps?"

"You keep talkin', boy and I'll cut your goddamn liver out and eat it." He suddenly looked queasy. "Soon's I get my stomach back," he groaned.

"You really feeling that poorly, Joe?" Rhodes asked, concerned.

"Worse."

"How about we find someplace you can get some more shut-eye?" Rhodes felt bad that Bonner was so hungover. It wasn't his fault, of course, but he still felt bad about dragging the old man out of bed so early.

"Need a little hair of the bear first." Bonner tried to spit out some of the foulness that clung to his tongue like he was born with it. He had no success. "Jesus," he mumbled. "Goddamn sweet Jesus."

"Don't you think you're a wee bit old for such nonsense?" Rhodes asked, unable to refrain from teasing Bonner.

"I'll be too goddamn old when I'm in my grave a month, and not a goddamn day before," Bonner grumbled.

Rhodes laughed. "I'll be certain to come along the day before and dig you up, just to see if you're still interested."

Bonner said nothing, but if the stare he fixed on Rhodes was a dagger, Rhodes would be six feet under right now.

They finally curled around the corner and then entered the saloon. It was still going strong; perhaps not quite as busy as the evening before, but roaring nonetheless.

By the time he had downed his second shot, Bonner was feeling a little better. "Now, goddammit, you can buy me some victuals, boy," he said firmly.

"Be glad to—so long as you don't eat as much as

you drank last night."

"Boy, you are plainly treadin' a fine line here."

"You don't scare me none, gramps. Old windbag like you."

They found a restaurant and stepped inside. A pleasant, though overworked young man took their order and hurried away, summoned by clanging pots and a shouting cook.

Rhodes and Bonner took their time eating. Rhodes was hungry and paid serious attention to his food. Bonner was still suffering from his hangover and picked at his food. "Goddamn," he muttered early on, "there ain't no one can mess up a good piece of meat like a goddamn Dutchman."

"Just shut your trap and eat. I ain't going to sit here all day waiting on you," Rhodes said calmly.

By the time he got a third mug of coffee in him, Bonner was ready to go to town on his food, false teeth clacking. "What do you got planned for today, boy?" he asked after shoving his empty plates away from him. He pulled out his pipe and fired it up.

"Reckon we ought to go see if Erastus needs any help."

"What's this 'we' shit?" Bonner asked, but he grinned.

"Hell, we're all in this together now. Even though we don't have any money tied up in their venture, we've been with 'em all along. We might as well see it through."

"You're too softhearted, boy," Bonner said. Then he grinned again.

Chapter Fifteen

Rhodes and Bonner wandered over to the hotel, taking their time to check out the sights. Intolerance was muddy, dismal even under the bright sun, odorous and boisterous. It was anything but dull. Tent houses and buildings stood side-by-side with ones of log or stone. Many of the buildings tilted dangerously, looking ready to fall over from their own weight. Small side streets and alleys straggled off at odd angles, taking people to nowhere.

The town seemed little different from yesterday, when the small group had ridden in. People still hurried about, gunfire erupted sporadically, fights broke out, gathered a crowd quickly, and ended fast, most often with the two combatants walking away together to toast their battle.

Rhodes noted more women and children on the streets, though, and more townsmen. He also was aware of the many businesses—besides the dozens of saloons, brothels, and gambling dens—lining the main street: at least three general stores, two dry goods stores, three groceries, a hardware store, gunsmith's, assay office, two doctors' offices, five barbershops, three blacksmiths, two newspaper offices, eight lawyers, a couple of Chinese laundries, one large, imposing bank and two smaller ones, and a plethora of restaurants.

It was a wild and wooly place, and Rhodes felt almost at home—as long as he had his pistols and his shotgun at hand. He glanced at Bonner. The old mountain man seemed somehow different, though Rhodes could not figure out why. "Something bothering you, old man?" he asked.

"Too many goddamn people for this ol' chil', goddammit."

"All these folks make you nervous?" Rhodes was surprised.

"Goddamn right they do. Why'n hell you think I stayed out here in these mountains or nearby for so goddamn long anyway?" Bonner asked rhetorically. "Hell, the beaver trade died out afore you was borned, and most of the mountaineers went off to some place or another where there was people about. But not all of us, goddammit. Ol' Gabe Bridger, he stuck it out as long as he could. Poor ol' bastard's half blind and finally had to give in and move to the States. Man, but he was a feisty son of a bitch in his prime."

A deep, resonant wistfulness in Bonner's voice made Rhodes glance sharply at him. Tears welled in the old man's eyes, and he was fighting them off. "You don't need to say any more," Rhodes said quietly. "It's none of my business and I ought not to've pried."

"Goddamn right," Bonner growled, finally managing to control his emotions. He was grateful for Rhodes's consideration. Most other folks would have been solicitous and made Bonner feel even worse. But Rhodes seemed to have a knack of knowing just what to do. It would never do to tell Rhodes that, though, Bonner figured. It'd most likely just give him a swollen head.

They went inside the hotel. A skinny old man

with a long beak of a nose sat behind the counter. He stood when the two men came in. He was unable to keep his distaste off his pinched face.

"What room's Mr. Flake in?" Rhodes asked.

"Twenty-two. But he's not there."

"You know where he might be?"

The skinny man shrugged and made a surreptitious movement, opening his hand.

Anger flared in Rhodes's chest. He had been having a good day, but it had soured on him. He reached across the counter and grabbed the hotelier's shirt with one big hand. He jerked the man forward. "The only thing you're going to get from me, you maggot, is broken bones. Now, you know where Mr. Flake might be?"

"He and the others went to breakfast," the man said, almost wetting his pants. "At Brindle's."

"Where's that?"

"Right next door." He pointed a quivering hand.

Rhodes released him. "Obliged," he said evenly, anger gone already.

Rhodes and Bonner went next door and spotted the group of Mormons. They each grabbed a chair and set them next to the table and sat. "Morning, folks," Rhodes said.

"Are you two hungry?" Flake asked.

"No, sir. Me and Joe ate already. We come to see what you have planned."

"Well, we're going to auction off the goods we brought in. We put up some signs yesterday afternoon." He chuckled. "Two store owners offered to buy us out, lock, stock, and barrel for a considerable profit, but I turned them down and told them to come to the auction. I figure we can do better by selling the goods piecemeal, but if the offer's right, I'd be glad to sell all to one buyer."

Rhodes nodded. "Sounds reasonable. Where and when?"

"At the livery where the wagon is stored. At noon today."

"You ain't wasting much time are you?" Rhodes said with a little laugh.

"Sloth is sinful, Mr. Rhodes," Flake said solemnly.

"I suppose it is," Rhodes responded flatly. He ran his index finger and thumb around his lips a few times. "You given any thought to what you're going to do for the winter?" he asked. It had not occurred to him until just now that while the Mormons would get a good price for the goods they brought in, they would also have to pay high for anything they bought in Intolerance.

"Not much," Flake admitted. "I want to sell our goods before I give thought to that. Why?"

Rhodes explained his reservations.

Flake nodded. "I've thought of that, and it does present a dilemma. However, I think that if we sell all the goods for the prices I believe we can get — and we sell off the big wagon and its team of mules, we should be all right. I checked some places yesterday since our hotel is asking a mighty dear price for such inadequate accommodations. There are few that are cheaper, but I have found a house — a shack, actually — that we could rent fairly reasonably. We also should have enough food and such in our stores to make it through the winter, unless it's extraordinarily long." He paused, then added, "Thank you, though, for thinking of us."

Rhodes shrugged. He felt responsible for the group. It was a ridiculous notion, and he told himself sternly not to do it anymore. "You going to need Joe and me to help out any?"

Flake nodded. In deadly serious tones, he said, "I

had hoped not to need you, because we're already so far in your debt." He sighed. "But . . . well, the marshal of Intolerance is asking a mighty dear price."

Rhodes looked at him quizzically. "Why?"

"I was told that the four previous marshals here lasted a grand total of twelve and a half weeks. Marshal Pritchard has been on the job two months, mainly, I think, because he hasn't been foolish."

"Damn," Rhodes breathed, more amazed than worried.

"Indeed," Flake answered.

"What's that got to do with me and Joe, though?" Rhodes asked after his wonder had passed.

"I don't trust the ruffians."

"That's wise," Bonner tossed in. He was leaning back in his chair tamping tobacco into his pipe.

Flake nodded. "Anyway, I had wanted to have the marshal watch over the sale to make sure nothing went wrong. And . . ."

"But the marshal wants too much money, so you want me and Joe to watch over things. That right?"

"Yes," Flake said tightly. He did not like asking Travis Rhodes to do any more for him. The young man had been a great help all along, and Erastus Flake was not a man who enjoyed being in another man's debt. Not that Rhodes had ever indicated he wanted any repayment. Still, Flake did not like asking for more help.

"I don't reckon that'd put me out any. How about you, Joe?" Rhodes asked, looking at his new friend.

Bonner shrugged. "Can't hurt none, I expect." He puffed on his pipe slowly, sending foul clouds of smoke spinning through the room.

"There, Erastus, all settled," Rhodes said. He stood. "We'll meet you over there just before noon."

He looked at Bonner again. "Come on, you lazy old fa . . ." he realized that the children were at the table, ". . . lazy old man," he amended.

"I was jist gettin' comfortable," Bonner complained.

"You get any more comfortable, you'll be snoring, and I'll have to pay the folks here rent money for you."

The children giggled, and Rhodes winked at them.

"Lord, Lord, why do I have to suffer such things?" Bonner said, eyes cast toward the heavens. He rose. "Woe unto you who have lost patience," he said quietly.

Rhodes didn't know who was more shocked, himself or the Mormons.

Bonner grinned and picked up his rifle, which had been resting against the table. "Well, come on, boy," he said with a grin. "You was the one all fired-up for gettin'."

As they hit the street, Bonner said, "You know, don't you, boy, that we could be up to our ears in trouble watchin' over this sale?"

Rhodes nodded. "I know." He paused, and shrugged. "What I don't know is why I'm so hellbent on helpin' these folks. I've tried to puzzle it out, but I ain't come to a conclusion."

"Maybe you're tryin' to replace your family," Bonner said evenly. He kept walking, and got a few steps before he realized that Rhodes was no longer next to him. He stopped and looked back. As Rhodes caught up to him, Bonner added, "And that ain't such a bad thing, all in all."

Rhodes shook his head in wonder. The more he considered the possibility that the statement was true, the more he knew it was. There was a lot

128

more to this rickety old man than met the eye, that was sure.

Rhodes grinned lopsidedly. "Then I ought to quit worrying about it and just follow the path where it leads, eh?"

Bonner nodded. "Just as long as you don't get to thinkin' them folks *is* your real folks," he warned. "They ain't, ya know."

"I'll keep it to mind."

They started walking again, and then Rhodes asked, "Where the hell're we going?"

"I don't know about you, but I aim to get a little more shut-eye." Bonner grinned. "I didn't get me a whole hell of a lot of sleep last night, and I ain't as spry as I once was."

"That's obvious," Rhodes said with a laugh. "But I reckon I could use a few more winks myself. Where?"

Bonner shrugged. "I reckon over where we left the horses and wagons. There ought to be an empty stall, or maybe the hayloft. Don't matter much to this chil' just where he lays his robe long's there ain't too much noise or people to come pesterin' me."

They told the stable man to wake them at eleven, if they weren't awake by then. Both figured that would give them time to have a bite to eat before keeping watch over Flake's auction.

Rhodes woke first, and lay there a few moments listening to Bonner's soft, wheezing snores, as well as the sounds of the stable and the town. He stood and stretched. Then he called quietly, "Time, Joe." Rhodes had learned on the trip to Intolerance that it was unwise to get too close to Bonner when waking him. One could never tell what would happen.

Bonner seemed to come awake all at once, eyes open and alert, hands reaching for weapons. Once he realized there was no danger, he almost slipped back to sleep, closing his eyes and settling himself.

"Come on, get up, you lazy old man," Rhodes said. Now that Bonner was more or less awake, he could be more free in his talk. He began brushing off the bits of straw and dirt clinging to his clothes.

Bonner growled, but his eyes opened. He pushed up, having a little trouble with it. "Goddamn rheumatiz," he snapped in irritation. He hated getting old, and sometimes wished he had been put under at the hands of the Blackfoot or some other hair-raising Indians.

Bonner brushed himself off, though not too much. It seemed to Rhodes that Bonner was unmoved by dirt.

Then they headed toward a restaurant.

Chapter Sixteen

A worried Erastus Flake was waiting at the barn for Rhodes and Bonner. The Mormon breathed a sigh of relief when he saw them. He hopped down from the wagon on which he had been watching for them and pushed his way through the milling crowd.

"Looks like you got yourself a mighty lively gathering," Rhodes said.

"I just hope they're not too lively," Flake said.

"Never can tell with a place like this," Bonner offered. As in all things, he considered himself an expert on such gatherings.

"You near ready to start?" Rhodes asked, ignoring Bonner.

Flake nodded absentmindedly. He was, Rhodes thought, a true businessman. He seemed harried enough to start pulling his hair out, yet Rhodes knew Flake would have it no other way. He just had to worry about every detail of business.

"Come, we have no time to waste," Flake said. He whirled and stomped toward the large barn. Rhodes and Bonner glanced at each other, shrugged and followed along.

Flake went into a small side door next to the barn's main double door. "Mr. Pace," he roared. "Mr. Pace!"

"What the hell do ya want with all yer hollerin'?"

Christopher Pace grumbled from over near the big freight wagon parked just behind a small, flatbed wagon just inside the double doors.

"It's time to begin," Flake said loudly.

"Hell, I been waitin' on you is all. Jeez."

"Well, wait no more, Mister Pace. Open the doors." He turned to Rhodes, Bonner, and Hickman, who had just materialized from the bowels of the barn. "Phineas will help me directly, bringing things from the freight wagon to the smaller wagon I'll be using as a podium. I want you two—" he indicated Rhodes and Bonner—"to keep a watch that no one steals anything, and that no one tries to get anything by violence."

"Tall goddamn order," Bonner said sarcastically.

Flake never heard him. He had already charged off, toward the opening barn doors. Pace and two of his workers shoved the smaller wagon outside. As Flake climbed up on the wagon, Pace and his men moved the big freight wagon a little nearer to the doorway.

"Ladies and gentlemen," Flake roared over the noise of the assembled crowd. When he had their attention, he said, "Welcome. And thank you for coming. I hope that we might offer you some things of value, of use."

"Just get the hell on with it," someone shouted from amid the masses.

"Very well." Flake paused. Then, "However, a little about the rules."

"Rules? What goddamn rules?" a man shouted.

"These rules," Flake said calmly. "The bidding will be over when I say it's over. All payments are to be made in gold, on the spot. No gold, no goods. And the auction will close when I say it closes." He paused, surveying the crowd. "I also have armed

132

men guarding the merchandise. Anyone who tries taking something will be shot down."

Everyone was now silent, waiting for the auction to begin. Flake gazed out like an emperor viewing his realm. He had stopped in the grocery stores and general stores yesterday. Much of what the stores had was equipment. Food was in short supply, especially flour, sugar, salt, molasses, and cornmeal. Flake, who had been a merchant most of his life, had figured on these goods being in short supply, and so when he had been doing his purchasing at Fort Laramie, he had made sure he had bought as much of those items as possible. Now it was about to pay off.

Hickman brought up a fifty-pound bag of flour and set it on Flake's "podium." The bidding began.

Rhodes directed Pace to bring up two smaller wagons and put one at each end of the wagon Flake was using. Rhodes climbed onto one and Bonner onto the other. With the height advantage, they could keep a closer watch on the crowd.

Rhodes kept sweeping the field with his eyes. He was only a little concerned that someone would cause trouble. The problem would really arise if a number of them tried to cause trouble. He began to grow bored after a while, as the stores on the big wagon dwindled.

He did, however, notice an attractive young woman in the crowd. She was, Rhodes figured, about seventeen. She had dusky brown hair streaming out from a calico bonnet that matched her dress. The dress did nothing to conceal her curvaceous figure.

He wondered about her, whether she had a husband, or a beau; and why she was in a place like Intolerance, standing with a decrepit old man.

133

Rhodes hoped the man was her father and not some husband she had been saddled with by a cruel stroke of fate.

Suddenly Rhodes spun and slipped off the wagon. He took two steps and knelt near the back of the big wagon. "You think a bag of salt is worth dying for, boy?" he asked quietly.

The boy, who was around fifteen or so, froze, not liking the feel of the double barrels of the shotgun brushing the back of his head. "No, sir," he whispered. He had slipped in—unobserved, he had thought—and grabbed the bag of salt. He was lying low, under the wagon, hoping for another opportunity to pop up and grab something else.

"What's your name, boy?"

"Andy. Andy St. John."

"How old are you, Andy St. John?"

"Be fifteen next month."

"You expect to reach that birthday, boy, you'd best change your thievin' ways. What the hell're you going to do with the salt? Sell it?"

"No, sir. I was gonna give it to my pa."

"He can't afford to buy it?"

"Not at the prices around here," St. John said simply.

Rhodes understood that, seeing how much breakfast had cost, and seeing what Flake was charging. "Your pa come on hard times?" he asked.

"Yessir."

"What happened?"

"He won't look on it kindly was I to say."

"I ain't going to tell him."

St. John was quiet for a little, then said, "We come out here so's Pa could work in the mines. Actually, he come out here first, a couple years ago, said he was gonna prospect and pan for gold and as

134

soon as he hit the mother lode, he was gonna send for us."

He quieted, and Rhodes figured he did not want to talk about it. It felt odd to Rhodes. He was only seven years older than Andy St. John, yet he had seen so much in life that it had robbed him of some of his youth. Rhodes shrugged. There was nothing he could do about that now. Hell, if the war hadn't come along, he might be doing the same thing St. John was doing right now. He moved the shotgun away from the young man's head. He had never even cocked it.

"Well, he never hit the mother lode," St. John finally continued, "but he did find some color. Enough to send for us. By the time we got out here, claim jumpers had got Pa's claim, and he was workin' for Ludwig and Macmillan."

"Who're they?"

"The big minin' company that come in. They're the ones brought in the two stamp mills up there. Anyway, that would've done us all well enough. Then Ma took sick. She passed on a couple of months ago. Pa took it pretty hard, and I guess he weren't thinkin' straight, and he got his leg stove all up bad gettin' it caught between two pieces of equipment. He couldn't work, so there wasn't no money comin' in. Soon's he was able, he went out and tried pannin' again. He found more color — it's darn near impossible not to around here, it seems — but not much more than'd keep us in flour at the prices the stores're charging."

"He better now?" Rhodes asked. He hardened his heart. The tale was one of woe, for sure, but Rhodes had been around long enough to know it could all be just that — a tale.

"Mostly. Still limps a lot, since his leg never got

135

doctored right. But the company don't want him back no more."

Rhodes rose. "Come on out of there, boy," he ordered quietly.

St. John did so and stood facing Rhodes. The teenager still held the sack of salt in his hand.

Rhodes stood there looking at the boy. He was almost Rhodes's height, but he had not filled out yet. He seemed all knees, elbows, and eyes, big round hazel eyes that were almost disconcerting to look at.

Rhodes made up his mind. "Listen to me, boy," he said, in his calm, reasoned voice, "and listen good. I find out you been giving me a load of shit here and I will hunt your ass down and make you pay in ways you can't even imagine." He paused to see if the threat had taken hold. It seemed to have. "Slip that salt into your shirt and get your skinny ass out of here."

St. John started to go, relief splashing across his thin, freckled face, when Rhodes reached out the shotgun, stopping him. "And you best not breathe a word of where you got it from. Understand?"

"Yessir," St. John said. There was no mistaking the relief in his voice.

"Git."

St. John slipped out the door like a wraith, and Rhodes climbed back onto his perch.

"I saw that, Mister Rhodes," Hickman said in one of his interminable trips between the two wagons.

"Saw what?" Rhodes asked innocently.

"Letting that boy make off with that bag of salt."

"So?" Rhodes asked with a shrug.

"Soon's I get a chance, I'm going to tell Brother Flake about it."

"It's your funeral," Rhodes said staring evenly back

at Hickman, who suddenly began to feel some uncertainty.

"What's that mean?" Hickman asked nervously.

"It means, Mr. Hickman, that if you say even one word about this, I'm going to pound you into ground."

"But . . ."

"When in the hell'd you get so goddamn sanctimonious?" Rhodes asked rhetorically in deadly cold tones. "How the hell do you know that I wasn't going to pay Erastus for it myself when this was all done?"

"But . . . I . . ."

"Phineas!" Flake bellowed for the third time. "Bring some more goods."

Hickman blinked at Rhodes and then turned. He hurriedly grabbed several tins of molasses and quickly went forward.

The mass of merchandise in the big wagon had already dwindled considerably. Rhodes went back to scanning the crowd. He spotted the attractive young woman again, and he let his gaze rest there for a little while. Looking at her, he could conjure up dreams of being married to her, of them settling somewhere a little less wild than Intolerance and raising a brood of kids.

As she had been before, she was standing with a man who looked terribly old. Or maybe he just looked overwhelmed by poor luck. The two had watched the parade of goods going to this person or that person, and each time something new came up for bid, they looked in a buckskin pouch. It appeared to Rhodes as if they never had enough in the pouch for anything. That was understandable considering that many store owners were bidding, and bidding high. That might make Flake rich, but the other people who would have to buy flour or what-not from the stores were going to be paying even higher prices.

Finally the man and young woman edged forward a little bit. Rhodes noted that the man limped. Seconds later, Andy St. John sidled up to the two and, with his back to Flake, showed the two something in his shirt.

Chapter Seventeen

A short, fat, dapper-dressed man moved up behind Andy St. John, the young woman, and the old man. He said something, at which he looked mighty smug. The others displayed a decent amount of distaste.

Flake's freight wagon was nearly empty, and yet the small group still seemed afraid to make any kind of bid. But as Flake called out that the last sack of flour was now open, the old man tentatively called out, "Ten dollars."

"Twenty," someone else shouted.

"Twenty-one," from Andy St. John's small group.

"Twenty-two," from the fat man behind them.

So it went, the little group raising the price by ever-smaller amounts, with the chubby townsman always upping the ante just a little more.

Rhodes hopped from his wagon to the freight wagon, and then to Flake's. He sidled up to Flake and said quietly, "Next offer that old man makes, you stop the bidding right then and there."

"But . . ." Flake said, looking at him in surprise.

"Just do it."

Flake spun and held out a hand. "Hold on a minute, folks," he said. He looked back at Rhodes and asked, "But why?"

"Because that fat son of a bitch behind 'em is going to outbid 'em no matter what they do."

"Why is that any concern of yours?" Flake was confounded.

"That old man, the girl, and boy look like they're up against it, Erastus. You know what that's like, don't you?"

"Well, of course, but . . ."

"Just call it your civic duty." Rhodes paused a moment. "I'll pay up whatever difference between what they pay and what you would've gotten."

Flake looked intently at Rhodes for some moments. Then he nodded. "There's no need for that." He turned to face the crowd again. "Now, folks where were we?"

The plump man shouted out the last figure he had given.

The old man looked into his little pouch. "Thirty-seven dollars and fifty-two cents," he said weakly.

As the chubby man began to open his mouth, Flake loudly, calmly and firmly said, "Sold!"

"Now wait a goddamn minute there," the chubby man shouted. "I was about to raise that bid."

"You're too late," Flake said flatly. He might be a businessman at heart, but he was afraid of no man. "I said at the beginning that the bidding was closed when I said it's closed. Next up for sale," he added, cutting off further protest.

The man, young woman, and youth came toward the wagon. As they went to hand Hickman the money, Flake called a halt to things out front and turned to Hickman. "There was a mistake in their bid, Phineas," he said evenly.

The old man looked stricken.

"Bidding should have stopped at twenty-five dollars."

140

"But, Erastus . . ."

"No buts now, Phineas. It was a wrong bid, and I'll not have any man calling Erastus Flake a cheat. Now if you're bound and determined to take that man's total of thirty dollars"—he winked at the old man—"then throw in that little sack of cornmeal we got back there and that one small side of bacon, too. I think there's a couple cans of that condensed milk back there. Put all that little stuff in a sack for 'em while I take their money."

Hickman looked at Flake like his friend had gone mad. Flake simply stared at him a moment. Hickman shrugged and went about his business. Flake looked down at the old man. "That'll be fifteen dollars, friend," he said quietly.

The man looked up, tears quivering in his eyes. "Thank you," he mouthed, afraid to say it aloud.

"Come on, get back to work," someone shouted from the small group of people still gathered out in front of the barn.

Flake ignored them as he took the money. "What's your name, friend?" he asked.

"Jim . . . Jim St. John." He paused, not sure whether he should speak again. He decided to try it. "My son, Andy. And my daughter, Hallie."

"Erastus Flake." He shook hands with both men and nodded to Hallie. "I must get back to work. Good luck to you."

"We've already had some, sir," the woman said. The old man took the sack of smaller items from Hickman, and then Andy St. John took the flour.

Flake was already back to work. But he was growing tired of it all. He called for Hickman to bring him three or four items to get rid of them more quickly.

Rhodes also was back at work, standing guard

from the open wagon. He watched as the St. Johns headed off down toward the street. From his vantage point, Rhodes could follow them for quite a distance. As he turned back to the front, he saw the chubby man walk straight away from the barn, heading toward an alleyway between a bakery and a brewery. He was moving fairly quickly.

Something about it puzzled Rhodes, and he worked on it. Then he started. He quickly jumped over to where Bonner waited, trying to keep himself awake. "You think you can keep an eye on things here, Joe?"

"I got nothin' else to do. What're you up to?"

"Ain't sure."

Bonner looked at him funny, but by the time he nodded, Rhodes was on the ground and walking swiftly away. Rhodes walked toward where he had last seen the chubby man. He stalked through the alley. At the far end, he stopped and looked each way. He suddenly wished he knew more about the town — and about the St. John family, mainly where they lived.

He didn't know any of that, though, but he was sure the chubby man was trying to head off the St. Johns before they got home, wherever that was. He wondered why for just an instant, but the vision of the beautiful Hallie St. John made him know why.

On a hunch, he went to his right, up the meandering mud street a little way. To his left was another alley. He glanced down it, and decided it was the right way to go.

Partway down that alley, another one branched off, and he spotted the heavyset man at the far end of the short alley. Rhodes wasted no time in heading that way, but he slowed as he neared the end. He eased up to it, and carefully peered around the corner to his left, then his right. There they were, on the small shady side street.

The chubby man had the three St. Johns up against the log wall of a house. Andy held both heavy sacks, looking frightened. The man had one palm on Jim's chest and the other on Hallie's, keeping them both hard up against the wall, and getting to feel a fair amount of Hallie in the doing.

Rhodes stalked up silently, putting a finger to his lips for silence when Andy spotted him. The youth's eyes were wide but he kept his mouth closed.

Rhodes whapped the chubby man a smart shot on the side of the head with the sawed-off shotgun. The man staggered to the side but did not go down. He did, however, remove his palms from Jim and Hallie St. John.

The chubby man whirled, face contorted with anger and pain. "What the hell'd you do that for, you goddamn fool?" he asked.

"Wanted to get your attention. Now that I have it, I might suggest to you that if you plan to try the laying on of hands, that you do it with someone other than the defenseless."

The man lifted a puffy, pale hand up to the side of his head. He looked at the fingers, now coated with blood. "Son of a bitch." He glared at Rhodes. "Do you know who the hell you're messing with?" he asked.

Rhodes shrugged. "Don't know and don't much care."

"I'm Hamilton Macmillan."

"Don't mean anything to me, boy," Rhodes said flatly. "All I know is you're a putrefying pile of horse droppings trying to take advantage of folks."

"My father owns the mine," Macmillan said huffily. "He owns the whole goddamn town."

"Watch your language around ladies, boy," Rhodes warned.

"I'll talk any goddamn way I goddamn well feel like goddamn talking," Macmillan said.

Rhodes held the shotgun in both hands. He jerked it forward, the muzzles slamming into Macmillan's stomach. The fat man's breath popped out and he doubled over. "Maybe now you'll watch your mouth."

"You're just goddamn lucky you have that goddamn scattergun in your hand," Macmillan wheezed.

Rhodes chuckled. "And just what would you do if I didn't have it?" he asked sarcastically.

"I'd beat the living hell out of you."

Rhodes laughed. He held out the shotgun. "Mr. St. John, would you be so kind as to hold this for me for a bit." It was not really a question.

"Sure," St. John said nervously. He took the weapon.

"Now, Mr. Hamilton Macmillan," Rhodes said easily, "let's see what you can do."

"What about those pistols in your belt?"

"They'll stay put. Now make your move, if you've got the gumption."

Macmillan straightened up, and grinned. He figured he had Rhodes now. They were about the same height, but Macmillan outweighed even the broad Rhodes by some pounds. He charged, swinging a meaty right hand.

Rhodes stepped up and blocked the blow with his left forearm. With a big right fist, Rhodes hammered Macmillan twice where the arm and shoulder came together. Then he stepped back.

Macmillan groaned and his right arm suddenly hung limply at his side. Hate glared hotly in his eyes.

"You still want to try something?" Rhodes asked

144

quietly.

Macmillan did not answer. He just stood there glowering.

Rhodes shrugged. "Now, I'm going to warn you just this one time. You bother these people again, and I'll tear that arm off for you. You got that?"

Macmillan remained mum.

"I asked if you understood me, boy," Rhodes said.

Something in that voice gave Macmillan pause, and for the first time he realized just how close to death he was. He nodded. "I understand."

"Good. Now git."

Macmillan shuffled off, holding his right arm tight to his body with his left hand. Rhodes watched until Macmillan was out of sight. Then he turned and smiled pleasantly at the St. Johns. "I'll take that scattergun back now, Mr. St. John," he said quietly.

"Thank you," St. John said weakly. He felt disgusted with himself for not being able to protect his family; nor even to provide for them.

"Name's Travis Rhodes. You want, I'll escort you folks home."

"I don't think that'll be necessary," St. John said stiffly. He might not be able to provide for Andy and Hallie, but he could at least turn down a demeaning offer of help.

"I'd rather he did, Papa," Hallie said.

St. John looked at his daughter sternly, and then suddenly realized that Hallie was interested in this young man. He wasn't sure how he felt about that. In some ways, if something were to happen between Hallie and the tough, wide-shouldered stranger, it would be good. She would be out of the house and so there would be one less mouth to feed. Rhodes also looked like a man who could offer him and his family some protection. That galled at St. John, but

145

it had to be considered. He was no longer young, and with his bad leg, he was hard pressed to accomplish much.

On the other side of the ledger, Rhodes did not look like the kind to set down roots in one place. He would hate to see something develop between Rhodes and his daughter, he would hate to see Hallie hurt when Rhodes went riding off. He sighed. Life had become too hard, too awkward.

"All right," he said. "If you want, Hallie."

"I would, Papa."

Rhodes strolled along with the St. Johns. He seemed to them to be just moseying along, but he was really very alert, eyes sweeping the path, surreptitiously checking alleys as they passed, windows and doorways.

The walk was short, and then the St. Johns stopped in front of a canted, shabby shack.

"Thanks, Mr. Rhodes," Andy said with a smile and a wave just before he went inside.

"I thank you, too," Jim St. John said. He was still embarrassed. He slipped inside to hide his shame.

"I'd be obliged if you were to let me come calling on you, Miss St. John," Rhodes said quietly.

She smiled brightly. "I'd like that, Mr. Rhodes."

"I'll be by tomorrow."

"Is ten all right?"

He nodded, then turned and walked away. He was almost stunned by it all. He had been smitten so fast that it still made his head whirl.

Chapter Eighteen

"You seem to be able to fool people into talking to you, Joe," Rhodes said to Bonner as they sat at a table in a saloon.

Bonner shrugged. "I got lots of gifts," he said, taking a sip of beer.

"About the only one you have is the gift of shelling out bullshit," Rhodes said with a laugh. He waited until the laughter had died down, then he said, "You heard anything of a Hamilton Macmillan?"

"Nope. Should I have?"

Rhodes explained his run-in that afternoon with Macmillan. "He claims to be the son of the guy who owns the big mine up the hill there."

"If he is, you could be in a deep puddle of shit, boy."

"Whoa, now I'm really worried." Rhodes snorted.

"I can tell." He paused for another mouthful of beer. "I suppose you want me to see what I can learn about this blubbery snot?" Bonner would prefer to stay just where he was.

"If you're up to it, old man."

"What're you payin' for all this work?"

"Hell, you don't know the meaning of 'work.' "

"Bah."

"That does raise another question, though,"

147

Rhodes said solemnly. "As you well know, prices ain't cheap in these parts, and I ain't got an unlimited supply of cash."

"You got any supply of cash?" Bonner asked pointedly, beer mug stopped halfway to his mouth.

"Not much."

"How much is not much?" Bonner set the mug down. He might act the crotchety old man — and even mean it more often than not — but when a friend was in trouble, he would help in any way he could.

"About twenty bucks or so."

"Around here, that ain't gonna last long."

"As if I haven't figured that out." He paused. "How about you, Joe? You got enough to keep you going a little?"

"Longer'n you. But not much." He had been broke before and it had never bothered him. But that was back in the old days, when a couple months' worth of trapping would give him enough money for one hell of a spree. And then he could get credit on supplies for the next season. But those days were no more; not for him, not for anyone. He might still be able to pull in some cash by slaughtering buffalo for the railroads, or just for the hides, but he was a couple hundred miles west and a couple thousand feet up for that.

He lifted his beer and stretched out his legs. He was too goddamn old, he figured, for worrying over such nonsense. Still, the talk had produced a gloom that settled over him. He could see that it had settled over Rhodes, too. Bonner drained his mug and set it down, then rose. "Be back in a spell." Cradling his Hawken with his left arm, he strode out.

Rhodes realized that he was sitting all scrunched up. He forced himself to sit back and relax. He sipped his beer. He decided that he would have to find a job somewhere, but he figured that shouldn't be too hard. There was plenty of work available for a strong young man with a willingness to work hard. Then he decided that he could let that wait a few more days. Or, he thought, perhaps he should just pack it in and head elsewhere. He had nothing to keep him here, and his prospects were certain to be better almost anywhere else.

A few hours later, too bored to sit and wait for Bonner to return, Rhodes finally got up and headed outside. He was feeling groggy from too much beer, too much gloom, too much smoke, and too much staleness. The night air helped clear his head a little. He headed off down the street, not sure where he was going, but he headed in the general direction of the livery. He figured he could stay the night there cheaper than just about anywhere.

He stopped at an intersection, and a small smile crossed his lips. He turned and headed toward the St. John's home. He stopped a few moments, looking at the place. Maybe there was something to keep him here.

He walked toward the livery again.

"Hey ol' hoss," Bonner said with a fair amount of cheer, moving into stride alongside Rhodes.

"What the hell're you so good-humored over," Rhodes said with a little irritation.

"Hell, it ain't good for a body to be so gloomful. Especially when I got news."

"Bad news, I figure."

"Just listen, then you tell me, you gripin' ol' son of a bitch." He spit tobacco and wiped the splatter off his lips with the back of a hand. "First off, that Macmillan feller you tangled with is pretty much a bag of wind."

Rhodes stopped and spun toward Bonner, staring at him in the dull glow of a lantern. "What?"

"Just what I said, goddammit. His ol' man's one of the owners, sure enough, but a small one, and he's back in the States. The uncle — Logan Macmillan — is the real boss in the minin' company. His pa sent the persnickety little bastard with instructions to his uncle to work his flabby ass off. Somethin' dear ol' uncle ain't been able to do as yet."

"So all that shit he gave me was . . ."

"Just what you said. He's a bully and his uncle ain't got a lick of likin' for him. Especially when it involves a young lady. From what I hear, if dear ol' uncle hears he's been botherin' that purty little thing, sonny boy might lose somethin' mighty precious to him."

Rhodes laughed in relief. He was not afraid of either Hamilton Macmillan or Logan Macmillan either. But at least now he wouldn't have to be looking over his shoulder every minute.

"That's the kind of news I like to get," Rhodes finally said.

"Thought you'd be appreciative," Bonner said smugly. "And there's more." He held out a pouch.

"What's this?"

"Take it."

Rhodes did. Slowly he opened it. Even in the dimness of the night broken only by a fluttering lantern, he could see the gold coins. "Where in hell'd this come from?"

"Your pay."

"My what?"

"Goddamn, you are knob-headed, ain't you? Jesus. You helped out them Mormon folks quite a bit. Fought with them, got 'em safely to Fort Laramie, helped out with the goods and all. They figured they was some in your debt."

"How much is in here?" Rhodes asked, still finding it hard to believe he had been blessed with such good fortune.

"Two, three hundred."

Rhodes whistled. Then he looked sternly at Bonner. "You ain't givin' me a line of bullshit now, are you, old man?"

"Like what?"

"Like maybe you had this stashed somewhere and are givin' it to me to make me feel better?"

Bonner produced another pouch and opened it. "My share of the gold for guidin' 'em up here and for helpin' out today and on the trail."

"Well, I'll be damned," Rhodes breathed.

"Then let's go get a head start," Bonner said gleefully.

"Head start?" Rhodes was confused.

"On bein' damned." Bonner cackled joyously. "I've gone a ways down that path already, but hell, there's a lot more trail to follow."

Rhodes laughed. "You go on, old man. I'll catch up to you tomorrow."

"You're gonna go see that purty little thing now, ain't you?"

"Not now. Tomorrow mornin', though."

"Filly-chasin' young snot," Bonner snorted.

"Just go on about your business, you scabrous old reprobate."

Rhodes watched a moment as Bonner swaggered off, and Rhodes smiled. He considered going to get a hotel room now that he had some cash, but then he decided against it. What with prices in Intolerance, he still didn't have enough to last out the whole winter, so any savings he could manage would be to his benefit. He turned and walked to the livery.

After breakfast the next morning, he stopped in a dry goods place and bought himself a new outfit, paying what for him was an outrageous sum. Carrying his packages, he walked to the nearest tonsorial parlor, where he had a shave, a hair trim, and a bath.

Clad in his new outfit of heavy denim pants, striped collarless shirt, bandanna around the throat, and a long, black jacket, he headed toward the St. John house. Hallie must have been waiting for him, he figured, since he had barely knocked when the door opened. He didn't mind—it showed she liked him and was looking forward to their time together.

She looked radiant to Rhodes. Her hair was washed and brushed to a sleek fineness. Her calico dress was old and faded, but it was clean and fit her very well. A bonnet hung by its string off the back of her head.

"Well, ma'am, what should we do?" Rhodes asked, as Hallie took his arm and they began strolling toward the heart of Intolerance.

"The first thing you should do is call me by my name, Mr. Rhodes."

"Only if you call me by my name, Miss Hallie."

She smiled, and he noticed that her upper lip curled up more on the right side than the left when she smiled. It didn't bother him in the least.

"All right, Travis." She paused. "I'd like a buggy ride, if we could do that?" Her bright blue eyes were wide with wonder, and worry. "It's been such a long time since I had me a buggy ride. Money's not been . . ."

"No need to talk of that, Hallie," Rhodes said earnestly. "You pa's had a run of bad luck is all. Every man has that of a time. He'll be back on his feet soon." He smiled. "And if it's a buggy ride you want, it's a buggy ride you'll get."

It did not take long to rent a buggy. Rhodes had Pace hitch up his mule to the buggy. As they rode through town, heading for the road away from the mines and stamp mills, Hallie suddenly looked distraught.

Rhodes noticed it, and his stomach tightened. "What's wrong, Hallie?" he asked.

"Oh, nothing," she said unconvincingly. She bit her lower lip.

Rhodes stopped the buggy in the middle of the street, eliciting a number of rude comments. He did not care. "We're not going another foot till you tell me what's botherin' you."

She shook her head, fighting back tears.

"All right, then, we'll go back. You don't want to be out here with me, I ain't about to force it on you."

"No!"

"Then tell me what's wrong."

"I was just thinkin' how nice'd be if we had us a picnic lunch with us."

"That all?" Rhodes said in some surprise. "Lord, I thought something was wrong. You want a picnic lunch, let's get us one." He pulled the buggy to the side of the wide street in front of Hornbeck's restaurant. Then he helped her down and they went inside.

"What can I do for you?" the waiter asked. Rhodes could not decide whether the man was just smug, or if he had an impacted bowel.

"Set us up a picnic basket," Rhodes said.

"With what?"

Rhodes decided the waiter was both smug and

had an impacted bowel. "Whatever Miss Hallie wants, you put it in there, then come to me and I'll pay up."

The waiter seemed as if he did not want to believe Rhodes, who simply glared at the man. The waiter got the message, and he turned. "Come with me, miss," he said.

Twenty minutes later, they were on their way again, equipped with a well-stocked picnic basket and a good heavy blanket. Rhodes turned off the main road onto a small trail that curled upward to the west. They went slowly, not wanting to overtax the mule, and because they were in no hurry.

They came to a meadow ringed with pines and aspens. A small creek tumbled out of the rocks along one side. Next to the rushing stream, on a shady patch of grass, Rhodes stopped. There was nowhere else to go anyway, this small meadow being ringed by peaks. Hallie got the picnic things out while Rhodes unharnessed the mule. He hobbled the animal and turned him out to graze. Then Rhodes took his seat on the blanket next to Hallie.

Chapter Nineteen

Rhodes took almost no end of ribbing from Joe Bonner over the next few days. The young man spent much of the time with Hallie St. John, enjoying himself more than he ever had. Most evenings, he hunted out Bonner in one of Intolerance's thirty-seven saloons, and once or twice he visited one of the fancy girls. He felt a little guilty about that, but he assuaged his conscience by telling himself that in doing so, he was protecting Hallie from his baser instincts and advances. Bonner even gave him a hard time over that, until Rhodes just wanted to pound his friend. Then he would calm himself and burst out laughing.

The day after the picnic with Hallie, Rhodes looked up Erastus Flake in the hotel. "I just wanted to stop by and thank you for all you've done for me, Erastus," he said quietly.

"On the contrary, Travis, we're still in your debt and will remain so for a long time to come."

"You don't owe me anything, Erastus. I didn't do all that much."

"Such modesty," Flake said with a laugh. "Anyway, we're glad to've helped you in some little fashion." He paused and then said, "Are you calling on that young lady you helped out at the auction?"

"Yessir. A fine gal she is, too, Erastus."

"She appeared to be all that and more, son." He lowered his voice. "If you need anything — money or some small amount of supplies — in order to win her over, don't you hesitate to call on me."

"Much obliged, Erastus." He could not believe his good fortune. "But I wouldn't want to leave you short."

"I don't believe that'll be a problem," Flake said seriously. "We made out better at the sale than I had a right to expect. Then we sold the freight wagon and team to the mining company for a tidy sum. We'll be moving into that place I told you about and will stay there for the winter."

"Sounds like you're all set up, then."

"I think so." Flake hesitated, unsure if he should say anything, then decided he had to. "Phineas and I have taken jobs with one of the merchants. That, too, will help us out." He stared straight into Rhodes's eyes. "Finding a job yourself might not be all that bad a thing. Especially if you are thinking of perhaps settling down with your young lady."

"I think such a thing is a bit early on both counts," Rhodes said with a laugh. "But I'll have to decide soon, I expect."

"Yes, well, thank you again, Travis, for all you've done, and don't wait to call on us if you need anything."

"I'll keep it in mind." The two shook hands, and then Rhodes left, eager to see Hallie.

A few days later, Hallie invited Rhodes to supper at her home. He gladly accepted. When he arrived at the house, though, Hallie seemed downcast. Rhodes figured it was because her family was in hard financial straits, but as they ate a sparse but tasty meal, Rhodes began to suspect something else

156

was bothering her. He tried to make light conversation, but none of the St. Johns were helping.

Finally he leaned back, irritated. He pulled two cigars out of a shirt pocket and handed one to Jim St. John. The old man looked pleased but guilty. Rhodes bit off the end of his cigar and lit it. "Now," he said, "just what's got you all so gloomful?" He liked that word, which he had heard Bonner use more than once.

"Nothin'," Hallie said lamely.

"Hallie," Rhodes said slowly, quietly, "I'm by nature a patient man. But when it comes to something botherin' someone I care for very much, I lose that patience rapidly." He paused for a few puffs on the cigar. "If it's a family problem, maybe I can help." He looked at Jim St. John. "There ain't any shame in needin' help of a time, Mr. St. John," he said earnestly. "We all need it. If you've encountered more difficulties, tell me. You never know but what I might be able to help you."

St. John looked at Rhodes, fear and worry in his eyes. He liked Rhodes considerably, though he had not shown it. He was still so embarrassed by his troubles that he did not want Rhodes to know how bad off he and his children really were. Still, he wondered, this might be the time to ask for some help. He nodded at Hallie.

The young woman took a breath, which Rhodes thought was quite interesting to watch. Then she said quietly, her cheek pinking up, "Hamilton Macmillan came by last evening."

"So?"

"He threatened Pa that if I didn't give in to his advances, he'd hurt Pa. Andy, too."

"That all?" Rhodes asked, surprised.

"Yes," Hallie said, flustered. Her life was about to

157

go into shambles and Rhodes looked and sounded as if he didn't care at all.

"Don't worry about it."

"But how . . . why . . . How can I not think about it?"

"Just don't," Rhodes said with a shrug. It was so simple to him. He couldn't understand how people clung to their worries like this. "He won't bother you again." He smiled easily.

Hallie smiled tentatively back. She could see in Rhodes's gray eyes that he was not making fun of her. He was just delighted to be in her company. She could never tell him that she thought about him in the same way. She only hoped that he could see her love for him in her eyes the way she could see it in his.

That set her heart aflutter with nervousness. She had not, in the few days Rhodes had been courting her, admitted even to herself that she cared for him so. It was a shock to her, but she enjoyed it, too. Still, she was worried that he might be playing her for a fool; that he might leave her soon. Seeing the warm, caring look in his eyes, she doubted that in her head, but her heart still worried.

"Now, how's about you and me takin' a stroll through town, Hallie?" Rhodes asked.

"Pa?" She looked at her father, who nodded.

It had rained for most of yesterday, and the ground had once more become a quagmire. The St. Johns had a small boardwalk out to the street. When Hallie and Rhodes got that far, Hallie stopped, looking at the mud. She was glad it was just about dark, since that would hide her embarrassment. She could never admit to Rhodes that this was her only good dress and shoes and she didn't want to get them covered with mud.

158

Rhodes had stopped and watched Hallie. He had noted that she had worn the same dress every time they had been together, and he figured it was one of only two or three she possessed. He also noted the distaste that lightly furrowed her usually smooth brow as she stood looking at the mud. Rhodes grinned and tossed away the cigar. He turned and suddenly scooped her into his powerful arms.

Hallie whooped in surprise at the move, but she gladly wrapped her slender arms around Rhodes's neck and leaned her head against his shoulder. She felt as if she were in heaven.

Rhodes figured Hallie couldn't weigh more than ninety pounds, and he had no trouble carrying her. Finally they reached the center of town, where there was a boardwalk in front of most of the buildings. Rhodes put Hallie down, and they strolled up one side of the street. Then Rhodes carried Hallie across the wide, muddy street, and they ambled down that side.

Rhodes felt good walking with the petite, beautiful Hallie St. John at his side. At the same time, though, he was worried. Not for himself, but for her. Intolerance was, after all, a rough-and-tumble mining town, where fights, gunfire, and other sorts of trouble broke out with mind-numbing frequency.

At the cross street down which Hallie lived, Rhodes picked her up again, and she nestled comfortably in his arms. He strode along, seemingly without strain. Just before getting to the St. John house he stopped.

Hallie looked up into his eyes in alarm. He smiled warmly, bent his head, and kissed her. Hallie was surprised, but then she responded as ardently as she could. When Rhodes pulled his head back, she asked nervously, "Did I do all right?"

Rhodes realized that for the first time in his life he tingled all over from the touch of a woman, and nodded. "Perfect," he said, voice husky. He started walking again. "I best get you home."

"Why?" she asked, worried and confused.

"So's I don't overstep my bounds," he said gruffly.

"Oh?" Hallie said, still confused. Then it dawned on her. "Oh!" Still, she demanded another kiss—one willingly given—when Rhodes placed her gently on her feet on the planks in front of her house. This one lasted a considerable while.

Then Hallie favored Rhodes with another smile that was dazzling even in the dim moonlight. "Good night," she breathed.

Rhodes nodded and turned, a little dazed. He headed straight for one of the saloons, jolted down a quick shot of whiskey, and then picked one of the painted ladies. He needed release.

Rhodes was saddling his palomino the next morning when Bonner arrived. "Goin' somewheres?" he asked, pointing to the horse.

"Just need to give him a little working out," Rhodes said flatly.

"Bullshit," Bonner said with a cackle. "Ain't you seein' your lady today? Or'd she finally get wise to your schemin' and toss you out?"

"You're a goddamn putrifyin' sack of buffalo droppings, ain't you?" Rhodes said, but there was no sting in his words.

"I've been told so by many a chil'," the still-cackling Bonner said. He sounded proud of the fact.

"One of these days you're going to go too far, old man," Rhodes offered, the threat feigned. He finished with the saddle and began working the bridle over the horse's head. "That fellah Macmillan was botherin' Hallie again," he said as he worked. "I'm

160

going up to the mines and have a chat with his uncle. Him, too, if he's stupid enough to be around."

"You want company?"

Rhodes shrugged. "Only if you ain't got anything else to do."

"I don't." With Rhodes's help, Bonner quickly saddled and bridled his horse, and they rode out.

It wasn't really all that far to the mine offices up the hill south of town, but it was a steep slope, and the horses really did need some exercise. They had been standing around for the better part of six days. But they could not find the office. They spotted a worker and waved him over.

"Where's the office?" Rhodes fairly screamed at the man. The roar of the stamp mills was deafening.

"Far side of town," the man bellowed back, pointing. "Next to the assay office."

Rhodes nodded. He and Bonner rode down the hill quickly, trying to get away from the noise. They finally found the office and dismounted, tying the horses to the wood hitching rail.

Inside, a bespectacled young man wearing a dark eye shade and with arm garters over his crisp white boiled shirt, worked at a large desk behind a thigh-high railing. There was little else in the room except a table on which maps were piled. At the back of the room was a door, which was closed.

The clerk looked up and asked, "Can I help you?"

"I'd like to see Mr. Macmillan — Logan Macmillan."

"He doesn't often receive visitors," the clerk said, looking with distaste at the two.

"Tell him it's about his nephew."

"Who shall I say is calling?"

"Name's Travis Rhodes."

The clerk nodded and headed toward the room at

back. He rapped on it, then went in. A few moments later he stepped back out, holding the door open. "Mr. Macmillan will see you now," he said.

Rhodes strode across the room and through the door, kicking it shut behind him, much to the clerk's chagrin.

Logan Macmillan was a wiry man of medium height, and a man who possessed a look of competence and command. His clothing was the best that could be had in Denver, or even St. Louis. His eyes were direct and his face clean-shaven. He stood and reached across the wide, polished oak desk, hand out. Rhodes took the hand and shook it.

"Sit," Macmillan said, waving to a chair in front of the desk. He settled into the plush leather chair behind the desk. The chair was so big it almost seemed to swallow Macmillan. "You're one of the men helped that Mormon fellow auction off the goods a few days ago, aren't you?"

"I am."

"Nice fellow. Flake was his name?"

"Yep. Erastus Flake."

"I bought his freight wagon and team after his auction."

"So he told me."

"Are you one of his people? A Mormon, I mean?"

Rhodes shook his head. "No, sir. I found 'em on the trail after they'd had some troubles. I just gave 'em a hand for a spell."

Macmillan nodded. "A drink?" he asked.

"Only if you're having one."

Macmillan smiled. "Hell, one little snort can't hurt, eh?" He pulled out a bottle from his desk and two glasses. He poured and then pushed one of the glasses toward Rhodes. He raised his own in a sort of toast. Rhodes reciprocated, and then they drank.

162

Macmillan corked the bottle and leaned back in the chair. "Now, sir, what do you want to tell me about my nephew?"

Rhodes could not miss the annoyance that had flitted ever so briefly across Macmillan's face.

Chapter Twenty

Rhodes chewed a lip a few moments, then said, "Your nephew has been casting unwelcome attentions on a . . . friend, shall we say. The young lady has quite plainly made known her displeasure at such attentions."

Macmillan looked serious, as if he were pondering some deep philosophical thought. He noted, though, that he apparently was not fooling Rhodes. He smiled a little sheepishly. "It's not the first time Hamilton's done such a thing," he said with a sigh.

"It may be his last." Rhodes spoke in his normal quiet tones, but the warning was clear.

Macmillan looked at him for a few moments. "You're the one who thumped the crap out of him, aren't you?"

Rhodes nodded.

Macmillan laughed a little. "Maybe the son of a bitch has more gumption that I thought. After that drubbing you gave him, he still pestered that girl."

Rhodes shrugged. "Gumption or no," he said, "he bothers her again and you'll be plantin' him in the boneyard."

"This is the St. John girl?" Macmillan asked, appearing outwardly to have no reaction to Rhodes's threat on his nephew.

"Yessir."

"And you are sweet on her?"

"Yessir." Rhodes felt no embarrassment at admitting it.

Macmillan nodded and sighed. "I'll do what I can," he finally said. "Hamilton is, I admit, a persnickety devil. To tell you the truth, Mr. Rhodes, I'm surprised as all hell that someone else hasn't kicked the crap out of him before this. It's my constant worry—that he will direct his attentions where they are not wanted and someone will kill him." He sighed. He seemed to do a lot of that when the talk was about Hamilton Macmillan. "Still he is my brother's boy and I have some responsibility for his behavior—and in keeping him safe."

"Tell him to stop botherin' people who don't want his attentions," Rhodes said flatly. "That'll keep him as safe as anything will."

"Indeed." Macmillan looked troubled. "I've done what I can to get him to become a man, but nothing has worked." He pushed himself up. Hands clasped behind his back, he paced. "I'll speak to him again," Macmillan said as he stopped pacing and faced Rhodes. "But I don't know how much good it'll do. He's a wayward young man."

"Wayward my ass," Rhodes said with no hint of humor. "He's a bully and a coward. The only reason he gets away with most of this shit is because he's your nephew. Most folks here need a job, and they figure that if they were to fight back against Hamilton, you'd fire them."

"That's always a possibility, I suppose, though I'd be more inclined to believe the townsman than I would Ham."

"They don't know that."

"I guess they don't." He ran a hand along his

smoothly shaven cheeks. "I'll see what I can do about him, Mr. Rhodes."

"That'd be wise, if you want him to go on living. I ain't one of the folks here who needs a job, and while I won't go to lengths to get on anyone's bad side, I have a lot less to lose here than many a man, and I ain't worried about incurring your wrath."

"I suspected that," Macmillan said with a slight smile. "Well, is there anything else I can do for you, Mr. Rhodes? A job perhaps?" He was only half joking, though he could always use a guard to keep the miners — and anyone else — from stealing Ludwig and Macmillan gold.

"That's a possibility," Rhodes said. "But not for me."

Macmillan looked at him, eyes wide in surprise, questioning.

"Miss St. John's pa."

"He the fellow with the game leg?"

Rhodes nodded.

"I thought he did work for us."

"Used to. Then he mangled his leg. He tried comin' back to work a while back, but he was told he wasn't needed, as long as he was gimpin' along."

"Must've been Winchell — Fred Winchell, the tunnel foreman — who told him that." He paused, thinking. "What kind of work can he do?"

"Nearabout anything he used to do, I suppose. He's got a limp, and that makes him a little less spry than some others, but you'll not find anyone more willin'."

Macmillan suddenly nodded. "I see no difficulty in this," he announced. "Tell Mr. St. John to report to Curley Benton in the mornin'. Curley's the foreman of the wagons. Mr. St. John can drive one of the ore wagons between the mines and the stamp mills. At his old wage, of course."

Rhodes nodded and stood. "I'm obliged, Mr. Macmillan, for your help and consideration."

Macmillan smiled weakly. "In most ways, I should be obliged to you, Mr. Rhodes." He paused. "Try to go easy on Ham, if you can. That's all I ask of you, sir." There was concern but no pleading in the man's eyes.

"I'll try," Rhodes said quietly. "That's all I can promise."

Macmillan nodded and held out his hand. They shook, and Rhodes walked out of the room. Bonner was regaling the clerk with bloody tales. Rhodes bit back his laughter when he saw the clerk's pasty, petrified face.

"Come on, you old coot," Rhodes said lightly. "You've scared the poor lad more than enough for one day."

As Rhodes and Bonner rode back toward the livery stable, Bonner said, "I almost forgot I had somethin' to tell you before, boy. I found us a place to stay."

"Boarding house?" Rhodes asked.

"Naw. Our own little shack."

"How much?" Rhodes asked suspiciously.

"Not a goddamn cent." He laughed. "Won it in a faro game last night."

"I hope you didn't win a place where we'll have to toss out a wife and a brood of young 'uns."

"Hell, what do you think I am, boy?" Bonner protested.

"I'll reserve judgment till I know a little more."

"Aw, pshaw," Bonner said. He leaned over the side of his horse and spit tobacco juice. "I went and checked it last night after I won it. It don't look much worse—and no better—than any of the others around here. It's kind of droopin' sideways some and there's holes big enough to ride a horse through, but it's better'n stayin' with the horses like we been doin'. It's got an old cook stove in it, so it'll keep us warm enough, I suppose."

"No family, though?"

"Naw. Checked that out, too. His wife and brood run off on him some months ago. Said she couldn't take it no more, what with all his gamblin' and drinkin' and whorin'."

Rhodes nodded. "Sounds like a right nice place," he said sarcastically. "Where is it?"

"Two streets over from your Miss Hallie's place toward the east, and half an alley north."

Rhodes nodded as they pulled into the yard fronting the livery stable. "I'm going off to Hallie's," Rhodes said. "I got some news for her old man."

"You mean to say you got no other reason for goin' over there?" Bonner asked. He laughed.

"Reckon I could find another reason," Rhodes said without embarrassment. He had given up being embarrassed by Bonner's crude jokes and such. He knew the old man was just funning him. "I'll meet you at the house after supper." He turned and walked the horse along.

At Hallie's, he dismounted and tied his horse to a stunted tree out front. Then he rapped on the door.

"Who is it?" Hallie asked cautiously, voice quivering with nervousness.

"Travis."

The door flew open, and Hallie smiled at him. "Come on in," she said brightly. She was relieved that it hadn't been Hamilton Macmillan who knocked. That was a constant worry. She also was just plain glad to see Rhodes. She had never thought she could fall in love with someone so fast. But she had. She vowed to tell Rhodes—soon—just how much she cared for him.

"You can quit your worrying now," Rhodes said as he took off his wide-brimmed hat and entered the house. "I talked to Logan Macmillan this morning, and he said he'll keep Hamilton away from you."

She looked skeptical. "Ham's not a man to take such advice kindly."

Rhodes shrugged. "I told Logan what'd happen if Hamilton bothers you again. He didn't like it a lot, but he understood it and he's willing—obviously reluctantly—to accept those consequences."

"I still don't know," Hallie said, worry wrinkling her forehead.

"Let's go outside a minute," he said quietly.

Hallie looked up at him, then nodded. She no longer found it necessary to ask her father for permission for these things.

Outside, Rhodes and Hallie went to the end of the boardwalk. Rhodes absentmindedly stroked his horse's mane. "You have to stop worryin' about this, Hallie," Rhodes said earnestly.

"I know, but . . ."

"Don't you think I'm capable of caring for you?" Rhodes interjected.

"Yes, but . . ."

"Do you think I'd let him—or anyone else—harm you?"

"No, but . . ." Her head was awhirl. She had lived in fear for so long that it was not easy to free herself of its lingering ravages.

"Do you doubt that I love you?"

"No, but . . ." She stopped, blue eyes wide and bright in the sunshine. "You what?" she asked. The fear inside her grew. She half suspected that she had wanted to hear those words and so had created them in her head. She was worried now that she would be rebuffed. At the same time, her heart sang with hope.

"I said, do you doubt that I love you," Rhodes said quietly and firmly.

"You've never said that before." She was so excited she could hardly stand still.

"I thought you knew. It ain't easy for me to say that."

A little chill wormed its way into Hallie's insides. "How many times've you said it before?" she asked.

"Once," Rhodes said with a small smile. "I said it to Netty Cornwall one time." He could see the hurt building in Hallie's eyes, and was sorry for it, but he could not resist. "We were about five at the time," he added.

It took a moment or two for that to sink in. Hallie's eyes widened again in surprise, then narrowed in anger. "Why you no-'count, overgrowed big ox," she said, hitting him in the chest with her small fists. "You rotten, grumptious, baitin' devil, you."

She planned to continue the tirade, but Rhodes swept her into the cocoon of his arms and pulled her tight to him. "There ain't anyone but you, Hallie," he said quietly as he stroked her soft, brown hair. "Never was before, and I expect there'll never be again."

"Ain't you gonna ask me to marry you?" she said into his shirt.

"One day, Hallie. One day." He paused, dreams of what life would be like with Hallie as his wife. "But

170

I've got to get myself set up first. Right now I don't have a hell of a lot of prospects."

"Well, find somethin' soon," Hallie whispered. "I don't want to wait till I'm an old maid before you take me to wife."

"Me neither."

"Good. Now kiss me."

"What about your neighbors?" Rhodes didn't much care for himself, but it might ruin Hallie's reputation.

"The devil take them," Hallie said firmly. She tilted her head back a little and waited.

Rhodes fulfilled her request.

"You comin' in for a bit?" Hallie asked when they parted lips.

"No," Rhodes said, a little befuddled by all that had occurred in the past five minutes. "I've got to go take care of the horse." Then he stopped, "Yeah, I will come in. I have something to tell your pa."

They walked into the small, shabby house, hand in hand. "Mr. Rhodes says he has somethin' to tell you, Pa," Hallie said.

Jim St. John looked from his daughter to his—he assumed—future son-in-law. "What is it?" he asked nervously. The news for the St. Johns had been bad for so long that he could see nothing else anymore.

"You're to report to a Curley somebody up at the mine tomorrow morning."

"Curley Benton?" St. John asked. Fear and hope fought for dominance.

"That's him."

"But . . . why?"

"Why do you think? You can't drive an ore wagon sittin' here."

"I'm hired on?" St. John asked, incredulous.

171

"Yessir."

"Oh, praise the Lord," St. John said, overcome. "I don't know how to thank you Travis. I—"

"No thanks are needed. All I did was to ask those folks to hire you on again, that's all. You'll have to show them you can handle it."

Chapter Twenty-one

Rhodes and Bonner spent a couple of days fixing up the old shack Bonner had won. It was not a great place, but with a little work, it was serviceable. They plugged most of the bigger chinks in the wall, repaired the chimney, made sure the stove worked, piled up some firewood, and stocked the cabin with such foodstuffs as they had been inclined to buy for now.

"Ain't exactly home, sweet home, is it, Joe?" Rhodes asked, laughing, as the two men stood looking at the outside of it.

"I been in a heap worse spots," Bonner said. "I ever tell you about the time I—"

"Yes, goddamn it," Rhodes said, laughing a little more, "About a hundred times."

"You didn't even know which tale I was gonna tell," Bonner said, feigning injured pride.

"It don't matter none," he ribbed his friend. He was determined to get back at Bonner for all the teasing Bonner had been doing about Rhodes and Hallie. He figured this was a good chance. "They're all the same. The great Joe Bonner conquers all—Injuns and bad men, outlaws and mountain men, grizzly bears and cougars." He was laughing even more now. "And all of 'em a pack of lies bigger than any I ever heard before."

"Such talk's likely to cut deep into an old man's pride," Bonner said, though he was laughing, too.

"You ain't got any pride—or decency either."

"Lordy, Lordy, I been cut to the quick," Bonner said. He was leaning against the cabin wall trying to catch his breath from laughing so hard.

"Come on, gramps," Rhodes said, still laughing, "let's go get us something to celebrate our new abode with."

"Now, *that's* the kind of tale I like to hear, boy. Plumb shines to this ol' chil'."

They walked softly down the relatively quiet side street toward the main section of town. Bonner carried his rifle, and had a Colt Dragoon revolver in his belt. Rhodes had both Whitneys in his belt and carried the shotgun. It was seldom when they headed toward the business district of Intolerance that they did not go heavily armed. Neither had had a call to use his weapons, and Rhodes figured that was because they were so heavily armed. A very light snow was falling and the temperature was not much above freezing.

They had come to calling one saloon—Hornbeck's, which was right next to the restaurant owned by Emil Hornbeck—their second home. It was not the fanciest saloon in town, but it was far from the worst, either. Hornbeck cut his whiskey a little less than his competitors did, and his girls were among the youngest and prettiest of all the Cyprians plying their trade in Intolerance. There were enough wheels, faro tables, poker games, and other forms of gambling to occupy most men, and he had a band playing once or twice a week. It was a comfortable place, and both Rhodes and Bonner liked it.

They grabbed a bottle at the bar and then worked their way toward the back where the tables not used for gambling were. The place was going pretty good, but there were a few empty tables. Rhodes and Bonner took one. Rhodes set his scattergun on the table, while Bonner rested his rifle against the table.

Rhodes pulled the cork and poured each of them a full glass of whiskey. The two had let it be known right from the start here that a shot glass was not a proper glass for drinking. Now that the bartenders all knew them, they would have two full-size glasses waiting for them.

Bonner took a healthy swig, and smacked his lips. Then he leaned back in his chair and crossed his legs at the ankle, resting his feet on the table. He held the whiskey glass on his stomach. Rhodes followed Bonner's example. They were quiet, listening to the cacophony whirl around them.

Rhodes almost fell asleep where he sat. Finally he roused himself from his lethargy and poured another drink for the two. As they sipped, Bonner looked at his friend. "Somethin' botherin' you, son?" he asked.

Rhodes shrugged. He didn't feel comfortable talking about it.

"You once told me that when a man needed some help that he could always count on a friend. You remember that?"

"I expect," Rhodes retorted sourly. "I must've been in my cups, though, if I said it to you."

"Hog shit," Bonner snapped. "You can't josh your way out of everything. Now, if you got somethin' troublesome stuck in your craw, boy, you best let it out."

"It ain't so much troublesome," Rhodes said slowly, feeling his way as he went along. "More of a puzzlement, I'd say."

"Troubles or puzzles, boy, it don't make no difference if it knocks you off your feet."

175

Rhodes smiled a little. "I've been smitten," he said quietly.

Bonner almost couldn't hear him what with all the noise in the saloon. "You're just worryin' about that now?" he asked in surprise.

Rhodes shook his head. "It's just that I aim to marry that gal, and that's got me all flabbergasted."

Bonner chuckled. "Thinkin' of gettin' hitched'll do that to a man."

"I know." Rhodes reached into an inner pocket on his long coat and pulled out a cigar. He lit it and sat puffing, his elbows on the table top, as he stared in Bonner's general direction.

Bonner fired up his pipe. "What're you gonna do about it, boy?" he asked when his pipe was emitting clouds of noxious smoke.

"I ain't sure. That's what's got me so puzzled. I know I got to get a job, but I ain't cut out for much."

"Don't fret on it, boy. The harder you look and press, the less likely it is that somethin'll come your way. Do like you do out on the trail, and keep your eyes and ears peeled."

"Reckon so." He puffed a few moments. "You think marryin' her's the right thing to do?"

"You love her?"

Rhodes nodded. "More than most anything."

"She feel the same?"

"She's said so, and I figure she's tellin' the truth."

"Then there ain't no more puzzlement, ya damn fool. You either marry her or you ride on off and forget about her."

Rhodes heard something different in Bonner's voice and he squinted at his friend. "What do you know about such things?" he asked.

For a long time, it seemed as if Bonner had not

heard Rhodes. But then he said, "Had me a Flathead woman once I was sweet on. I was just fairly new to the mountains then and didn't know my pizzle from lodgepole. Our brigade stayed with a village of Flatheads one time, and I met White Plume. Goddamn if she wasn't the purtiest thing this ol' bastard's ary set his eyes on. Goddamn, but she did shine."

His eyes behind the veil of smoke were distant, wistful, and filled with pain. Rhodes sat silently, knowing instinctively that he was hearing something that Joe Bonner had never told anyone else, something he had kept bottled up for thirty years or so.

"Well," Bonner finally went on, "I didn't have more'n the 'skins on my back, so's there was nothin' I could give her ol' man for her. Still, I waited every day down by the crick for her to come along. She come along but didn't do nothin' for a couple days. I was feelin' mighty glum, but then one day she did stop. And everyday after, too, till we pulled out."

He stopped again and tossed back some whiskey. "Anyways, she told me she'd wait for me till the next spring. She told me that if I was as great a hunter as I liked to think, that I'd have a heap of plews to give for her."

The noise of the saloon seemed far away, dim, and indistinct. Rhodes still waited in silence, puffing evenly on his cigar. It took several minutes before he realized that Bonner was not going to say more. "So, what happened?" he asked quietly.

"She was carried off by Blackfoot. Her ol' man got together a war party right off and they chased after them Blackfoot. Caught 'em and whipped the shit out of them fierce bastards, too. But they found White Plume's body in the Blackfoot camp."

"Jesus," Rhodes breathed.

Bonner nodded. Rhodes watched him, and he could see the old man working through the pain, forcing it back down into that dusty crevice of his brain where he had kept it all these years. Bonner finally smiled. It was a small one, but a real smile nonetheless. "So, boy," Bonner said gruffly, "don't you piss on this here chance. You might nary get another'n."

Rhodes suddenly felt much better. He had no more questions about what he would do about Miss Hallie St. John. He relaxed.

An hour later, a quartet of men entered the saloon and headed for the bar. Rhodes would have paid them little mind, just as he had everyone else who had entered or left, except that they seemed somehow familiar. He sat there, eyes on the men, as he paged through his memories, trying to fix where and when he had seen them. He was sure he had.

"Somethin' else botherin' you, boy?" Bonner asked.

It took an effort to leave off trying to recall things, and answer Bonner. "You see them four just come in?"

"Which four?" Bonner asked, looking in that direction.

"The young fellah with the white hair and those with him."

Bonner nodded. "Yeah. So?"

"I swear I know them boys from somewhere."

"Durin' the war maybe?" Bonner asked, turning back to look at Rhodes. "You see lots of folks at such times, and not really know most of 'em."

Rhodes shrugged. "Maybe so." He relaxed and sipped some more whiskey, but he continued to stare at the four men. Suddenly the four began laughing, and the one facing the man with the white hair suddenly became visible.

Rhodes started. He had been leaning back on the chair, but now he snapped forward. "Jesus," he said, anger knotting the word.

"What'n hell's wrong with you this time, boy?" Bonner asked in some irritation. He had listened to enough gloomy talk — and made enough — to last him a good long while. He was not up for more.

"Those four. I ain't met any of 'em, but now I know where I know 'em from. Three of 'em are the ones who waylaid the Mormons on the way out."

"You sure?"

Rhodes nodded. "We got their description from some fellah ran a tradin' post down there a ways. The one with the white hair is Orson Mackey. The little ratty-lookin' fellah's Clyde Laver. The dandified one with the scar on his face is Floyd Decker. I don't know the other."

"What're you fixin' to do, boy?"

"I expect I ought to pay them a visit and mention to them the error of their thievin' ways."

"There's four of 'em, and ain't but one of you," Bonner reminded him.

"You gone and got so old you don't like a little fracas, old man?"

"I could still kick your fat ass any day, sonny." He paused. "You plannin' on bringin' 'em to Marshal Pritchard?"

"I expect. If he ain't interested, we can stash them someplace and let the vigilance committee handle it from there."

"Got it all figured, have you?" he asked.

"Near enough."

"You expect them boys to just get all aquiver with fear when you tell 'em you gonna throw 'em all in jail?"

"Well, I guess they could do that," Rhodes said

contemplatively. Then he grinned a little. "Of course, I don't expect it." He absentmindedly patted the scattergun on the table.

"You're a nervy little bastard, ain't you?" Bonner said with admiration. It was one of the reasons he liked Travis Rhodes.

Rhodes shrugged. It was something he never questioned. He had absolutely no fear of dying, or of going into battle. It was one of the things that made him so deadly when he was in a fight. It wasn't that he wanted to die, it was just that he didn't care one way or the other. His fate, he figured, was not in his hands, therefore he would not worry about it or fear it.

Bonner drained his whiskey glass. "Well, hell, boy, let's go'n get it over with." He stood and lifted the rifle.

Rhodes also finished his glass of whiskey as he grabbed the scattergun. Side by side, he and Bonner headed toward the four men.

Chapter Twenty-two

Rhodes and Bonner came up to the four men from the door side of the saloon, having skirted the whole barroom floor. With the door almost directly behind them, the two would have the light behind them. That would give them at least a little bit of an edge in cutting down the odds.

Orson Mackey turned, as the unknown man said something to him. The two other outlaws also turned.

Mackey was clad in a citified suit, with vest and string tie. He wore a good-quality brown derby. The suit and the big scar carving itself across his face set Mackey apart from the others quite a bit. The unknown man was wearing a butternut shirt and pants made of ducking. A battered hat rested on his head. Laver and Decker were clad in black denim pants, collarless shirts of a fancy flower pattern, and vests. Laver wore a worn gray derby, and Decker a Stetson with the front brim pinned to the crown.

"Something I can do for you fellows?" Mackey asked politely.

"You can come along peaceable to the jail house and wait there till I round up the law," Rhodes said.

Mackey laughed. He seemed to be enjoying himself. "Surely you can't think I'd do something like that for no good reason. You aren't the marshal here, are you?"

"Nope."

"Then why should I acquiesce to such a ridiculous demand?" Mackey asked. His words and voice were utterly calm and polite, but danger lurked in the dark brown eyes.

"Won't be no skin off my ass to put a slug or two into your carcass."

"That wouldn't be nice."

Rhodes shrugged, unconcerned.

Mackey was irritated. Usually his politeness lulled men into a false sense of security. If that didn't work, a glance at the scar and the flat, deadly eyes was enough to convince most to move on. This one showed neither inattentiveness or fear.

"What's your name, friend?" Mackey asked.

"Travis Rhodes. My partner's Joe Bonner," Rhodes said never taking his eyes off the four men.

"Well, Mr. Rhodes, just why is it that you want to run me into the jail house?"

"Among other things, horse and mule theft, robbery and intimidating folks."

"And when was I supposed to have taken part in this wave of crime?" An audience was growing, and he liked that. He could play an audience better than many stage performers could. He was warming to his role.

"Couple months ago, back near the Platte River." Rhodes knew he was losing the advantage. Mackey was too smooth, and his three companions were content to let him hog the spotlight and throw the law off.

"I've never been to the Platte, Mr. Rhodes," Mackey said evenly.

"Bullshit," Rhodes said. He pointed toward the man's chest. "You mind tellin' me where you got that locket?"

"From me dear, departed mother."

"Mind if I have a look at it?"

"Me mother'd be very put out with me for allowin' such a thing." Mackey patted the locket on his chest.

"I ain't going to ask you but this one more time to let me see that locket," Rhodes said calmly.

"Or?" Mackey was still smug.

Rhodes snicked back the hammers of his shotgun. He could not see that the question needed more of an answer.

Mackey was sweating now. He was not afraid, but he had no desire to die, and at this range, that scattergun would tear him to shreds. It was not a pleasant thought.

Bonner, who was standing partly sideways so that he could watch both the outlaws and the door, suddenly said, "Pritchard's comin'. Erastus is with him."

Suddenly Laver screeched, "That's the bastard we robbed! He's gonna finger us!" He went for his pistol and snapped off a shot.

All hell broke loose all at once. Marshal Wade Pritchard shoved Erastus Flake hard, sending the Mormon falling to the side. Then Pritchard went for his own revolver.

"Stupid bastard," Mackey muttered. He was still afraid to move with that scattergun pointed straight at his chest.

Floyd Decker pushed Rhodes hoping to get a

little leeway for gunplay. He also had sense enough to know that Mackey could not help his companions while Rhodes held that shotgun on him.

Rhodes fell a step to the side. Mackey went for the revolver at his waist. He managed to almost get it out when two loads of buckshot splattered a goodly portion of his torso all over the bar.

Rhodes dropped the scattergun and yanked out one of the Whitneys. Without seeming to be aware of doing it, he swung in a slight crouch and fired all five shots he kept chambered in the weapon. Two hit Decker in the back, as the outlaw made for the door.

Rhodes swung back, noticing that Bonner was firing his Colt pistol and that Flake and Pritchard were down. Rhodes fired at Laver, who apparently had been hit already and drilled him twice. His fifth shot missed, and tore out a chunk of the bar.

Dropping the pistol, Rhodes grabbed the other. He whirled just in time to see a tomahawk-clutching Bonner charging toward the unknown man, who was fleeing. Bonner let go some kind of war whoop.

Marshal Pritchard was on the floor, hurt bad, as far as Rhodes could see, but he managed to get an arm up and tangle the fleeing man's legs a little. As the man tried to right himself, he heard the wild screech behind him. He partly turned, just in time to catch Bonner's tomahawk on the side of the head. The blow ripped off a large hunk of the man's skull and sent it skittering across the floor. He stood, as if he didn't really know he was dead. He fell, landing partly on Pritchard.

Suddenly all was silent, except for the drip of broken bottles. The saloon patrons began easing out from behind tables and chairs.

Rhodes made no effort to check on Mackey. No one could live through the double blast of the shotgun he had taken. So shredded was his torso that there might not be enough left for the undertaker to work with. He knew he wouldn't have to check on the unknown man either. He did go and check on Decker and Laver. Both were dead. Each had been hit at least three times.

Rhodes turned and headed toward the door. Bonner was helping Flake up. Then Rhodes and Bonner knelt alongside Pritchard. He, too, was dead. Rhodes counted seven bullet holes in the man's body.

"Tough ol' bastard, weren't he?" Bonner said.

"Sure was. Too bad such a man's got to get killed by such scum." He paused. "You hurt?"

"Nary a scratch. You?"

"Got winged once. Here." He looked at his left arm as he pointed to it. "Well, hell," he said in some amusement. "I got winged twice."

"Christ, I've cut myself shavin' worse'n that."

"Me, too." Rhodes realized Flake was looming behind him. "You all right, Erastus?"

"Only a scratch. Marshal Pritchard shoved me out of the way as the gunfire began."

A winded, puffing Logan Macmillan pushed into the saloon so fast that he almost tripped over Bonner and the marshal's body. "Jesus," he said, still panting from the run here from his office, as he looked at the carnage. He stepped fully inside the saloon. Bonner stood and moved away from Pritchard's body as Macmillan kneeled there to look the corpse over.

Finally he stood, looking sternly at Rhodes and

Bonner. "You mind telling me what went on here?"

Rhodes shrugged. "We were aimin' to arrest those four back there." He pointed with his thumb.

"Why?"

Flake explained it all.

"Why didn't you just go get Marshal Pritchard?" Macmillan asked.

Rhodes shrugged again. He slid his pistol into his belt. "Seemed like a good idea to just mosey on up and arrest them before they could start any trouble. We planned to hold 'em till Wade showed up."

"And?" Macmillan looked mean and gruff.

"And, then Wade came in," Rhodes said, weary of answering questions. He had been trying to do some good here, and now Macmillan was trying to twist it all around and place the blame on him.

"I was with the marshal," Flake interjected. "As soon as we stepped in the door, that man"—he pointed to Laver's body—"screamed something about the law and then begin shootin'. Marshal Pritchard pushed me out of the line of fire, and even as I was falling, I could see him get hit twice. He started firing back as soon as he could." Flake shook his head. "If he had not taken the time to push me to safety, he would've been able to fire some seconds sooner. It might've saved his life. Instead, he made sure my life was spared."

"Wade was that kind of man," Macmillan said sadly. "He was not only the marshal, he was my friend." He turned mournful eyes on Rhodes. "My apologies, Mr. Rhodes," he said quietly.

"No need, Mr. Macmillan." He turned toward the bar when Dexter Fairchild, the undertaker came in. He stopped and picked up his pistol and

186

put it in his belt. Then he got his shotgun. As he lifted it, he thought of something. He knelt next to Mackey's body. There, on the shreds of flayed flesh and splintered bone, was Flake's locket. It was covered with blood but otherwise unharmed. He lifted Mackey's head by the hair, worked the locket over the head and then dropped the head.

Rhodes turned and walked to Flake, who was watching with some interest as Fairchild puttered around Pritchard's body. "You might want this, Erastus," Rhodes said, dangling the locket's chain from one finger.

Flake looked at it as if he didn't recognize it. Then his eyes widened. "My locket," he said, gingerly taking it. "Who had it?" he asked.

"Mackey."

Flake looked over there. "He's in a rather grisly state, isn't he?"

"Couple loads of buckshot in the chest'll do that to a man," Rhodes said dryly.

Flake pulled out a handkerchief and wiped the blood off the locket. "It's unscathed," he said in wonder.

"Sort of a minor miracle, eh?" Rhodes said.

Flake glanced at the Gentile, but saw no indication that Rhodes was ridiculing him. "Indeed. Most wondrous."

"Anything else of yours they might've took and not sold?"

Flake thought for a minute. "Possibly some small jewelry items, I suppose."

"We're going to check through those fellahs' pockets and such, Mr. Macmillan," Rhodes said. "See if they have any more of Mr. Flake's loot."

Macmillan nodded.

187

Rhodes did most of the lifting and moving of bodies. Not only was he younger and stronger, he also was more inured to bloodshed and the results of such violence. They were just going through Laver's pockets, the last of the four, when Macmillan strolled up. He shook his head at the uselessness of such gunplay. "Find anything?" he asked.

"A ring of Mrs. Hickman's and a pocket watch of mine."

Macmillan nodded. "How much money are they carryin'?"

Rhodes stood and wiped off his hands on a piece of cloth the bartender had thrown to him. Then he bent and picked up a sack into which he had been placing all the money he had found. "Three hundred seventy-two bucks plus some change, if I counted right."

Macmillan nodded again. "Dexter, come here," he said, looking toward the undertaker.

The short, rotund jolly man came up. He looked like anything but an undertaker.

"How much to bury Wade? Top-notch everything."

"Fifty bucks, I'd say. Get the best casket, silk lined and all. The best embalming. A small stone, but a nice one. Even a small service."

"Travis, give him fifty out of that sack."

After Rhodes had given Fairchild fifty dollars, Macmillan asked, "How much to bury the rest of this rabble, Dexter?"

"I assume you don't want the best for them," Fairchild said with a bright smile.

"Not quite," Macmillan said dryly.

"Twenty bucks ought to be enough. Plain pine coffin, no services, no stone."

"Give him another twenty, Travis." He paused. "Make it twenty-two and whatever loose change is in there. That'll even things up." When that was done, he said, "Keep the rest, Travis. You, the old man there, and Mr. Flake can split it."

"Be glad to," Rhodes said with a grin. He counted out the gold and silver coins onto the bar. When he had three neat stacks, he handed one to Bonner, and another to Flake. He swept up the third heap for himself.

Chapter Twenty-three

Rhodes was shaving, the lower half of his face covered with lather, when a knock came at the door. "Who is it?" he called, as his hand rested on a nearby revolver.

"Logan Macmillan."

"Come on in." He watched the door in the mirror. When he was sure it was Macmillan, and that he was alone, he went back to shaving, sliding the straight razor smoothly over the stubble.

"This the best you can do?" Macmillan asked with a little smile, waving a hand at the room.

"Well, it's small and cramped, but it's home," Rhodes said dryly.

Macmillan took a seat in a rickety chair at a matching table. Neither seemed very steady, so when Macmillan sat, he did so gingerly.

Rhodes finished shaving and wiped his face off with some sacking. Then he turned toward his visitor. "What can I do for you, Mr. Macmillan?" he asked, more than a little curious.

"I talked a little more with Mr. Flake last night after that fracas over in Hornbeck's. He seems to have a mighty high opinion of you, Travis."

Rhodes nodded and reached for his shirt, which was hanging from a bedpost. He began pulling it on.

"A number of other folks in town feel the same."

"Speak your piece, Logan," Rhodes said. He wasn't angry, but he was not fond of people who didn't just come out with whatever it was they wanted to say.

"All right," Macmillan said with a weak grin. "Since Marshal Pritchard has crossed the divide, we need a marshal. And I thought that . . ."

"I thought you said all these folks had good opinions of me," Rhodes interjected, now a little annoyed.

"They do, but what does that . . ."

"You were going to offer me Pritchard's job, weren't you?" When Macmillan nodded almost meekly, Rhodes continued. "If all those folks seem to be of favorable opinion of me, just why in the hell are they sendin' me to my doom?"

"But they . . ."

"You went through, what, five, six marshals in six months? How long did the longest one last? Two months?"

Macmillan sighed. "All that's true. But you know as well as I do that Intolerance needs a lawman. Preferably a good, strong, fearless one. Man who takes this job can't be afraid of death. I saw you last night after all that was done. Nine men of ten would've been sick at what went on. You looked like it was just another day in a saloon."

"What's your interest in this?" Rhodes asked. He suspected that Macmillan wanted him to be a private lawman to police his mines.

Macmillan grinned. "I'm the mayor."

Rhodes was speechless for some moments. "You keep that fact mighty quiet," he said finally. He went back to buttoning his shirt.

Macmillan shrugged. "Folks who need to know,

191

know. I'd get every idiot in the mining district bothering me at every hour of the day or night if it got spread around." He paused. "Now, what do you say?"

Rhodes tucked his shirttails into his pants. "What're you offerin'?" he finally asked.

"Fifty bucks a month, plus half of all the fines you collect. The rest of the fines go into the city treasury."

"Like last night?"

"Like last night. We'll get you a newer, better place to live, paid for by the city. You'll be allowed up to three deputies — you can pick anyone you like. And," he tacked on with a small smile, "you'll get the best goddamn funeral money can buy when the time comes."

Rhodes smiled at that, too. "Mighty generous." He paused. "What about Pritchard's deputies?"

A sour look crossed Macmillan's face. "Wade was down to only one by now. He quit last night, right after Wade was killed. Said the thirty bucks — or even fifty — wasn't worth the fuss."

Rhodes nodded, understanding the man's reluctance to take on such a position.

"So what do you say, Travis? You'll take the job?"

"What about supplies?"

"All you need for the job, plus living. Paid for by the city."

Rhodes mulled it for a few minutes. It sounded reasonable, but he still was skeptical. "Who's paying me?"

"The city."

"Not Ludwig and Macmillan?"

"No, sir." Macmillan seemed almost offended. "You will be the marshal of Intolerance, not a guard for Ludwig and Macmillan. Unless . . ."

Ah, here it comes now, Rhodes thought.

". . . you want to take that as a job in addition to the marshal job. Or instead of."

Rhodes was nearly disappointed that his suspicions were unfounded. "I don't do any work for you, is that right?"

"That's right." Macmillan paused. "That's another reason I keep quiet about being the mayor. Most folks'd think you — or any other marshal the city hired — was a company man."

"You got an office?"

"Yep."

"Jail?"

"Behind the office."

"Judge?"

Macmillan shrugged. "A couple of the older lawyers act in that capacity sometimes." He smiled again. "You'll be the final judge in many of the infractions, Travis. Somebody's breaking the law — or even what you *think* is the law — you arrest them, jail them, fine them, or run them the hell out of town."

"Gives me a lot of power."

Macmillan nodded. "Another reason why we're selective with the men we hire as marshals. Not only does he have to be good with a gun and with his fists, he has to be a fair-minded man; one not easy to rile. You're such a man, I believe." Macmillan shut up, allowing Rhodes some time for thinking.

Rhodes paced the room a little, working it over in his mind. There was little to keep him from taking the job. He was not afraid of death, and it would give him something sort of stable as a job which meant he could propose to Hallie. Still, he had suspicions that there was more to this than Macmillan was letting on. That and the fact that the marshals lasted so short a time in Intolerance. Hallie would

193

not be happy about that, he was certain.

But, he thought, if he took the job with the idea of keeping it just through the winter, Hallie might be agreeable. He hoped so anyway. However, he would not tell Macmillan it was for him only a temporary job. He would worry about that when spring came.

"Looks like you got yourself a marshal, Mr. Macmillan."

"Great," he said. He stood and pulled a star from his jacket pocket. He came forward to pin it on Rhodes's shirt.

"A gold badge?" Rhodes asked, surprised.

"What else would we use in a town whose sole industry is in gold?" He stepped back, patting the badge to sort of settle it. "Come on, I'll show you to your office."

Rhodes, who had not put on his backup pistol under his shirt because Macmillan was there, hesitated. He would feel odd going out without it. Then he shrugged, and put on his long, black coat. He still had the two Whitneys in his belt and the scattergun. He grabbed the shotgun and went outside into the cool afternoon.

The marshal's office was just north of what could be considered the center of town. It was set amidst all the troublesome spots in the city, for the most part. It was surrounded by saloons, brothels, gambling parlors, two discreet opium houses, hardware stores, and billiard rooms. It would be nothing if not lively, Rhodes figured.

Macmillan walked past the office, though, toward the house just to the south of the jail and slightly behind it. Macmillan led the way inside. It was empty except for some basic furniture, and it smelled freshly washed.

194

"I had it cleaned and emptied last night," Macmillan said. "For you, or for whoever took the job."

Rhodes nodded and prowled through the place. The house was two rooms—the outer one was kitchen and dining room, the rear one a bedroom. The bedroom contained a wood four-post bed on which was a thin blanket and a quilt. There was also a small table and side chair, two lanterns on the walls, another on the table; a chest of drawers on which were a basin and pitcher, and a large wardrobe chest. There were no windows in the bedroom, which Rhodes felt was wise. No one could raise the hackles of people more than a marshal, and to have windows where someone could blast him easily was not too wise.

The kitchen dining area had a sink with a pump. "That work?" Rhodes asked, pointing.

"Sure does. Might need priming every once in a while, but it works."

There was a flat work surface, a pantry, a dining table, and a hutch with a small supply of dishes, cutlery, and other household items.

"Wade didn't often use any of the kitchen stuff," Macmillan said. "He preferred to eat out. For a while, though, he had a woman come in every day to do the cleaning and cooking."

Rhodes nodded. "Well, we best go and see the office now," he said.

The office was bigger than many Rhodes had seen, but not too big. It was made of stone. Wood framed the doors and windows, which had real glass. Inside, there was a small anteroom, that contained two chairs and a small cast-iron stove in a corner. The door was of good, solid wood and there was one window, barred. It was separated from the office by a short railing across its width. The railing had one small, swinging gate.

The rest of the office consisted of a big desk and its chair; one other chair; a weapons rack containing two shotguns and a Henry repeating rifle, a wood bulletin board next to the weapons rack; a small wood rack for hanging the cell keys; a cot and another small stove on which a large coffeepot sat. At the back of the office ran iron bars with a door of the same. Behind were three cells, running widthwise. Each was perhaps ten feet deep by eight wide. There was a very small slit for a window in the rock wall of each cell at the back.

"Not fancy, I grant you," Macmillan said. "But serviceable."

"I expect it'll do." Rhodes was having second thoughts about this. "You know, don't you, Mr. Macmillan, that I have no experience at being a lawman?"

"Makes no difference. You have what it takes to do the job. I'm not worried about it, nor is the city council. And so you shouldn't be."

Rhodes nodded, some doubts lingering.

"Well, I must bet back to my work, Travis. You need supplies or anything, go to Burgmeier's. He'll put them on the city's bill. He gives you a hard time, come see me. You need information or anything, also come see me. Any questions?"

"Expect not." He paused. "Oh, one. You have deputy badges?"

"Should be in the top right-hand drawer of the desk. Have some folks in mind for the job?"

"One anyway."

"The old guy, Bonner? That his name?"

"Yessir."

Macmillan looked skeptical. "Isn't he a little long

in the tooth for such a job?"

"You need to ask that after last night?"

Macmillan smiled and nodded. "No, I suppose I don't. Well, it's your choice. Oh, and, by the way, deputies get thirty a month. Most of the other marshals also let their deputies have half the fines they collected, too. Some allowed the deputies to keep one-fourth, with you getting one-fourth and the city the other half. Again, that's up to you."

He paused, thinking. "As for supplies, deputies get what they need for the job. No personal supplies." He grinned conspiratorially. "Of course, there's nothing to really say that you couldn't get some personal supplies for yourself and then decide you really didn't need them after all and give them to your deputies." He winked. "But you never heard that from me."

"Hear what?" Rhodes asked with a chuckle. Maybe this job wouldn't be so bad after all, he thought.

"All right, Mr. . . . rather, Marshal Rhodes. You're on your own." Macmillan strolled out and headed back to his own office.

Chapter Twenty-four

Rhodes stood for some minutes, not moving, staring out the window and wondering if this wasn't really a dream — or nightmare. It certainly didn't seem real to him. His left hand came up and brushed the cold metal of the badge. What a year it had been, he thought. His enlistment had been up two months before Appomattox, and he was released from the army. Here he was, little more than six months later, the marshal in a town of perhaps two thousand people.

He shook his head, turned, and walked to the desk. He sat and began pulling open drawers, wanting to see what was there. He found the deputy badges and tossed one onto the surface of the desk. There was little else in the drawers except junk, most of which he picked up and tossed into the stove. Then he stood and grabbed the rings of keys and tried them all, including the one to the weapons rack. He checked each weapon. None was loaded, and he could find no ammunition in the desk. He would have to rectify that.

Then he pulled the wanted posters off the bulletin board, where they had been stuck up by a thin dagger. He sat again and leafed through the papers. Several of them were quite old, and he tossed them aside. They would do well to get a fire started, he figured. He smiled when he came across posters for Orson Mackey, Floyd Decker, and Clyde Laver. Those he decided he would keep, if simply for his own edification. He didn't think he would be able to claim the four hundred dollars—two hundred for Mackey and one hundred each for his two companions—anytime soon. He would, however, consider trying to do that.

The only other time he stopped was when he came across a wanted poster with a fifteen hundred dollar reward. Rhodes studied it for a moment. Dalton Turlow certainly had a list of crimes—Rhodes figured he would have to keep his eyes peeled for Mr. Dalton Turlow. Fifteen hundred would get him out of this job and go a real long way toward setting up a household with Hallie. He sighed and stabbed the posters back into the board with the knife.

Rhodes picked up the deputy badge—it was also of gold—and stuck it in his shirt pocket. With scattergun in hand he stepped outside. Hardly anyone paid him any attention, but he felt considerably self-conscious anyway. He put that from his mind as best he could.

He wondered what to do first. He wanted to get moved into the house he had been given, go tell Hallie, hire Bonner, get supplies for the office and for the house. He grinned, thinking that maybe this marshaling job was a lot harder than he had imagined.

As he walked, eyes automatically sweeping around, alert to danger, he decided that he had to tell Hallie first—unless he spotted Bonner. He didn't, and soon was knocking on the St. Johns' door. Andy answered the door and grinned. "Oh, Sis," he said making the second two syllables.

Hallie was delighted to see him—until she spotted

the gold badge on Rhodes's chest. She suddenly frowned.

"I thought you'd be pleased," he said lamely.

"Pleased at what?" Hallie demanded, eyes snapping fire.

"That I got a job. Now we can . . ."

She wasn't interested in hearing any more from him, and her loud, angry voice overrode his quiet one. "What kind of job is that? Huh? Tell me that then, darn you. A job where you ain't gonna live more'n another couple of weeks. You call that a job? And you were fool enough to think I'd be pleased with such nonsense? What's wrong with you, you big dummy?"

She had to stop for breath, and Rhodes quickly jumped into the breach. "Now, just calm down a minute, Hallie," he started. He stopped when he heard Andy snickering. Rhodes turned narrowed eyes on the boy. "Don't you have some chores to do, boy?" he asked.

"No, sir," Andy said with a grin.

"I'll find some for you, but I don't think you'll like 'em all that much."

Andy's eyes widened, but he still grinned. He hurried outside.

The lull had allowed Hallie to get her wind back, and she started off on another tirade. "Calm down, you said. You expect me to calm down when the man I love, the man I want to marry and raise a family with, the first man I ever loved, and hopefully will be the only one I'll ever love, when you come in here and tell me you've just taken a job that's like you committin' suicide right here in front of me? You expect me to calm down after that. Didn't you get enough of bloodlettin' last night, well, didn't ya?"

"But—"

"But my eye, darn ya. I heard what happened last night down in that sink of degradation. Guns going off all which ways, and you standin' there in the middle of it all. Now you want to take a job where you have to do that each and every day . . ."

"It ain't going to be everyday. It'll—"

But Hallie was not done yet. "I thought you loved me, you fool. I really thought you did. I thought you were gonna take me away from all the gunfightin' and such."

"Dammit, Hallie," Rhodes finally said in exasperation.

"No, Travis. No. Damn you. Damn *you*." She was gasping and sobbing and shaking some.

Rhodes wondered whether he should embrace her. Then he shrugged. It wouldn't hurt to give it a try, he supposed. He wrapped his big, powerful arms around her. She did not really resist, but her body was as stiff as a board. He continued to hold her.

"You think you can let me speak my peace now?" he asked quietly.

She shook her head, getting tears on his shirt.

"Well, I'm going to speak it anyway. After I've done that and you want me to go, I'll go."

Hallie said nothing. "I took it because it pays well, and I aim to lay low. I'm not going to go out looking for trouble. I didn't tell them that I was going to quit this job after the winter. But that's what I aim to do. Soon's winter lets up and spring's here, I aim to marry you, girl, and we'll go off somewhere else. That's if you still want me then."

Hallie pulled away, and he let her go. "No," she sniffed, "that's if you'll still be alive." She looked miserable.

"Well, that's my plan. I gave 'em my word, and I can't go back on that."

"Oh, yes you can," Hallie said dabbing at her running nose with the end of her sleeve.

"No I can't," Rhodes said firmly. "Maybe I ain't the best man in the world at anything, but I got pride. Givin' someone my word's the best I can do. I go back on my word, I'll not be the man you fell in love with."

"Yes, you will. And you'd be alive."

"I'd as rather be dead than to go back on my solemn word, Hallie. And if I did, I *wouldn't* be the man you fell in love with. You know that well's I do. You should've been able to see what happens to a man who's got no more pride left with your father the last couple months. There wasn't a thing he wouldn't try to do for you and Andy, even grovel. And he wasn't half the man he was when your ma met him, I'd wager."

Hallie knew it was all true. But knowing it did not mean she had to accept it. "You men and your pride and your word. It's stupid."

"No it ain't, Hallie. A man can be dirt poor, not have nothin' of his own, but he gives his word to someone, he'll be expected to live up to it. That shows the real measure of a man."

"But I'm scared, darn it all."

"I understand that," he said. "But there's dangers every day. Look at your pa. He was a healthy, hale man, until that accident changed him. I bet you've seen a difference in him since he's been back working. Haven't you?"

"Yes." It sounded small, forlorn.

"But he could get in another accident easy up there. The walls could cave in on him, or he could fall off a wagon and go under. A man can die a thousand different ways just going about his daily business. Surely you can see that."

"I can," Hallie admitted. "Don't mean I agree with it, or like it. I'm still scared. Your walking outside and getting killed is somethin' folks can accept. But you takin' this job makes it seem like you're lookin' to get yourself killed early."

"I ain't."

"Oh, I know." She dabbed at her eyes and nose with her sleeve again.

Rhodes stood there feeling more awkward than he ever had. He took off his hat and twirled it idly in his hands. "Well, Hallie," he finally said slowly, "things're up to you now." He paused, but got no response. "I love you more'n anything, Hallie, and I want you to be my wife someday. But if you don't want me, I'll understand." Actually, he wouldn't understand, but he would live with her decision.

"I don't know," Hallie said, still sobbing.

"You have to make up your mind."

She looked up at him, eyes flecked with red, and swollen all around them. "Maybe it's you who has to make up his mind. But maybe you've already done so."

"What's that supposed to mean?"

"Well, it seems you don't love me enough to give up your job. You've chosen it before me."

"Maybe that's the way it is," he admitted. "But I'm a man of my word. I gave it to the city to do this job. And, whether you want to admit it or not, I gave you my word, too."

"How?"

"By tellin' you I loved you. It's as true now as it was the first time I said it. I also gave you my word that I'm coming asking for your hand as soon as I was settled into a job."

"A job with prospects, I think you said."

Rhodes shrugged. "Whatever. I got a job now, and one that pays pretty well. I come over here so you could share my joy at being considered good enough to hold such a responsible position."

"Good enough at what?" Hallie demanded, her anger, fear, and worry not lessened an iota. "At killin'?"

"I hope there's more to this job than killing," Rhodes said simply. "Anyway, I figured that now I had a job, I was going to come ask for your hand in marriage. Maybe set a date in the spring."

"You'll be dead long before spring." Hallie felt icy fear rushing through her veins.

"Why do you say that?"

"You know why," Hallie snapped. "The longest a marshal has ever made it in Intolerance is two and a half months."

"I'm not like those others."

"Cocky, aren't you?"

"At times," Rhodes admitted. "But I'll say this, if I wasn't so cocky and so sure of myself, I'd never have met you. And," he added pointedly, "you'd have been victimized by fat Ham Macmillan. That what you want? To be his woman?" He sucked in a breath, anger beginning to eat at him. "You have to know that he'd never take you to wife. He'd just use you and drop you like an empty food tin."

Hallie shuddered. "I might's well just give in to that anyway."

"How can you say that?" Rhodes hissed. He was as mad as he ever had been in his life.

"You keep that stupid badge and you're gonna be dead long before we could get wed. Then where'll I be? Huh? Easy pickin's for Ham or some other schemin' man with no morals or conscience."

Rhodes didn't know what else to say to her. He was worn out, it seemed, from the arguing. But he could not even consider reneging on his deal to become the marshal of Intolerance. He'd as soon shoot off a foot.

He waited a little in silence, then asked, "You want to see me any more, Hallie?"

It took a long time for her to answer, and Rhodes agonized over it. "I don't know," she finally said. "I really don't know, Travis."

Rhodes nodded, steeling himself against what he figured was his impending loss. It was like amputating a limb — better fast and quick, rather than waiting for the lingering rot of gangrene.

"Well," he said, putting his hat back on, "I'll be over to my office" — how odd that sounds, he thought — "if you take it to mind to see me again." He paused, the acid roiling in his stomach. "If you don't, I wish you well, and I hope you find someone more accommodating to your wishes."

He could not bring himself to say goodbye to her. He simply spun and left, striding past a shocked, worried Andy St. John, who watched him as he walked away.

Chapter Twenty-five

Hovering between rage and despair, Travis Rhodes stalked the streets of Intolerance. The bright, cold sunshine did nothing to raise Rhodes's spirits. He noted it, and that autumn was fully here. He walked proud and erect, almost daring someone to challenge him. No one did, though several people acknowledged the new marshal with a wave of a tipped hat. He returned those greetings politely. After all, he had given his word to do this job and acting politely toward the townsfolk was part of that job.

He went back to his office, but decided he was not happy there. He still had things to do, things he had put off in his rush to proudly show off for Hallie. He put on his long frock coat, locked the door behind him, and headed toward Hornbeck's saloon. As he suspected he would, he found Bonner sitting at a table toward the back regaling a bunch of wide-eyed saloon patrons with his feats of daring-do.

Rhodes grabbed a beer from the bartender, who informed him that it was on the house. Rhodes nodded thanks and strolled back toward Bonner. He sat a little back from the small crowd gathered around the old mountain man and listened halfheartedly. Even that much was good medicine for him. Bonner almost never failed to perk him up with some tale telling.

After a little, Rhodes crooked a finger at Bonner. The old man finished up his tale, accepted the applause and the offer of drinks—for later—and sent everyone away. Rhodes picked up his still half-full mug and walked to Bonner's table.

Bonner almost choked on his own beer when Rhodes's coat gapped open in the front and Bonner spotted the gold badge.

"Jesus, Mary, and Joseph," he muttered. "My friend, gone over to the other side. Will wonders never cease?"

"Just close that flapping hole of yours," Rhodes said more tartly than he had planned.

Bonner noted it but said nothing for now. He sipped some beer. "So, boy, why'd you come on over here and break up my little parley?"

"A parley is when two or more people speak," Rhodes said in more near usual tones. "What you were doing was sitting there spoutin' off."

Bonner laughed. "I expect I was." He finished his mug and waved for another. The bartender brought it and another for Rhodes, took away the old mugs, and disappeared behind his bar again.

Bonner hunched over the table, and slowly turned the beer mug in front of him. "Now, boy," he said sternly, "what's put the bug up your ass this time?"

"This," Rhodes said, tapping the badge.

"How'd you ever get trapped into wearin' that piece of shit?"

Rhodes explained it tersely but thoroughly, including Hallie's reaction. When Rhodes was done, Bonner said nothing for a little while, just continued staring down into his mug of beer.

Finally, Bonner's head came up and he grinned a little. "You're in a deep puddle of shit, ain't you, boy?" He cackled wildly.

"Goddammit, Joe," Rhodes hissed. His anger rarely flared, but it had done so not long ago at Hallie's house, and it was renewed now. "How dare you make light of all this."

"Pipe down, goddammit." Bonner paused, still chuckling. "Hell, you was the one brought all this down on yourself. Wasn't me forced you to take that goddamn thing. And it wasn't your little lady made you take it neither."

There was nothing Rhodes could say to that. It was all true. It didn't lessen his annoyance any. He sulked for a few minutes, but managed to start coming out of his funk. Suddenly he grinned just a little.

Bonner, who had been watching Rhodes, wondered what was up now. "Somethin' strike you as humorous all to a sudden?" he asked suspiciously.

Rhodes pulled out the deputy's badge. He placed it on the table and pushed it across the table with an index finger. "Take it," he said quietly.

Bonner recoiled as if snakebitten. "You gone plumb goddamn *loco*, boy?" he asked, high voice quavering with indignation.

"Just take it," Rhodes said.

"No goddamn way. Not this chil'. I'd as soon have my ass smeared with honey and be set down in a cave with a griz."

Rhodes laughed despite himself. "Take it." A note of friendly warning entered his voice.

"There ain't nothin' you can do or say gonna make me take that goddamn thing," Bonner said firmly.

"You either take it, or I'll run your ass into the calaboose."

Once again Bonner looked stricken. "You'd do that to an old friend like me? A man in his dotterage? I'd not last a day in that hole before I'd pass on to the Great Spirit, brokenhearted and havin' missed out on the final years that'd rightly be mine."

"Is there never any end to your bullshit?" Rhodes asked with a small laugh. The fight with Hallie less than an hour ago seemed far away.

"Nope," Bonner answered, laughing.

Rhodes waited out the laughter, and then grew serious. "I'd be obliged if you were to take the badge, Joe. There's nobody in Intolerance I can trust, except you. And nobody I'd rather wade into battle with."

"All this puffery's gone make me puke," Bonner growled. But he reached out and picked up the badge. He turned it in one callused hand.

"Put it on," Rhodes encouraged. When Bonner showed no inclination to put it on, Rhodes said, "You get paid thirty a month, and half the fines you collect." He paused. "And, since I get a house for being the marshal, you get the old place all to yourself."

"Well, la-de-da," Bonner said sarcastically, but a grin hovered on his lips.

"Well, this might convince you," Rhodes said. "When I come in here just now, bartender Mike over there told me the beer was on the house. I suspect that's a regular thing."

"I guess I might's well take it," he said finally, " 'cause I just know you're gonna pester me till my dyin' day, if I don't."

"That's a fair assessment," Rhodes said frankly. "Instead of puttin' that badge on now, though, I expect we ought to get you some new duds."

"I ain't wastin' none of my hard-earned specie on some goddamn city clothes."

"You don't have to use your money. Come on."

They finished their beers and headed for Burgmeier's. There Rhodes bought himself several shirts, some long johns, a new pair of boots, bandannas, socks, and pants. They got about the same for Bonner, though the old man grumbled.

Once that was set up, Rhodes bought all the metallic cartridges he could find for the rifle and two shotguns in the weapons rack. He considered buying two new pistols, ones that used metallic cartridges, but he decided against it. He was familiar with his Whitneys, and the availability of metallic cartridges was not assured.

Rhodes made arrangements to have everything delivered to either of the houses or the office. Then he told Bonner to hit the tonsorial parlor for a shave and a bath, if nothing else.

"Goddamn, boy," Bonner grumbled. "I ain't had a bath in a coon's age. I don't see why I ought to have one now."

"Just do it, or I'll drag your ass over there myself and hold you in the water."

While Bonner was taking care of his ablutions, Rhodes wandered back to the office and began putting supplies away. He started a fire in the stove as much to ward off the chill as to make a pot of coffee.

Eventually, Bonner came by, growling and snapping. He looked like a new man.

"Hell," Rhodes said with a small laugh, "you don't look half as old as you really are. Lookin' like that, you might even be able to romance some sweet young thing." Even as he said it, he knew he shouldn't have. All it did was remind him of Hallie. He shook himself out of the doldrums.

"You gonna get any more deputies, boy?" Bonner asked. "With just the two of us, we're gonna be hard pressed."

"Yeah, I've thought of that. But I ain't sure who."

"Didn't Pritchard have any deputies?"

"I asked about that and was told that he had several for a while. One got killed over in Dockery's saloon. Another had the shit beat out of him one night. He quit, and one of the others soon followed. The only one left quit last night, as soon as he heard Pritchard had been killed." He sighed. "I'm allowed to have three deputies, but I don't know anybody but you, Erastus, Phineas, Hallie's old man, and her brother." *Damn,* he thought, *everything I do or say brings her back to mind.*

"Erastus is probably too old, though he ain't near as old as I am," Bonner said. "He just ain't as spry."

"That's true. You've been more active than I suspect he has." He paused. "What about Phineas?"

Bonner shrugged. "He's young enough, but I don't think he's got the balls for it."

"I'd thought the same." He sighed. "You know anybody? Hell, you've met most of the town already."

"Met a lot of folks, but I can't say as I know any of 'em. Not well enough, anyway, to put my trust in 'em."

"Well, I expect it's just going to be me and you for a spell. Maybe with winter comin' things'll quiet down." He didn't really believe that, though.

They went about their job with a minimum of fuss. There was always something for them to be doing. With a city the size of Intolerance and a population of rough-and-tumble miners, vagabonds, travelers, gold seekers, and outlaws, they were kept busy enough.

For the first week or so, Rhodes tried to be everywhere at once. Bonner finally set him down and said, "You can't do it all by yourself, boy. Now, lis-

211

ten, I know you're still sweet on that St. John girl and want to show her you're good at your job—and sock away some money for later—but you're gonna run your ass ragged."

Rhodes, bleary-eyed from lack of sleep, nodded.

"Good, now go on home and get some sleep."

After that, both Rhodes and Bonner were a lot more judicious with what they bothered people about. They were wary around drunks, because one never knew what one of them might do. And they made a concerted effort to keep people from hurrahing the town with gunfire. For minor infractions, a fine of a dollar or so was enough, or maybe letting a friendly drunk sleep it off in a cell.

It soon got to a point where the town was fairly docile, or as much as could be expected. Those who had seen the gunbattle between their lawmen and the four robbers had passed the word on to others, usually embellished a bit more with each retelling. Most of the men in town quickly concluded that Marshal Rhodes and Deputy Bonner were hard men, and ones not to be trifled with.

The two lawmen made friends among the townsmen and merchants, but found no one they could be able to trust to be another deputy. Andy St. John had pleaded several times with Rhodes to allow him to be a deputy. He always slipped away from home and headed to the office—Rhodes had not seen Hallie since the day he was named marshal.

"You're too young, boy," Rhodes said each time Andy pleaded.

"I'm as old as you were when you went off to the war," Andy said in response every time.

Rhodes would always growl at him. "War ain't some kind of game, boy. It's dirty and hard and nasty." He felt inadequate to describe the horrors he

212

had seen.

Andy would go away depressed each time, but a day or so later would be back to try again. Each time Andy popped into the office, Rhodes would ask after Hallie. The youth's answer was always the same: "She ain't mentioned you, Marshal. But I figure she's thinkin' on ya at times."

Rhodes would always ask, too, if Hallie was being bothered by anyone. The response was always in the negative, except once.

"Ham's been by the house a couple times. He ain't come to the door or nothin'; just rides back and forth, like he's waitin' for Hallie to come out or somethin'."

Rhodes nodded, face tight with anger. He had no opportunity to go looking for Hamilton Macmillan that day, and early the next morning, Hallie showed up at the office.

"Can I talk with you, Travis?" she asked quietly.

Heart pounding, he nodded and indicated she should sit. He did, too.

Chapter Twenty-six

"I'd like to make a complaint against someone, Marshal," Hallie said meekly.

Rhodes felt as if he had been slapped in the face. As he reached for a piece of paper and an ink pen, he managed to cover up the despair he felt. He dipped the nib of the pen into a bottle of ink and, with the pen poised over the paper, asked, "And who do you want to make a complaint against Hal . . . Miss St. John?"

"Ham Macmillan," Hallie said so quietly that Rhodes had trouble hearing her.

"What's he done?" Rhodes was struggling to maintain a rigid officiousness. He felt sure he was succeeding to some extent.

"Well," Hallie said haltingly, "he's not done anything really, except to always be around where I am. He walks back and forth in front of the house, when I'm there. He never comes on our property. He follows me when I go to one of the stores or to church of a Sunday." She paused.

"Is there more?" Rhodes asked, mouth dry.

Hallie nodded glumly. It took a few more seconds before she spoke again. In the interim, Rhodes could hear the wall clock he had brought in ticking away like a metronome.

"He's become more bold the past few days," Hallie finally said. "Not that's he's really bothered me . . ." She felt a fool for having come here. Macmillan scared her with all his spying on her, but it sounded silly when she spoke of it like this, as if she were some little girl scared by the wind.

"Go on," Rhodes said, still trying to keep his composure.

"Well, he's had some little gifts delivered to the house, with notes. All proper, of course, but still, I'm afraid of him, and I've told him so." She hesitated a moment. "And, since you . . . I . . . we . . . parted company, he's become more bold in followin' me. He's even taken to talking to me almost like he was speaking to himself when I walk down the street or somethin'. He's usually only a few feet behind me. Close enough I can hear him, but not so close as to arose suspicions."

Rhodes waited for more, but there was only silence. He looked up, and knew right away it was the wrong thing to do. He had never felt such hurt inside as he did now sitting there looking at Hallie St. John. For a man who was utterly fearless in battle, the feeling was eerie.

"Is there anything more, Miss St. John?" he asked. Despite himself, hope sprouted in his chest.

Hallie hesitated, then said, "No. No, I don't think so." She rose.

"I'll need you to sign here," Rhodes said, pointing his pen at the paper. "That means you agree that what you've said is here on the paper. Sort of makes it official."

"Of course." Hallie took the pen and quickly scrawled her name. She handed Rhodes the pen back. "Thank you for any help you can give me, Marshal." She was stiff, proper, prim. No one seeing her now would think that a spark of love lingered inside her.

Rhodes also rose. "I'll do what I can, Miss St. John," he said, every bit as formal as she. "I don't know when I'll be able to get to it, though. With only Deputy Bonner and me, we're hard pressed to keep up with things." He tried to smile but could only bring forth a pale imitation of the real thing.

"I understand, Marshal." Hallie left, leaving Rhodes to his heartache.

For quite some time, Rhodes sat there, eyes fixed on the paper before him. He was still sitting there when Bonner came in sporting the coat he had paid to have made for him. It was of finely tanned buckskin and reached almost to his knees. It had fringes down each sleeve and along the yoke, had a pocket on each side at waist level and sported buttons made of elk antler. Bonner wore it open, allowing him access to his pistol, and Rhodes could see the pocket inside over the left breast and two others at waist level.

"She come to take you back?" Bonner asked lightly. Then Rhodes looked up, and Bonner almost cringed at the look on Rhodes's face. Silently, he went to the stove, grabbed a mug from one of the hooks on the wall and poured himself some coffee. He sat in the chair which was so recently used by Hallie St. John, and he put his feet up on Rhodes's desk.

Bonner sipped for a few minutes, then said rather harshly, "You best get over that gal, unless you're aimin' to get yourself kilt in a hurry."

"I've tried, Joe. Damn if I haven't, but . . ."

"I know how you feel, boy, but you keep moonin' over that gal, and you're not gonna keep your mind on business. That's sure to be fatal."

216

Rhodes nodded. After a while he managed to shake himself out of his lethargy somewhat. He folded Hallie's complaint neatly and slipped it into the inside pocket of his jacket. Hefting his shotgun, he said, "Keep a lookout on the office for a while, Joe, will you."

Bonner looked at him through squinted eyes. "You ain't gonna do nothin' foolish now, are you, boy?" he asked.

Rhodes almost smiled. "No." He paused. "Not yet anyway." He left the office and strolled down the street, peeking into every one of the better saloons, looking for Hamilton Macmillan. He was not to be found on the one side of the street, so Rhodes crossed and headed back up the other side. He thought for a moment to stop in to talk with Logan Macmillan, but then decided that could wait. He wanted to talk to Hamilton Macmillan first.

Hamilton was supposed to be at work up at the mines at this time of day, but Rhodes knew that the man seldom was there. He preferred spending his time in saloons, brothels, and gambling halls.

Almost halfway back to his office, Rhodes found Hamilton in the Mountain Belle saloon. It was one of the three very fancy saloons in Intolerance, and its prices correspondingly high. Rhodes had been in the place only a couple of times, all since he had become marshal and all related to his official duties. The Mountain Belle was not for working stiffs. It was for men like Hamilton Macmillan, and his uncle, Logan. And it was for people like Lucky Pete Corrales, who had hit it rich. Corrales had spent the bulk of his time — and money — in the Mountain Belle, until he was broke again and left to find his fortune one more time.

The Mountain Belle had real doors, with real stained glass in them, instead of cheap wooden batwing doors. Rhodes turned the knob and went in. As usual, it was like entering another world. Where most of the saloons in Intolerance were raucous and rowdy, the Mountain Belle more often than not was sedate and quiet. It was disconcerting to some.

He spotted Hamilton right off, sitting at a table near the back, surrounded by three of the high-class soiled doves employed there. Rhodes nodded at the bartender and to the shotgun-toting guard sitting in a chair at the top of the stairs. Both returned the salutation.

Rhodes started across the saloon, feeling self-conscious as he always did when he came in here. For one thing, it was so quiet as to be unnerving. But part of it was the figure he presented. He sort of felt like he was not supposed to be in here. Since becoming marshal, he had tried to keep neat and clean. He now had several pairs of trousers and shirts, so he didn't have to wear the same thing every day, except for his coat. But still, he could see in the mirror that he looked out of place in his nice outfit as well in the saloon. A man five-foot-eight and weighing close to two hundred twenty pounds was not going to cut a svelte figure no matter how well dressed.

He stopped at Hamilton's table. He waited precisely two seconds for acknowledgment. When it did not come, he said, "Take a walk, girls."

They looked from Rhodes to Hamilton, who mouthed the word "stay."

"Now, girls, or I'll haul you all in for having expired licenses."

They left, but in no great hurry. Rhodes reached into his pocket and produced the piece of paper. He dropped it on the table in front of Hamilton. "Read it," he ordered.

"No," Hamilton said flatly.

Rhodes had the shotgun in his right hand. With his left, he scratched at his newly shaven neck. Then he shrugged. "Suits me. Get up."

"Why?" Hamilton looked surprised, and a little afraid.

"Takin' you to jail."

"What the hell for?"

"Disobeying the marshal in pursuit of his duties."

Hamilton snorted. "You can't take me to jail."

"Oh, yes I can," Rhodes said, not angrily. "I had planned for you to be there one day, but you've just gotten yourself two days now. Would you like to try for three?"

Hamilton glared. "I ain't going willingly," he said with a sneer.

"That don't bother me neither." He paused. "You do remember what happened the last time you gave me a hard time, don't you?"

Hamilton could feel the pain in his shoulder joint at the remembrance. "Yes," he said tightly, anger flaring.

"Then get your fat ass up and headed on to the jail," Rhodes said evenly. "You give me any shit on the way and I'll clean your plow for you."

Hamilton stood and began walking across the saloon. His face was beet red from anger and humiliation. He turned and headed stiffly up the street toward the jail.

"You're gonna regret this, goddamn you," Hamilton sputtered angrily when Rhodes had placed him in a cell. "You can't do this to me. I'll have my uncle fire your ass and then get some of his mine

219

workers to kick the shit out of you. Goddamn it, you just wait and see."

"You keep mouthing off to me, boy, and I'm going to put a dent in your head." When Hamilton sat on the cot in the cell, still glaring at Rhodes, the marshal said, "You're a damn fool, boy, you know that? You could've saved all this humiliation and embarrassment if you'd only done what you were told."

"Piss off, goddamn stinking son of a bitch."

"Trouble with you, boy," Rhodes said easily, "is that you keep getting yourself in trouble and then try to blame it on others." Rhodes sighed. "Well, I guess there's no call to keep talking at you. You're too damned stupid to listen." He turned and hung the keys on a peg. "Keep an eye on that big bag of wind back there, will you, Joe?"

"Sure. Where're you goin'?"

"Down to talk to Logan."

Bonner nodded. "You want I should thump him a few times while you're gone?" he asked, his cackling laugh erupting.

"Only if he asks for it."

Logan Macmillan's clerk nodded when Rhodes entered the office and quickly went to inform Mr. Macmillan that the marshal was here, then waved Rhodes in.

"Morning, Marshal," Logan said with a smile. They shook hands, and Rhodes sat. "Now, Marshal, what brings you here? Not trouble, I hope?"

"Afraid so, Logan. Not real bad, though."

"My nephew?" he asked.

Rhodes nodded. "He's been bothering Miss Hallie again. She and I . . . Her and . . . Well, there's been a fallin' out between us." Rhodes was acutely embarrassed. "Anyway, Ham thinks that now he can move in on her, though she's still rejecting his attentions."

"So where do things stand now?"

"Miss Hallie signed out a complaint against him this morning. I went over to serve it on him just a little bit ago, and he gave me sort of a hard time and . . . Well, he's locked up now."

"For how long?" Macmillan was not very surprised.

Rhodes shrugged. "I told him two days for disobeying my orders. I ain't figured out yet what to do about Hallie's complaint."

"Can I bail him out?"

"I suppose you can get one of the lawyers to write you up a paper to do that, but I'd not recommend it." He paused, wondering if he should proceed. Then he decided he should. He was not afraid of Logan Macmillan or Hamilton Macmillan or anyone else for that matter. "His kind won't learn anything if they always get bought out of trouble. A couple days in jail might just open his eyes."

Logan laughed. "I doubt that, son."

Rhodes smiled in response. "Yeah, me, too. But it's better than him—or you—buying his way out."

"I agree." Macmillan tapped his fingers on the desk a few moments, then asked, "Why'd you come here to tell me this?"

"First, I figured you ought to know. But also to warn you." Rhodes still felt uncomfortable among the privileged classes, but he was not afraid.

"And?"

"And . . . if he continues to be a pain in my ass, I'm going to thump him good and hard. Especially if he keeps pestering Hallie."

"But if you and she are no longer . . . courting?"

Rhodes shrugged. "It hurts like hellfire to not be

courting her no more," Rhodes said frankly. "I don't know as if that hurt'll ever go away, but that's something I'll have to deal with on my own. She wants some other man, she can have him, much as that might hurt me. But if she don't want someone and he keeps pestering . . ."

"I understand," Logan said. "You mind my asking why you and Miss Hallie have gone asunder?"

"I don't mind," Rhodes said. He tapped the gold star on his chest.

Logan nodded. "You could give it up."

"That's what she wanted me to do."

"Why didn't you? I would've understood."

"I gave my word to take this job. I can't go back on my word."

"Life can get hard for a man with such principles."

"I expect." Rhodes stood. "Well, I've taken up enough of your time, Mr. Macmillan. I just wanted you to know what was going on with Ham."

"I'm obliged for that." He was about to rise to shake hands with Rhodes, when he snapped his fingers. "Wait, son. Sit again. There's something I need to tell you."

Confused, Rhodes did so, twirling his hat in his hands.

Chapter Twenty-seven

"You know that we're stockpiling gold bullion in the First Mining and Mercantile Bank?" Mr. Macmillan asked.

"I'd heard that, but nothing official. What's that all about, and what's it have to do with me?"

"Our last two shipments were fairly small, comparatively speaking, and both were hit by thieves. It's been difficult to get men to ride along with gold shipments because of that, so we ended up storing it in the bank."

"And?" Rhodes asked suspiciously.

"And, it's not as big a secret as we'd like it to be." Macmillan paused, drumming his fingers on the desk. "There's plenty of men who'd kill for the haul of gold we have sitting over there right now. Including the ones who robbed our earlier shipments."

"And?" Rhodes's suspicions were increasing.

"We expect you to do your duty and make sure that gold stays safe until we can ship it out a week from tomorrow."

"I thought you said I didn't have to do any mining company business."

"You should know better than that, Marshal. Granted, that gold belongs to Ludwig and Macmillan, but what would happen to Intolerance if that gold was stolen? That'd not only hurt Ludwig and Macmillan, but everyone—*everyone*—else in town."

Rhodes nodded. "I expect you're right on that."

"In addition, we have hired plenty of men to guard the gold when we haul it out. They'll start coming into town in the next couple of days. With those men—plus the fact that we're moving it so close to winter, we're hoping we can get the gold out to Denver, and do so without loss of men. You won't have anything to do with that—unless you want to volunteer for it and make some extra money."

"I'm busy enough," Rhodes said with a little regret. "And, I expect I'm going to be even busier the next week. That's all I need is a bunch of gunslingers riding into Intolerance with some cash in their pockets and a few days to blow off steam."

"It should be interesting," Logan Macmillan said dryly. He paused. "Anyway, I wanted you to know that the gold was there, and what would be happening with it. I also wanted to alert you to the expected arrival of men to guard the shipment."

Rhodes twirled his hat a little more as he sat thinking. "What makes you think someone'd try robbing the bank if there's that much gold in there?" he finally asked. "Hell, all that gold in bullion won't be easy to transport."

Mr. Macmillan nodded. "Right. But if you get a dozen men or so, and each grabbed two bars, they'd be set up for a long, long time." He paused and sighed. "I don't really expect the bank to get robbed—that's never happened. But there's a first time for damn near everything. I also wonder if maybe Dalton Turlow and his men—they're the bastards who've hit us the past couple of times—might try hitting the bank this time, instead of the caravan, since the wagons will be so heavily guarded this time."

"I guess that makes sense," Rhodes admitted. "I saw a poster on this Turlow fellah. There's a big price on him."

Macmillan nodded. "I don't know where he came from, nor do I give a damn. All I know is that he and his men—I've heard sometimes as many as two dozen, though usually some fewer—have hit us several times, and I'm getting damned sick of it." He paused. "That poster on him is old, Travis, and after his most recent robberies, I'll give ten thousand in gold to the man who brings him in. Or kills him."

"That's a fine passel of cash," Rhodes said with a whistle. "Does anyone know about that reward?"

"Most folks in Intolerance. Hell, enough of 'em would've been happy with the fifteen hundred. More than a few tried to earn it. The boneyard down at the end of Ludwig Street is now the home for all who were foolish enough to try."

Rhodes nodded. "How about these men you've hired to guard the shipment? You know anything about them?"

"Not much. I've had the Pinkerton people check them out as much as possible. I'm fairly certain they're trustworthy."

"Well, I expect your gold's safe enough in the bank, Mr. Macmillan, but I'll keep an eye out, especially after some of the gunmen you've hired start showing up."

"I ask no more." Logan rose and held out his hand. "Another couple of weeks, and we'll be in the clear on this."

That afternoon, Rhodes went out and deputized Phineas Hickman, as well as a townsman named Sean Malone. He also unofficially deputized Andy

St. John, mostly so that he could have the young man watch over the office and the cells. That would free up Rhodes and his three deputies to handle the extra business they would have to handle.

As expected, strangers began arriving the next day. Most were conspicuously armed, but kept out of trouble. Few men in Intolerance — townsmen and miners for the most part — wanted to tangle with the hard-eyed newcomers. All of them made a stop at Logan Macmillan's office soon after arriving, and then were on their own. Rhodes had had some papers printed up laying out some of the basic rules he expected to be followed. Things such as no gunplay, no hurrahing the town, no prodding of locals into gunfights, keeping away from townswomen. Macmillan was to hand out a paper to each man as he arrived.

Some of the gunmen knew each other, and took to sticking together. Others kept to themselves. Several saloons were staked out by the gunmen, and few townsmen bothered them.

Rhodes let Hamilton Macmillan out two days after jailing him. Before unlocking the cell door, Rhodes read Hamilton the complaint filed by Hallie. He opened the door and warned, "Don't go near her or her house."

"Oh?" Hamilton sneered. "What're you going to do, lock me up again?" He stepped out of the cell and Rhodes punched him in the stomach, doubling him over.

"That, boy," Rhodes said coldly, "was a taste of what I will do to you if you bother Hallie again or if you give me any more lip. Now move." Rhodes expedited Hamilton's movement with a kick to the rear.

Hamilton staggered outside, still partly doubled

226

over. Several townsfolk saw him and laughed.

"Lordy, do you believe the stupidity of some men?" Bonner asked as he poured coffee for them both.

"It amazes me every time."

Things remained relatively quiet in Intolerance. There were the usual fistfights, drunks, petty thefts, and such to keep Rhodes and his deputies busy, but they were not overtaxed. Indeed, the presence of the hired gunmen seemed to make the town a little more quiet. The gunmen, knowing that they would probably be blamed for any trouble, often kept the locals from doing things that would bring the law running.

But it was too good to last.

Just before dark of the next day, Rhodes and Bonner were sitting in the office, passing the time. Both were bored. Hickman and Malone were off getting supper. Andy St. John was home.

A burst of gunfire brought Rhodes and Bonner to their feet. It had been a time since someone hurrahed the town.

"Damn, I went and spilled my coffee," Bonner grumbled.

Rhodes smiled. "I guess one of us ought to go see who's breaking the peace," he said.

"You go," Bonner suggested. "I'm too old for such shit." He grinned.

"Old fart." Rhodes reached for his scattergun.

Suddenly the door burst open. A twelve-year-old whom Bonner knew only as Billy slammed to a stop, gulping in air. "Shootin'," he gasped. "Men shootin'. Killed old Cyrus."

Rhodes and Bonner did not need to hear any more. They dropped their cups and grabbed scatterguns. Rhodes jerked open a desk drawer and yanked out a handful of shotgun shells and stuffed them in his pocket. While doing so, he moved out of the way. Bonner grabbed some, too, and dropped them into a big outside pocket of his buckskin coat.

Then the two were outside and running like hell toward the gunfire. It was almost dark, and so the lanterns lining the main street were lit, as were the lanterns in the saloons and shops. That and the dying sun gave the two lawmen enough light to see by. The outlaws were down at the far end of the main street, and were just getting ready for another ride through Intolerance.

Rhodes and Bonner stopped, puffing a little, in the middle of the street approximately halfway through Intolerance. Both threw their shotguns to their shoulders as the horsemen galloped toward them. Rhodes was just about to pull the trigger, when the riders pulled to a noisy stop about ten yards away, breath clouding in the cold air.

Rhodes lowered his shotgun. "I'm Marshal Travis Rhodes," he said calmly but loudly. "You boys are breaking the law here, and I'm duty-bound to bring it to a halt."

He got no response from the mounted men. "I'd be obliged if you boys was to put them weapons away and go on about your business peaceably."

That got a response, but not the one Rhodes had wanted. The men started laughing. One, a man clad in black with a face that had suffered a heavy case of smallpox, said, "You're going to take on all seven of us?" He and his men laughed at the wit.

"I ain't aiming to take on anybody if I can avoid it," Rhodes said evenly. The town seemed almost eerily quiet. " 'Course, you want to start some trouble, I'll finish it for you."

"Ooh, now I'm tremblin'," the same man said with a sneer.

"What's your name, boy?" Rhodes asked.

"Clovis Pennington," the man said arrogantly.

"Why don't you get down from that horse, Mr. Pennington, and come on over here for a chat?"

"Not of a mind."

"I'd be obliged if you was to do that for me."

Pennington was about to retort, but something in Rhodes's voice had given him pause. He grinned and dismounted, holstering his Colt as he did. "Now, Marshal, what can I do for you?" as he swaggered toward Rhodes, a sneer on his lips.

Rhodes creased Pennington's forehead with the scattergun. Pennington's eyes rolled up and he teetered, but he did not fall. Rhodes grabbed the man's revolver and tossed it to Phineas Hickman, who had arrived moments before.

"I don't take insults lightly, Mr. Pennington," Rhodes said calmly. "And your insults've landed you in jail for a day or two. Mr. Hickman, please see that Mr. Pennington arrives at the jail."

"I ain't walking there, boy," Pennington snarled.

"Then you'll be dragged there, for one way or another, you're going to the calaboose."

"Son of a bitch," Pennington mumbled, but he began walking up the street, with Hickman, pistol out, right behind him.

Rhodes had never fully taken his eyes off the other six men. "Any of you others care to dispute my rules?"

"Hell, Marshal, we was just funnin' some," one of them said. "We don't want no trouble."

All six put their pistols away. In silence, they turned their horses and rode down the street. Rhodes and Bonner stood, watching.

Suddenly the outlaws wheeled their horses and

spurred the animals. Pistols in hand once again, they rode hell-bent for the two lawmen.

Rhodes waited as long as he could, then loosed both barrels of buckshot from his scattergun. Horses reared and whinnied in fright. Rhodes heard Bonner's shotgun going off. Two men fell in the dusting of snow. A woman to Rhodes's right screamed.

Rhodes tossed his shotgun down and snatched one of the Whitneys from his belt and fired until it was empty. More gunfire ripped out, and others screamed. Another horseman fell, as did a horse. Rhodes felt bullets tugging at his clothes, but he did not flinch. This was just like Spotslyvania, where the lead had come like hail. Now, as then, there was no escaping it, so there was no reason to duck and flinch.

Rhodes pulled his other Whitney and blasted away. But now the three men who remained on horseback were fleeing, racing like hell out of Intolerance. Rhodes quit firing and watched for a few moments, making sure the gunmen really were gone. He finally shoved both Whitneys into his belt and picked up his shotgun. He brushed dirt off the scattergun as he turned to Bonner.

"Oh, Jesus Christ, no," he moaned when he saw his friend lying in a puddle of blood in the middle of the street.

Chapter Twenty-eight

Rhodes walked woodenly toward Bonner and knelt at his side. The old mountain man was dead already, face frozen in a rictus of anger. He had been hit five times that Rhodes could tell, and at least three of those would have been fatal.

Rhodes was sick with hatred. Though he knew Bonner would have been pleased to go under fighting, Rhodes could not accept that. Not here, not now, not at the hands of a bunch of saddle bums.

"Let me in there, dammit, Marshal," Dr. Henry Fermin said, trying to shove Rhodes out of the way.

"You're too goddamn late," Rhodes said flatly. He felt wetness on his cheeks and wondered where it came from.

Fermin knelt and with one quick glance knew Rhodes was correct. He stood again. "Well, I'll go see if any of those others needs my services."

"No!" Rhodes roared. He jerked to his feet and grabbed the doctor by the shirtfront. "No, goddammit. Joe's dead, and those bastards are going to be dead, too. I ain't letting you patch them up." He shoved Fermin away from him angrily and knelt again. He didn't know why; there was nothing he could do for his friend.

Rhodes felt hands on his shoulders and a gruff

voice say, "Come on, Travis. Leave him be now. He's at peace. Leave him."

Rhodes allowed himself to be pulled up. Without thinking about it, he grabbed the shotgun. "I'll be all right, Erastus," he said. "Thanks for your help."

"I did nothing," Flake said quietly as Dexter Fairchild, the undertaker, arrived.

"You do him up real good, Dex," Rhodes said to Fairchild. "Good stone and all."

Fairchild nodded. He thought it only proper, and he knew he would be paid either by the city, or by Rhodes himself.

In a daze, Rhodes walked up the street, oblivious to the people around him. He looked in the window of the jail and saw Hickman and Sean Malone sitting rigidly in straight-back chairs. Malone faced the door, shotgun at the ready; Hickman faced the cells.

Rhodes put his hand on the door, but then pulled it back. He moved on around the side to his house. He dropped the shotgun on the table, and his two Whitneys right after it. Then he slumped into a chair and sat, head in his hands. He thought of nothing and everything, ideas banging around like ricocheting bullets.

He didn't know how long he sat like that, but he finally roused himself enough to fill a coffee mug with whiskey and gulped it down in three swallows. Then he went back to sitting, staring into nothing.

Sometime later, Flake showed up with Bonner's few possessions that he carried on him. He set them on Rhodes's table, opened his mouth to say something, but didn't. He simply turned and walked out, easing the door shut behind him.

Rhodes didn't know how long she had been there, but he slowly came to be aware that Hallie St. John

232

was sitting next to him, one arm around his shoulders. He allowed her to pull his head down toward her and rest it on her soft shoulder.

Finally, she said, "Come on, Travis, you need to go to bed and sleep." She gently tugged at him.

Like an automaton, he rose, lurched to the bedroom, and flopped onto his bed. Hallie lifted his legs, one at a time and set them on the bed. She pulled off his boots. Standing back, she wondered if she should do more. She wanted to, but her upbringing made it difficult. She bent and kissed him softly, tasting the whiskey and stale coffee that lingered on his lips.

"Do you want me, Travis? Here? Now?" she asked quietly. She felt sullied in doing it, but at this moment she was ready, even willing, if it would help Rhodes.

Rhodes's eyes opened and he stared listlessly at nothing for a few moments. Then his eyes focused on Hallie. "No," he whispered. "Not like this." His eyes closed again. He fell asleep, and began to shake, as if he were cold.

Hallie stood there looking at Rhodes for a while, then she gingerly lay on the bed and pulled Rhodes as tight to her as she could. She wanted him to draw from her strength, from her warmth.

Hallie awoke in a panic, thinking she had done something terrible. Then she realized she was still fully clothed—and Rhodes was not there. As she rolled off the bed, she thought of how hard it would be to explain this to her father, even though nothing had happened. She was glad nothing had happened, but she also regretted it.

She stretched as she walked into the kitchen area. Rhodes had a pot of coffee ready and was frying bacon in a pan. She walked up to him and pressed her cheek against his right biceps. Then she shooed him to the table. "This's woman's work," she told him sternly.

They ate silently, but finally Hallie had to ask, "What're you gonna do now, Travis?"

"Going after 'em," Rhodes said coldly.

"You can't."

"The hell I can't."

"But . . ."

"Hallie," Rhodes said wearily, "you told me awhile back that you didn't want me because of this job. I can't see why you came back now, unless it was to nag me about its dangers again. If that's the only reason, you best go on back to your pa and find yourself a city man. If you come back 'cause you still love me and want to be with me, you got to let me do this."

"But I—"

"There ain't no middle ground here, Hallie. You're either with me and support me, or you leave for good."

It took Hallie perhaps a second to decide. "I'm yours, Travis, for as long as you're al . . . as long as you want me."

Rhodes nodded. He was all efficiency now, unafraid, his grief shoved into a compartment in his brain where he could take it out later and examine it, if he wanted to. "I want you to go fetch old Mrs. Kimball, and tell her I want to see her now. Then you best go tell your pa where you were. He'll be worried sick."

Hallie nodded. She wondered why he wanted Mrs. Kimball. That old fool was a crab. "You going to be all right while I'm gone?" she asked, hand on the door handle.

Rhodes nodded.

"You're not gonna leave on me before I get back, are you?" She was terrified that that's what he planned.

"I'll be here."

Hallie left, and Rhodes sat and began cleaning, oiling, and loading his shotgun and the two pistols. Before he was halfway through, Mrs. Kimball rapped on the door. When she came in, Rhodes stood. "You made Joe's buckskin coat, didn't you?"

"Yes," she answered timidly. She was usually a busybody, but now she was terrified.

He held up his own frock coat. "Can you put two big pockets inside this—like you did for Joe? And maybe some fur lining?"

"Yes."

"Can you have it done by the noon hour?"

"If I work very hard."

Rhodes reached into a pocket and pulled out a five-dollar gold piece. He flipped it onto the coat. "Do it," he said flatly.

He was almost done cleaning his weapons when Hickman arrived. "What're you plannin' for today, Travis?" he asked. "Sean and I are tuckered out, but we'll stick there as long as you want."

"You check Pennington over good to make sure he ain't carrying a hidden gun?"

Hickman nodded.

"Get Andy and tell him to take a spell at sitting in the office. I'll be over directly."

Finally he finished, just about the time Hallie returned. "Stay here, Hallie," he warned bluntly. "Don't you come over to the office for anything. I'll be back soon."

Andy seemed glad to see Rhodes. "He been giving

you a hard time?" Rhodes asked, pointing at Pennington.

"Some."

Rhodes nodded. "Let them other two boys go."

Andy did not think to argue. He simply got the keys and opened the two end cells. He got a little scared as he walked from one to the other and Pennington reached out, trying to grab him. But he kept his composure and finished his business.

When the two prisoners had left—fled was more like it—Rhodes lay his shotgun on the desk, followed by his two Whitneys and his knife. He made no move to leave behind his backup pistol. Last, he pulled off his short wool coat and set it on the desk. "Open the cell door, Andy," Rhodes said icily.

"What?" St. John asked, incredulous.

"You heard me. Open that cell door, and then lock it behind me."

"You gone *loco*, Travis?" St. John asked, eyes wide.

Pennington said nothing. He could not tell whether this was a good thing or bad. He was beginning to think the latter, seeing how angry Rhodes was, and how mean his eyes were.

"No, I ain't gone *loco*, boy. Now do what I told you." He paused. "Once you do that, you might want to go take a walk. And lock the door behind you so I ain't disturbed."

St. John gulped and nodded. He had no plans of going anywhere. He wanted to see what Rhodes was going to do. He opened the cell door. Rhodes stepped inside and then St. John closed and locked it.

Pennington forced a cocky look onto his face. "Well, well, the big, bad marshal's come to rough me up some, eh?"

"I come to kill you, boy," Rhodes said bluntly.

Pennington suddenly felt a little queasy. It was one thing to face a maniac when you were on the back of a horse and had six men with you. It was another to take on a man as solidly built as Marshal Travis Rhodes in the close confines of a small cell.

"You were such a tough guy when you were with all your goddamn cronies," Rhodes said chillingly. "Let's see just how tough you are, boy."

"Hey, come on now, Marshal," Pennington said in placating tones, "I didn't have nothin' to do with what happened to your friend. I was in here."

Rhodes clumped forward, backing Pennington into a corner. Suddenly Pennington threw a desperation punch. It hit Rhodes's wide chest and bounced off. Pennington began to sweat, knowing he was in deep trouble. He threw another right fist at Rhodes's head.

Rhodes blocked the punch with his left arm, and then smashed his right fist into Pennington's right side, low. A rib snapped and Pennington gasped.

Rhodes stepped back, letting Pennington fall. "Get up, boy," he hissed.

"I can't," Pennington groaned.

"Let me help you, boy." Rhodes grabbed Pennington's right arm and tugged. Pennington screeched, as the movement caused the broken rib halves to grind together. But he got to his feet, and tried to kick Rhodes in the groin.

"That'll never do," Rhodes said after stepping out of the way. Then he grabbed Pennington's right arm again, this time in both hands. He jerked it down as he brought his leg up fast. The two lower arm bones snapped like twigs. Pennington screamed and turned frightened eyes on the monster in the cage with him.

Rhodes moved forward and proceeded to throw

punishing fists at Pennington. Never in his whole life had Rhodes been this enraged, and he took every bit of that rage out on Clovis Pennington. After just a few minutes, Pennington was reduced to a moaning, quivering mass. That still did not end the barrage of fists.

Rhodes never heard the frantic pounding of the door but St. John finally felt he should let Logan Macmillan, Hickman, and Erastus Flake in.

The three men poured into the office, and Logan grabbed the keys. He jerked the cell door open. He and Hickman managed to pry Rhodes away from Pennington. Chests heaving from the exertions, Logan and Hickman shoved Rhodes against the barred wall of the cell and held him there.

Eventually, the light of reason came back into Rhodes's eyes. Seeing it, Logan nodded to Hickman. They released him. "You all right, Travis?" Logan asked.

"Yes."

"Go on out of the cell now." As Rhodes did, Logan turned and looked at the pulpy mass that had not long ago been a man. He was still breathing, but Logan knew there could be nothing to do for him—except perhaps shoot him to put him out of his misery. Logan was not so inclined. He turned and walked out of the cell.

Chapter Twenty-nine

Rhodes plopped into the seat at his desk. His face was hard and unforgiving.

"You got a bottle?" Mr. Macmillan asked. When Rhodes nodded, Logan went rooting through desk drawers until he came up with a half-empty bottle. He pulled the cork and tossed it on the desk. "Here," he said, holding out the bottle. "Take a swig of this."

Rhodes shrugged and took the bottle. He poured some whiskey down his gullet, not really tasting it. He handed the bottle back.

Logan had a drink. He held it out to Hickman, but the Mormon refused. Logan shrugged and set the bottle on the desk. "Mr. Hickman, please go find Dexter Fairchild and bring him over here for Pennington."

When Hickman had left, Logan turned to Andy St. John. "You watched that?" he asked.

"Yessir," he whispered. The youth looked stunned, as if he could not comprehend what he had seen. He was sure he no longer wanted anything to do with being a lawman. He looked down at the silver badge Rhodes had made for him, and then he touched it. He almost tore it off and threw it down, but something stayed his hand. He wasn't sure what.

"You all right, son?" Mr. Macmillan asked.

"I think so, sir," St. John said. He was trying mightily to keep from throwing up.

"Think you could clean up the cell — after Pennington's taken out?"

"I think so."

"Good. Go on and get a pail, some water, and some kind of soap. By the time you get back, Pennington should be taken care of."

The boy nodded, eyes still wide. He ran out, glad to be away from the smell of blood, death, and fear.

Inside, silence grew, as neither Logan nor Rhodes felt the need to say anything. Both men did reach for the bottle on occasion. After a few minutes, Logan brought out cigars and handed one to Rhodes. After lighting the cigar, he sat on the corner of Rhodes's desk, facing the door. He had no desire to stare at Rhodes's rock-hard features or Pennington's battered remains. Through the window, Logan could see a crowd gathering in the autumn chill. Many people pointed fingers at the marshal's office and jabbered loudly. Most could not have known what had gone on in there, but they were sure to have a heap of speculation.

Not long after, Hickman returned with Dexter Fairchild and two strapping young men. The two young men carried a cheap pine casket. They went straight to the cell in back. With Fairchild watching over them, the two young men reached for Pennington.

"Jesus!" one of the men said, jumping back. "Son of a bitch ain't dead."

"Tut, tut, Mr. Hornsby," Fairchild said. "If he's not dead now, he will be by the time we get him back to the office. Or would you rather sit here and watch over the unfortunate soul until he succumbs?"

"No, sir."

"Good. Then pick him up and put him in the casket. He won't bite."

"Jesus, I gotta get another job," Hornsby said.

"Sure feels funny catchin' up a warm one, don't it?" the other youth said as the two reached for Pennington.

Hornsby nodded. "I can't recall gettin' one's been pounded so much either."

"Less chatter and more work, boys," Fairchild said. As usual he seemed cheerful.

It did not take long before the big, young men were marching out, coffin on their shoulders. Gawkers crowded around them, until Hickman and Malone, who had come into the office just moments ago, had to go out and clear a path for the "funeral procession."

While the onlookers were distracted by the coffin, Andy and Hallie St. John slipped into the marshal's office. With quiet determination, Andy headed for the cell with his pail and began cleaning. Hallie stood in the corner by Rhodes's desk, one hand on his shoulder.

"I see you two are seeing each other again," Logan said, looking from Rhodes to Hallie.

Hallie nodded tentatively; Rhodes said nothing.

Mr. Macmillan sighed. "Now what?" he asked.

Rhodes shrugged, as if only an idiot would ask such a question. "I'll go after the others. The ones who got away."

"That wouldn't be wise, Travis."

Rhodes looked up at Logan in surprise.

"The gold," he said quietly.

"Fin and Sean can watch it."

"It's your job. You're the one in charge."

"Bringing killers to heel's my job, too."

The way those others were riding, they were out of

your jurisdiction in minutes. They come back here, you can arrest 'em. Until then, you're supposed to stay here and watch over the bullion in the bank. You gave me your word to do this," Logan warned.

"You're right, I did," Rhodes said with a nod.

"Well," Logan said expansively, "now that that's decided, we can all get back to work." He smiled in sympathy at Rhodes. "You can take the rest of the day off, Marshal, to see to your friend's funeral."

"Thanks," Rhodes said sarcastically.

"What do you want us to do now, Travis?" Hickman asked.

"You boys get any sleep last night?"

Both Hickman and Malone shook their heads.

"Go on home, then, and get some shut-eye. I'll stick it out here and handle whatever comes up."

"You think they'll be back?" Malone asked. His voice held no fear, only curiosity.

Rhodes shrugged. "Don't see why they would. Out of seven of 'em, four're dead." He paused. "Unless they come back with some friends," he added flatly.

"They do that," Malone said, "maybe I can get in on the action." He seemed put out that he had missed the gunbattle. With that, he turned and headed outside.

Minutes later, Andy finished cleaning the cell and came out into the office with his pail. He still looked green.

"Best go on home, boy," Rhodes said quietly. "Get some rest." Rhodes looked up at Hallie. "Why don't you go with him."

"Don't you want me here?" Hallie asked nervously.

"I have things to do. Come by and we'll have supper together." He was worn down by all that had happened in so short a time.

"All right." Hallie patted Rhodes's shoulder, wishing there was something she could say or do to help him. But there wasn't, and she knew it. Quietly she went outside with Andy, who left the pail of bloody water behind.

Rhodes sat there for a while, puffing on the cigar, taking occasional swigs from the whiskey bottle. He felt deflated, like someone had taken all the air out of him. Finally he pitched his cigar into the pail and then stood. He stretched and yawned, annoyed, angry.

Fairchild returned, knocking on the door and then entering quietly.

"What can I do for you, Dex?" Rhodes asked.

"It's about your friend—Mr. Bonner."

"What about him?"

"We need to know what he should wear to his final reward. The clothes he was wearing are quite bloody, but we could use them, if you wish." He quieted, waiting.

Rhodes thought for a few moments. "I'll stop by directly, Dex. Unless you need it all right this minute."

"No, Marshal, I can wait a bit." He paused. "Also, when do you want the burial to be?"

"I can't see any reason for waiting. Late this afternoon, just before dark. That all right?"

"Fine. That'll give us enough time to do a bang-up job."

Fairchild's ebullience was annoying to Rhodes today, but Rhodes managed to refrain from criticizing. Fairchild could not help it; it was just the way he was.

Rhodes left on the heels of Fairchild, heading for the shack he and Bonner had shared not so long ago. Rhodes went inside and lit the lanterns. He began piling Bonner's belongings on the old bed.

He had not been at it long when he heard the door creak, and then quiet, soft footsteps. He pulled one of his Whitneys and spun to face the door to the front room. The Whitney was cocked and his finger was on the trigger.

Only a fraction of a second, less than a heartbeat, kept Hallie St. John alive. Shaking from almost having killed the woman he loved, Rhodes eased the hammer down. Hallie stood in the doorway, fascinated fear frozen on her face as she watched him.

"I came to help you," Hallie said, voice still wavery from fright.

"How'd you know I'd be here?" he asked, his voice almost normal.

Hallie noted that fact, and she figured Rhodes was coming out of his funk. It would be a while, and rightly so, before he was over it completely. "I just knew is all," she said with a small shrug.

Rhodes nodded and went back to gathering Bonner's possessions. There wasn't too much — Bonner's old, single-shot muzzle-loading pistol; a small, well-used Bible; a scalp; several knives; a pair of dice made from old lead balls that had been squared off; a deck of cards; a photograph taken not long ago of Bonner with an Indian woman and a child; some old clothes. Not much for a man's whole life, Rhodes thought.

Rhodes put some of the items in an old sack and handed it to Hallie. "Take that to my house. I'm takin' these other things to Fairchild's."

Hallie nodded. Both left, he going one way, she the other. At Fairchild's, Rhodes handed the undertaker a fair-size buckskin bag. "Things I want Joe buried in," Rhodes said gruffly. "That and his coat."

Fairchild nodded. As Rhodes left, the undertaker unpacked the bag, finding the old, worn buckskins

244

Bonner had been so fond of wearing, the flintlock pistol, a wood-handled butcher knife, a beaver trap, a twist of tobacco, a well-used pipe, and the scalp. Fairchild looked askance at the latter, but then decided it was not his place to judge what others took to the other side.

Old Mrs. Kimball was inside Rhodes's house, when he returned. She and Hallie were sitting, each with a cup of coffee in front of her. When Rhodes entered, Mrs. Kimball jumped up, as if she were doing something wrong.

"No call for you to get up, Mrs. Kimball," Rhodes murmured quietly.

"I brought your coat back, Mr. Rhodes," she said, sitting again. "It was a fast job I did, but a quality one, nonetheless."

"I'm obliged. Was what I gave you before enough to cover everything—new material, your time?"

"Oh, yes, Marshal. More than enough. I feel like a thief for taking it."

"You earned it, ma'am."

Rhodes put on his best shirt, one he had just gotten that day at Burgmeier's, and new pants, then his refurbished frock coat, his marshal's badge shiny against the coarse black cloth. When he was in the store, Rhodes could see no need for restraint, so he had also gotten himself a somber, flat-crowned hat, and new, calf-high boots.

He stepped outside, stopped, and looked around again. It was, he realized, a beautiful early winter day. The afternoon was waning rapidly, but the sun still gave off plenty of light and some feeble heat. The day was cool, turning to cold and crisp. He walked toward the livery stable.

"What can I do for you, Marshal?" the livery man, Pace, asked.

"I want Joe Bonner's old mule. That cantankerous beast he used to ride all the time."

Pace nodded. "You want him saddled?"

"Nope. Just lead him out here."

Pace returned in minutes with the animal. "It's a godawful shame to waste such a beautiful day on a funeral," he said

Rhodes nodded. He had thought the same himself. He led the mule outside and walked quickly to the St. John house. Jim St. John was still up at work, but Hallie and Andy were waiting. They were dressed in their finest somber outfits, Andy with his silver badge on his only jacket. He looked almost funny. The jacket, his only suit, had been bought two years ago, and was small across the shoulders and in the arms. The pants were a little better, but not much.

Together the three headed toward the cemetery, still towing the mule. Along the way, Phineas Hickman, Erastus Flake, and Sean Malone joined the procession. They were almost the only ones at the graveside service. The only others were Preacher Moss; Irish Maggie, a soiled dove; and Logan Macmillan. Fairchild and his two helpers waited patiently a discreet distance away.

Moss kept the service short, then Rhodes went and knelt beside the open coffin. Old Joe looked pretty good, Rhodes thought. Maybe not really realistic, but enough like his cantankerous old self so's no one'd notice too much. Rhodes drew in a ragged breath. "So long, you nasty old fart," he whispered. "You raise some hell wherever it is you're going." He almost smiled, as he heard Bonner's old cackling laugh in his head.

Rhodes stood and nodded. Fairchild's two helpers came up and quickly, with no fuss, nailed the top onto the coffin. Then they eased the coffin into the grave, using ropes. Rhodes tossed in a handful of dirt onto the coffin and then stepped back.

When the undertaker's helpers had filled in the hole, Rhodes nodded again and gave each a dollar. They left, until only Rhodes, Hallie, and Andy were left. Rhodes went and got the mule from where he had left it tied to a tree. Stopping with the mule right over Bonner's new grave, Rhodes calmly drew his pistol and shot the animal in the head.

The mule made a strange noise and fell heavily, kicking some. Rhodes knelt to see if the mule needed another bullet. He didn't. Rhodes stood, feeling as if a great weight had been lifted from him. He even smiled for real this time. Old Joe was watching from wherever he was, and he approved of what Rhodes had done for him.

Chapter Thirty

Rhodes was saddling his palomino just before midnight when Hickman materialized. Rhodes had heard him coming and waited quietly with a pistol in hand. When he saw who it was, Rhodes put his pistol back into his belt and went back to saddling the horse.

"Where're you goin', Travis?" Hickman asked.

"Out after the three bastards that got away."

"You told Mr. Macmillan you wouldn't do that."

"Did I?" Rhodes asked, unconcerned.

"You did," Hickman said firmly. "I was right there when you did, too."

"I never promised him any such thing."

"But I heard—"

"You heard him say that I gave him my word to stay here instead of chasin' killers."

"Yeah. And then—"

"And then all I said was, 'You're right, I did.' That's all. I just agreed that I had said that. I never promised him today that I wouldn't do it."

"That's splittin' some fine hairs, there, Marshal," Hickman said.

Rhodes shrugged. "Right now I don't give a tinker's damn what I said to Mr. Macmillan or what he thinks I said to him. All I care about right now is catching the sons of bitches who killed a good man."

"You want company?" Hickman asked.

Rhodes looked over the horse at Hickman, showing some surprise.

Hickman saw the look and half-smiled. "I know we've had our differences, Travis," Hickman said bluntly. "But that don't seem to matter much right now. I think back on it, and you gave me and Erastus far more help than would've been expected from a Gentile. From a fellow Saint, we might've expected it, but certainly not from an outsider."

He paused and spit into the hay on the floor. "I thought all along that you were helpin' us just to take somethin' from us. I didn't know how or why," he added with a shrug. "Worse," he added, "I was jealous. I thought maybe you were going to try to steal Minerva away from me. Though you never said an unkind word to me or an untoward word toward Minerva, I was afraid of that.

"And I was jealous of you directly, too. You're a strong man, good with your fists and with your guns. I was just filled with jealousy, and I've not been as good a friend as I could have been because of it. But I've come to see recently that there's no reason to be jealous of you. I can admire some of your traits and maybe wish that in some ways I was more like you. But to let the green monster eat at me, blind me to another man's worth, that's unspeakable. I'd . . . Well, dammit, I'd like to . . . I don't know . . . make it up somehow . . ."

"That's admirable, Fin," Rhodes said seriously. "But I reckon I got to do this one alone." He paused to slip the bridle over the palomino's head and shove the bit gently into the horse's mouth. "Besides, you'll be a lot more valuable here than out there. With me gone and Joe dead, you'll be the main lawman in Intolerance now."

Hickman nodded. "There anything you need?" he asked.

"Just watch over Hallie for me."

"I'll do that."

"Obliged." Rhodes hung a bag of supplies over the saddle horn.

"You know it's snowin' again?"

Rhodes nodded as he tied his bedroll to the back of the saddle. Then he pulled on his frock coat and mounted the horse. "I'll be back in a couple days, I expect. Try to hold the lid on things here." Rhodes rode out of the stable, and walked the horse along the almost quiet streets of Intolerance.

Snow was falling steadily, if not thickly, and the temperature hovered around freezing. The wind whistling up the empty canyons made it feel colder. Rhodes was glad he had the fur-lined coat, and thick, warm gloves.

There was really only one way the gunmen could have gone when they left Intolerance. But five miles on, the road forked. One road wandered northwest and then cut due north through Berthoud Pass and on down the valley toward the Colorado River. The other turned southwest and into a wilderness of sharp canyons, steep cliffs, thick pine forests, and God knew what else.

Rhodes stopped at the fork, gathered some fire-wood, and made some coffee. The temperature had plummeted, and Rhodes didn't like just sitting here. But he could see nothing in the pitch black. He had gotten this far simply by letting the palomino follow the road on its own.

When the light finally broke, feeble in its grayness, Rhodes packed up and pondered which way to go. The more heavily traveled road beckoned, but Rhodes thought that it might be too obvious a way to take.

On the other hand, with snow coming regularly, heading into the unknown, probably deadly area seemed foolhardy. He opted for the well-known road, figuring the outlaws would probably head for Denver where they could hole up for the winter.

It was still snowing and seemed to be coming thicker and wetter. The wind had picked up, but the temperature still hovered somewhere around zero, Rhodes figured. The heat of his rage warmed him, and kept him going.

Sometime in the afternoon with the wind ferociously whipping the snow at him, Rhodes began the climb up into Berthoud Pass. He had no idea of how far into the pass he was when a particularly savage blast of wind knocked him off his horse, and slammed the palomino onto its side.

Rhodes managed to get up before the horse and he made a desperate lunge, barely grabbing the reins before the horse got completely away. But the whinnying horse bolted anyway, dragging Rhodes along in the deep, drifted snow. Rhodes bounced and hopped, hands and shoulders aching from trying to hold on. He was soaked from the snow, and had to keep spitting out clods of snow so he could yell at the horse to stop. Not that his bellowing had any effect on the horse.

All the galloping through the deep drifts began to tell on the horse, and it slowed quite a bit. Gathering up his reserves of strength, Rhodes jerked himself upright and flung himself into the saddle just as the palomino bolted again. The combination of deep snow, Rhodes's weight, and his calm, soothing, familiar voice brought the horse to a stop. The animal stood there, big sides bellowing in and out.

For the first time in his life, Rhodes began to doubt himself. He doubted his abilities, his sense, and his wisdom. None of that, though, would get him out of this trouble. He dismounted and wrapped the reins tightly in one big fist. He walked into the hellish roaring wind, staggering through mushy snow that was two feet deep already. He managed to find some rocks and a few twisted, gnarled old trees almost up against the mountain-side. He worked into the boulders and trees, relieved that much of the wind was blocked out. It did nothing to raise the temperature or keep out the snow, though.

He tied the horse to one of the trees and then he leaned back against a boulder. He was puffing almost as much as the horse. He was in deep trouble, and he knew it. Trouble was, there wasn't a damn thing he could do about it. Not in a blizzard. He would have to wait it out, and hope it didn't last too long or get more severe. He figured that as a last resort, he could kill the palomino and keep himself alive on the horse meat. That would make it mighty hard to get back to Intolerance, but if forced to it, he would do what he needed.

After two days—give or take a half a day—the blizzard wore itself out. Rhodes breathed a sigh of relief but did not venture out right away. He managed to scrape up a little more firewood and made himself the last of his coffee and the last of his bacon. He also managed to scrounge up a little feed for the horse.

After eating, and finishing off his coffee, he packed up. "Well, old horse," he said quietly, "time we was gone home." He saddled the horse. Just before pulling himself into the saddle he looked up at the dark, gloomy clouds. "I'll avenge you yet, old man." He rode out slowly.

Rhodes wanted to rush back to Intolerance, to get out of this infernal weather. But the horse had been hard used, and Rhodes could see no benefit to pushing the palomino any more than was necessary. He made a camp that night on the side of the trail amid the thick pines. Here a little grass remained under the trees. The horse went to grazing right away. Rhodes built a fire and watched the palomino still trying to nibble up any greenery it could find.

"Well, at least one of us has something to eat," he said. He soon climbed into his bedroll and went to sleep.

It seemed to take forever to get back to Intolerance. In an effort to help the horse even more, he walked alongside the horse as much as he rode, if not more. But finally the town was in sight, and the thumping from the mills could be heard.

He pulled himself wearily into the saddle and began the last long walk. As he entered Intolerance, he sensed something unusual. It took him a little while to realize what it was. The few people outside stopped and were staring at him. There was not a single friendly face among them. Rhodes wondered what had gone wrong.

The ride to his office seemed almost as interminable as the time on the trail had been, what with everyone gawking at him. Not only had he not seen a friendly face, he had seen some hatred.

Instead of going straight to the livery, as he had planned, he went instead to his office. He dismounted out front and tied the palomino to the hitching rack. There was no one in the office, that he could see through the frosted window, though it looked as if the cells were occupied.

Curious, he went inside. "Where's Deputy Hickman or Deputy Malone?" he asked the four prisoners. They all looked at him and shrugged.

He shook his head, and turned, ready to head out again.

Hickman burst through the door. "I just heard you were back, Travis," he puffed.

"What's going on here, Fin?"

"Nothing," Hickman mumbled.

"That's a crock of shit, Fin, and you know it. I come ridin' into town and see everybody looking at me like I just killed their mother or something, and you tell me nothing's wrong."

"Macmillan's been spouting off about you," Hickman volunteered.

"What's Ham Macmillan got to be mad at me about? At least now."

"Not Ham—Logan."

"You best tell it, Fin. Fast and plain."

"I . . ."

Logan Macmillan charged into the office. "So, you're finally back, eh, Marshal?" he said more than asked. His voice was thick with sarcasm.

"What the hell's your problem, Logan?" Rhodes asked, his own temper beginning to simmer.

"My problem? You want to know what *my* problem is? Well, goddammit, I'll tell you what my problem is. My problem is you, you hardheaded, stupid son of a bitch. That's my problem."

"You're this angry 'cause I wanted to go get Joe's killers?"

"No, goddammit. I'm angry because you, goddamn you, disobeyed my orders and went—"

"Whoa, boy, right there," Rhodes snapped. "I disobeyed your *orders?* You don't give me any orders."

Logan was livid but he managed to gain some self-control. He spoke in measured tones, as if weighing each word. "True, but I had *asked* you not to leave just yet because of the gold over at the bank."

"So?"

"So, goddammit, Dalton Turlow and his men were here while you were wandering around the country-side on your merry little quest."

"And?"

"And, they made off with a good goddamn portion of the gold."

"When?"

"The morning after you left."

"How many of them?"

"We counted ten, though there might've been a dozen."

"How much did they get?"

"More than half a million." Logan's face was red with anger, and grew more red with each question.

"That's a pretty good haul—weight-wise."

"Yes, goddammit, it was a good haul. They used two goddamn wagons pulled by eight mules each."

That seemed mighty strange to Rhodes, but he just filed the information for later, when he could examine it at his leisure. "Nobody chased 'em?" he asked. "Hell, outlaws slowed down by two wagons full of gold couldn't have been going very fast."

"We got a posse going and gave chase, but those bastards killed three of 'em. The posse decided they'd be better off back here in Intolerance."

Rhodes nodded. To him things did not quite add up, but he couldn't figure out what. He was not gifted with logic at the best of times, he figured, and now, what with being tired, underfed, and cold, he didn't want to think at all.

"All right," Rhodes said. "Fin, take my horse over to the livery. Have Pace wipe him down good and then fill him with oats. Have the palomino saddled and ready to go in two hours. Round up Malone to—"

"Sean's quit, Travis," Hickman said, embarrassed. "After the robbery, people started making fun of him and me. Sean couldn't take it, and quit."

"And you?"

"I'm a Saint, Travis. We've been persecuted from the beginning."

Rhodes nodded. "All right, see if you can round up Andy then. You and him go get me enough supplies for maybe two weeks and load 'em on my old mule. Think you can do that?" he asked. "Or do you want nothing to do with me either?"

"I'll get it done."

"Just what are you figuring to do?" Logan asked as Hickman headed for the door. Hickman stopped and looked back, intent.

"I'm going after them."

The older man laughed. "You're a card, Rhodes. You really are."

"I don't see that there's anything so funny here."

"Let me ask you this, Travis. Did you get the other ones?"

"Nope." The word was filled with shame and anger.

"Hell of a lawman you are," Logan said nastily.

Rhodes reached up and touched the gold star. "You want it back, you can have it."

"Nope. No, sir. Not at all," he said, laughing again. "I want to see the great marshal in action. So does everyone else." Logan walked out, still laughing.

"It's been that bad, Fin?" Rhodes asked.

Hickman nodded. "You want me to send Andy over? And Hallie?"

"If they ain't afraid of being seen with me. If they are, tell 'em to stay where they are. No reason to have them made fun of. Oh, and just one more thing. See if somebody from Hornbeck's can bring me some supper. I'd hate to have to sit in that damn restaurant with everyone gawking at me. Most of 'em probably would sit there hoping I'd choke on a chicken bone."

"A suggestion?" Hickman said.

Rhodes shrugged. "Anything that'll help."

"I'll send Minerva over to your place here. She can cook something for you and won't anybody have to be gawked at."

"Thanks, Fin," Rhodes said wearily.

Chapter Thirty-one

Rhodes kept his head high and his back straight when he rode out of Intolerance, despite the hoots, catcalls, and malevolent stares thrown his way. He could have taken a roundabout way, over on the eastern edge of town, where there were few people, but he refused to do that.

He was in a bitter, foul, festering humor as he walked the palomino down the main street. He fought back the urge to grab the scattergun and start blasting some of these smug, scornful townsfolk. He decided that such a thing would not do, but he vowed that when he brought the Turlow gang to justice he would come back here once more. With luck, he would leave Intolerance then for the last time. Whether he would leave alone that time or not depended on Hallie St. John, though that looked even more doubtful than the idea of succeeding at his hunting down the Turlow gang.

Hallie had come to the house while he was eating his supper. She looked confused, hurt, worried. She glanced askance at Minerva Hickman, but then she sat across the table from Rhodes.

A moment later, Minerva said flatly, "I expect you two want to be alone." She paused. "There's more biscuits and potatoes, Marshal, if you're still hungry.

You need anything else, send someone to fetch me over at the house."

Rhodes nodded. "I'm obliged, ma'am."

"Why?" Hallie asked in a plaintive whisper after Minerva had left. "Why'd you have to go and leave like that?"

"It was my duty," Rhodes mumbled with a mouth full of beefsteak and biscuit.

"Your duty was here, Travis. Here."

"No it wasn't."

"Yes it was, darn you. You're the marshal of Intolerance, not a county sheriff or a federal marshal. Your job doesn't stretch outside the city limits." Her voice was rising in tone and pitch.

Rhodes shrugged. "That might be, but if I had been here when that gang robbed the bank, I would've gotten a posse up and rode after 'em."

"Yeah, so?"

"So, I'd be riding out of Intolerance—my jurisdiction. That's all I was doing when I went after those others. They killed a man—no matter that he was my friend, he was a lawman for the town, and was gunned down while he was trying to do his duty. That's why I went after those three. There ain't no one, includin' you, who can tell me I did wrong in that."

"I suppose not," Hallie said grudgingly.

"It doesn't matter now anyway," Rhodes said, punctuating his quiet remarks with jabs of the biscuit in his hand.

"Why not?"

"I've got to go after the robbers now."

"By yourself? That's suicide. Get a posse up and go after 'em."

"You think there's any man—except maybe Fin or

259

Erastus—that'd join any posse that I was forming? I'd have as much luck trying to fly."

"Don't do it, Travis," Hallie said earnestly. "Please don't. Just forget about them. Quit your job, and let's go away someplace."

"I can't do that, Hallie." He sighed. "I've got to get the robbers, and then go after the men who killed Joe. Then, if you still want me, we can go away someplace."

"That's likely to be a long, long time, Travis. I wait for you, I'm liable to end up an old maid soon."

"It won't take long," Rhodes said confidently.

"How can you say that? How? You were gone three days and found no sight of Joe's killers. You waited out a blizzard, and more snow'll be comin' any time."

Rhodes shrugged as he shoveled more food in.

"And what're you gonna do if you catch up to 'em? There was ten or twelve of 'em robbed the bank. I've heard that Turlow has even more men at his beck and call. What can you do alone against all those men?"

Rhodes had thought of that and come to no conclusion. Most importantly, he had to find them first, then he would decide what to do about them. He knew one thing, though—after the humiliation Turlow's gang had caused him, there were going to be at least several of his men that would never make it back for a trial.

He would not tell that to Hallie, though. He just said quietly, "I don't know, Hallie. I really don't."

"What about me, then?"

"What about you?"

"You're gonna just up and leave me here, alone, with Ham Macmillan still to bother me."

"He been pestering you?"

"No, not since you arrested him that time. But I know he's around, and he'll know you're gone. I expect he'll come around then."

"Fin'll warn him off. Just go tell him."

"I don't want Fin. I don't want Ham. I want you, darn it. Don't you understand?"

"I understand. I want you, too. But some things got to come first." His voice was a dull monotone.

"But . . ."

Rhodes put his fork down and stared into Hallie's eyes. "Hallie, we can sit here and argue over this till the end of time. But it ain't going to change my mind, and it ain't going to make what I have to do any easier." He paused, wondering how much he should say. He didn't want to seem weak in her eyes.

"What I need most from you right now is your full, undivided support, if you can give it. It'd help me a whole lot to know I got one person in all of Intolerance that I can trust and count on. One person who gives me a reason to come back to this goddamn place."

"I don't know if I can do that, Travis," Hallie said honestly, tears streaming down her face.

Rhodes popped the last piece of beefsteak and biscuit in his mouth. He chewed slowly, feeling the twisted knot of loss growing in his belly. When he swallowed, he said quietly, "I reckon you best go then, Hallie, if that's the way you feel. It'll be better that way—for us both."

"But . . ." Hallie blubbered, looking at him with red-flecked eyes.

"There's no more to say, Hallie. I can understand your feelings. I don't have to like 'em, but I can understand 'em. Go now. Go and find yourself a decent, hard-workin' man. I ain't worth you givin' up your dreams and your wants."

Hallie was crying full out now, her shoulders shaking with the fury of her sobbing. Rhodes stood and walked into the back room. He picked up Bonner's old percussion Hawken in the fringed buckskin case. Rhodes had never been all that good with a rifle, but he thought it might come in handy. He grabbed the shot pouch and powder horn, too.

He heard the front door open but not close. He looked through the doorway into the kitchen and could see the front door swinging open. Beyond it, Hallie St. John ran, stumbling and slipping on the snow and ice. With a sigh, he went to shut the door but saw Fin Hickman coming.

"You got everything I asked for?" Rhodes asked.

Hickman nodded. He held out a sack. "Why more pistols?"

"If I catch these boys, there's a good chance I'm going to be a wee bit outnumbered."

Hickman nodded. "I can still ride along with you."

Rhodes shook his head. "No, you got to take care of things here. Like a wife and kids. There's no call for you to be out in the middle of the winter hunting down men."

Hickman nodded. He felt almost useless, but he knew he would have his hands full here. "All right, Travis. Andy and Erastus are down at the stable, packin' the mule and all. You sure two kegs of powder're gonna be enough for you?" He smiled weakly. "Or maybe too much?"

"There's always that." Rhodes reached into the sack and pulled out two .36-caliber navy-style Colts and a box of metallic shells for them. He loaded each pistol with five rounds. He dumped the rest of the cartridges from that box into his outside coat pockets. The three other boxes of cartridges he would put into his saddlebags.

He put on the frock coat. Inside were two pockets, one on each side, over the breast. Into each, Rhodes slid one of the Colts. Then he buttoned the coat, which since Mrs. Kimball had added a warm lining of fur, was a little snug, but not too uncomfortable or confining.

Hickman glanced out through the window. "They're comin'."

Rhodes nodded. He slapped his hat on and held out his hand. "I'm obliged for all you've done, Fin," he said as they shook hands.

"It's me who's grateful, Travis." He paused. "God go with you."

"He'd be welcome company, though I'm not sure He'd be happy with the quest He'd be accompanying me on."

"It's a just cause, Travis. Never doubt that."

Rhodes nodded. He pulled on his gloves, picked up the extra boxes of shells, and went outside. No one said anything as Rhodes put the cartridges into his saddlebags. He pulled himself into the saddle. He looked at Hickman, Flake, and Andy St. John. He started to say something to them, but realized he had nothing to say. He touched the brim of his hat, and turned the horse's head. Then he began the long, tortuous walk through Intolerance.

Once outside of town, he stopped and pulled off his gloves. He tied one bandanna around the top of his hat and under his chin, covering his ears. He tied another around his face, just under the eyes.

It was colder than anything Rhodes had ever experienced; a cold that reached down inside a man and drew out the marrow of his bones. It was a raw cold, too, that lay damp and wicked on a man, sucking the life out by inches.

He looked up at the heavens. "Do your worst,

Lord," he said, breath clouding before his face despite the bandanna, " 'cause you're the only one's going to stop me from findin' those men."

He pushed on and in short time he was at the fork again. He stopped, for no other reason than to take a look around. The landscape was bleak, barren. Even the rocks seemed frozen. There was no question about which way he could go. He had been up the road to Berthoud Pass when the bank was robbed, and no one had come by him. That meant Turlow's men had to have gone the other way.

Rhodes clucked to get the horse started again, and within an instant jerked back on the reins. "Son of a bitch," he breathed.

All—well, most—of the questions that had been preying on his mind now had been answered. If the gang had robbed the bank that morning after he had left, and he had passed no one on the road, then they must have been in Intolerance already. Or hiding near enough that word could be gotten to them within a short time.

It also meant that someone in Intolerance was in cahoots with them. There was a goodly number of roughnecks, scalawags, and outlaws in Intolerance, but it would have to be someone who knew what was going on throughout town; someone with connections. Someone like Logan Macmillan. Rhodes could not believe, though, that Logan Macmillan would be involved in any of this. It just did not make sense. It did make sense, however, that someone like Hamilton Macmillan might be involved. He often spent time in saloons that could be considered low places, and he was an arrogant young man who had been forced to live under his uncle's hard thumb. Such a thing might make a prideful man want to lash out at those he considered were keeping

264

him down. Someone like his uncle, Logan Macmillan, and the Ludwig and Macmillan Mining and Mineral Company. And revenge on the marshal wouldn't hurt, either.

"That snot-nose bastard," Rhodes muttered. He turned the horse down the smaller road that led to . . . he was not sure where. He only knew that it had to be where the robbers had gone.

Only one question remained for him now: Logan Macmillan had said that a posse was formed and chased after the outlaws. Three of the men in the posse had been killed by the outlaws. They could not have gotten far or Rhodes would've heard the gunplay.

He shrugged and rode on. It was not important now, and there could be any number of explanations. He knew enough to raise some hell when he got back to Intolerance. He smiled grimly as snow began falling again. Now he had one good reason for going back to Intolerance.

"Come on, there, horse," he said, suddenly eager to be on the move. It was not so much that he felt pressure; it was more that he just wanted to get this part of things over with and then go finish it off back in Intolerance.

Chapter Thirty-two

It took Rhodes eight days to find the outlaws. It wasn't that they had moved so far, it was because Rhodes had had to check every canyon, draw, and forest he came across that would be big enough to allow in two heavily loaded wagons. That and the off-and-on snow served to slow him considerably.

Even worse, though, he thought frequently, was the cold. It was bone-numbing. He hated making camp at night because of it, but even more, he hated waking up in it. Each day, it seemed as if his bones and joints had frozen overnight, and they creaked and groaned with each movement. He even came to appreciate the snow that fell more often at night, since when it covered his bedroll some, it held out the cold a little.

In another interminable canyon — this one cutting southwest off the trail — Rhodes became more alert. He felt somehow that his quest was almost over. As he had in each place he had checked, he moved forward slowly, inching around bends, stopping to survey each little clearing for what might lie beyond, waiting in trees beside the trail to see if anyone was coming.

Rhodes could not tell from the trail if anyone had been this way in a while. In the eight days since he

266

had left Intolerance on his latest quest, it had snowed at least some every day. Plus there had been some sleet, which crusted over the top of the snow. Still, for some reason, he was sure he would find who he was looking for somewhere in this long, jagged gash in the earth.

The ragged, rough trail looked off into nothingness to his right, but the path was certainly wide enough to allow a freight wagon down into the canyon. The trail began to flatten, though it still went up and down hills. Rhodes was sure he was getting near the bottom of the canyon, and he had begun to doubt his hunch that this was the place, when he came around another bend in the trail and stopped. He was on a hillside, looking down into a snow-covered mountain meadow. At the far end of the meadow were three buildings—a cabin with a thin plume of smoke curling out of the chimney, what looked to have been a barn, and a sideless shed. The shed had two large wagons, their backs covered with canvas.

Rhodes stayed there a few moments, looking around. To his right—roughly west—the side of the mountain ran steeply from the meadow to an unseen peak. Pines clung with stubborn obstinacy to the rocky mountainside. To his left, the mountainside was less sheer, and in some places flattened into small plateaus.

Rhodes pulled off the trail to his left and wound his way through the pines. Twenty yards on, he found a small flat spot. Boulders were piled in jumbled confusion on all sides but the mountain one. Rhodes stopped, looked around and then nodded grimly. It would do well for his base of operations. He dismounted, legs protesting from the cold, and tied the horse and mule to a tree. He knew he had to care for the animals soon, but first he had to see to a fire.

Rhodes gathered firewood quickly. He would need more of it soon, but this would get him going. He started a fire in a miniature tunnel in the boulders. It was situated so that it could not be seen either from the cabin or the trail. If someone down in the meadow saw the smoke, Rhodes figured, he would think it was nothing more than clouds or mist clinging to trees and hugging the mountainside.

Once the fire was going, he put on his coffeepot. Food could wait, but he needed some hot liquid in his belly. While the coffee was heating, he unsaddled the horse and unloaded the mule. He quickly but thoroughly curried each animal and made sure they could find some feed among the trees. Then he went and had a cup of coffee while food cooked.

Done, he moved around the boulders until he was in a spot bare of trees and boulders, which gave him an unimpeded look down at the outlaws' hideout.

The meadow that spread out from the base of the hill was only about fifty yards across from his position. The meadow was longer to his left and right than it was straight ahead, but not by much. Rhodes thought he could see the trail leave the meadow slightly to the left of the barn, but he could not be sure. A stream tumbled down off the rocks in a small waterfall to the right of an empty corral just to the right of the house. Scattered about the grounds near the house were gold rockers, and other mining equipment. A falling-down sluice box ran from the creek toward the house.

As Rhodes watched, a man came out of the house. Rubbing his hands together against the chill, he hurried to the barn and went inside. Though the man was bundled up in a bright wool coat, Rhodes thought he looked at least a little familiar. He reached through the buttons of his coat and pulled a sheaf of papers from the coat's breast pocket. He looked at the pictures drawn on the wanted posters, nodding when he came on one he thought was the man who had just gone into the barn — Charley Bartlett, a small-time cardsharp and gunman. Rhodes put the papers away. Minutes later, Bartlett came out of the barn and half-ran back to the house and inside.

Rhodes kept watch throughout the gloomy afternoon, taking frequent short breaks to go around the boulders to warm himself at the fire. Occasionally, too, he would grab more wood and toss it on the pile near his fire.

Throughout his watch, he wondered what he would do. He had no certainty that all the robbers were here, but after having spotted Bartlett, he knew at least some of them were. Whether they were all here or not, Rhodes knew he was vastly outnumbered. His first task, he decided, would be to see just how many men he faced. For all he knew, Turlow had taken most of his men to go rob someplace else, leaving only a couple of men here. Rhodes didn't think that likely, but it was a possibility that if true would simplify his task considerably.

Another major problem he would have to overcome was finding a way for him to sneak up on the house. He could see no easy way to do it. Behind it was the creek, which tumbled along the base of a short, sheer cliff. Rhodes could see no way to get up on the cliff and maybe ease his way down on a rope. To his right was a waterfall, cutting off access to that side of the house. On the other side, the mountain crowded hard by the meadow. Rhodes figured he might be able to make his way down there that way, using the barn to partially hide his descent, but that was a chancy proposition. The mountainside there was steep and covered with broken rock that was coated by snow and slick ice.

He figured his best bet would be to wait for dark and then move across the open meadow. But that, too, presented problems. For one, if the clouds broke, allowing the moon to provide some light, he could be seen from the cabin. In addition, if he went when it wasn't snowing, his tracks would be seen through the snow as soon as it got to be light. If he went while it was snowing to cover his tracks, he might not be able to see anything.

He pondered his dilemma over another cup of coffee near evening. It was almost full dark now. He finished the coffee, and then stood, mind made up. He grabbed his shotgun and checked it. He wrapped the triggers and hammers in a small piece of fur to keep the powder dry and to make sure the gunlock did not freeze up. Then he headed toward the trail. He worried a little about his tracks leading into and out of the forest at the side of the trail, but he figured no one would be using the trail now. Besides, the tracks should be covered up quickly if it started snowing again, which seemed probable.

He moved along the side of the trail as it dipped down toward the meadow. As it flattened, he slipped off to the right, along the base of the mountain. He followed that as it curved around toward the waterfall and the house. He thought he would freeze to death as he felt the spray of the waterfall on his face, and he moved as fast as he dared, trying to build up a little body heat. The stream down on the flat behind the house was frozen over the top. All the while, Rhodes could see odd lines of yellow light thrown across the snow field by the light shining

270

through the gaps in the cabin's log walls.

Rhodes finally flattened himself against a back corner of the cabin. His face was still freezing, but under his coat he was sweating. He turned and peered through a crack in the wall. He could see very little of the inside of the cabin, but he counted at least six men. He moved along the back wall of the cabin, stopping to peer inside at each opportunity. At the other end of the cabin from which he had started, he stopped again. Altogether, he had counted fifteen men, and he figured there were a few more he hadn't been able to pick out.

He slid across the small open space between the cabin and the shed and barn. Inside the shed, he looked under the tarpaulin of each of the two wagons. Sure enough, they were filled with gold bullion. He checked the barn, too, and found sixteen mules and almost two dozen horses. He also spotted some grain. With a mischievous grin, he grabbed a burlap sack and filled it from the barrel of grain.

He moved out, back the way he had come, carrying the shotgun in his right hand, and the sack of grain over his left shoulder. It took a while to get back to the trail, since he was still moving slowly and deliberately. It was snowing again, but not heavily, and down here the wind was quite a bit less ferocious.

As Rhodes turned off the trail toward his camp, he stopped. Something didn't seem right to him, but he could not figure out what. He leaned against a tree to give himself time to catch his breath — and to think.

It came to him slowly, but then he nodded. There was a fresh set of tracks going toward his camp. He set the grain down carefully, and moved ahead slowly, angling a little toward the mountainside. As he neared his camp, he spotted another horse, saddled, standing near his horse and mule.

He inched away from the animals and more toward the far side of the camp, from the trail. He stopped, seeing a man sitting at the fire, warming his hands and watching the path he had taken into the camp. His back was toward Rhodes.

Rhodes unwrapped the shotgun carefully and stuffed the fur into one pocket. He considered just blasting the man, but he did not want to do that. For one thing, he wasn't sure just yet that the man was one of Turlow's men. For another, the gunshot would alert those in the cabin, though Rhodes could get around that by using his knife. But mainly, he wanted the man alive to question him. It would be much easier gleaning information from someone who knew what was going on than in him sneaking around trying to spot things.

Rhodes watched for a few minutes, wanting to make sure someone else wasn't around, though he had seen nothing to make him think anyone else was here. He began to step out into the small clearing but caught himself before he moved.

He rested his scattergun against a tree and pulled out the piece of fur. Holding it around the rowel of one spur, he eased the spur off and placed it down in the snow. He followed the same procedure with the other. It had not occurred to him to do this before, but down by the cabin it had not mattered so much. With the sounds of a fire, men talking and laughing, plus the insulation of the cabin walls, he had had no fear of giving himself away then. Now, however, it was a different story.

He picked up the shotgun again. With a deep, silent, frosty breath, he moved ahead swiftly, confi

272

dently. Two yards behind the man, Rhodes said quietly, "Howdy."

The man spun going for his holstered pistol all in the same move. He was surprised, but he covered it well. However, by the time he was halfway up and his revolver halfway out, Rhodes was only a foot and a half behind the man.

Rhodes lashed out with the scattergun, holding it in two hands, like a batter in one of those baseball games he had seen during the war. The man caught the shotgun's two hard barrels square across the forehead. He sank down like an icicle over a fire, until he was just a pile of rumpled clothes and useless limbs.

Rhodes took the man's gun and pitched it out of the way. Then he got some rope, which he dropped on the ground next to the man and rolled him over. "I'll be damned," he muttered, rage flaring suddenly and very hotly in his chest. There was no need to check the face against the wanted posters he carried. This man was not among them. He was, however, one of the men who had fled when Joe Bonner had been gunned down on the main street of Intolerance, Colorado Territory.

Chapter Thirty-three

Rhodes waited for the man to regain consciousness — after trussing him up and gagging him. But Rhodes was in no mood for patient waiting, so he melted some snow and dashed it on the man's face. It took two tries, but finally the man began showing signs of regaining consciousness. The man blinked some, trying to figure out where he was, but finally he was conscious, though Rhodes figured the man must have a splitting headache.

"You fully awake, boy?" Rhodes finally asked.

The man mumbled something.

"Just nod, or shake your head, you damn fool."

The man nodded.

"Good. Now in a minute or two, I'm going to ask you some questions. In order for you to answer, I'm going to have to take the gag off you."

The man nodded vigorously.

"However, that also opens the possibility of you screaming for help."

No nod this time, but Rhodes could see the hope in the man's eyes.

"I figure that even an idiot like you can puzzle out the fact that if you scream for help, I'm going to blow a hole in you big enough to drive those wagons full of gold through it. Because by then, I won't have any more need for secrecy." The hope in the man's eyes dimmed and died. "Now, if you're cooperative, I don't see why I can't just haul you back to Intolerance under arrest, even if you are the son of a bitch who killed ol' Joe Bonner." There were times when being quiet-spoken with a calm, reasonable tone and cadence worked for Rhodes instead of against him. He was pretty sure that he had the man convinced that he could put away his sorrow at a friend's loss — and any desire for revenge. "What happens there'll be up to those folks. How's that sound?"

The man nodded. He knew he had no choice right now. But if he kept alive, there was always a chance to jump the lawman somewhere, especially when there were eighteen men down in the cabin.

"All right, let's give it a try." Rhodes cocked the shotgun and pointed the weapon at the man's chest as he reached over to untie the gag.

The man spit a few times then sighed. "How's about you untie me, too, man? I'm gonna freeze to death like this."

"You're close enough to the fire. What's your name?"

"Who's askin'?"

"If you sass me even one more time, I'm going to put the gag back in your mouth, and then I'm going to do some very painful things to you." Rhodes had spoken very distinctly, wanting to make sure the man knew just exactly what trouble he was looking at. "Now, what's your name, boy?"

"Simon Hungerford."

"What're you doing out here, Simon?"

"Lookin' for some friends," Hungerford said glibly.

"And you expected to find them in my camp?"

"Hell, I didn't know it was your camp. I figured it was theirs."

"There was only one horse here."

Hungerford shrugged. "Figured the others was gone off somewhere."

"You didn't know that horse — one that was so distinctive — didn't belong to your friends?"

Hungerford shrugged and smiled weakly. "Hell, half my friends are horse thieves. One of 'em could've just stolen it."

"That, Mr. Hungerford, is about the first true thing you've said." Rhodes sighed. "Now, what's Turlow planning to do with the gold?" He could see in Hungerford's eyes that he had scored a solid hit.

"I . . . I . . . I don't know."

"It's not bad enough you're a goddamn liar, you're also a poor goddamn liar."

"Christ, man, I don't know what the hell he's gonna do with the goddamn gold. I'm gonna get me my share and head for Californy."

"That makes some sense." Rhodes paused. "I'm not very patient these days, Mr. Hungerford. Being cold all the time, and having sores on my ass from riding so much and losing a friend has made my temper shorter than usual. So what I want you to do, is to tell me all about it. How it was done, who did it, how it was planned, and who in Intolerance was behind it."

"You know someone in Intolerance is behind it?" Hungerford asked, surprised.

Rhodes nodded. "I figure it's Ham Macmillan." The look in Hungerford's eyes was almost startling. "It's not Macmillan?"

"It's a Macmillan all right, but not Ham."

"Logan?" Rhodes was incredulous.

"Didn't know near as much as you thought, did you, man?"

276

Rhodes shrugged. "Now that I'm aware, tell the rest of it."

"You wanna hear what I got to say, you're gonna have to untie me and get me some hot food and coffee."

"What I'm going to do is start breaking some of your bones."

Hungerford's eyes flashed hotly, but one look at Rhodes's wide torso and the big, meaty fists at the end of arms that looked powerful even hidden under the coat, convinced him that Rhodes could do as he said.

"Damn, you're a son of a bitch, ain't you?" Hungerford muttered. "All right. Logan told me and some of the boys to ride into Intolerance and start raisin' a ruckus, which we did. That's when you and that old far . . . that old man come out. I didn't want to go back after we started ridin' away, but Luther, he made us do it. I didn't mean for that old man to get killed. I didn't even know it till you said it just now."

Hungerford actually looked a little sad, but Rhodes figured it was more because he knew he was going to die soon rather than any remorse. Still, if the knowledge that he was going to die oiled Hungerford's tongue, Rhodes figured so be it. Or, if Hungerford was unburdening his soul in an effort to gain some leniency with Rhodes, that was even better. He'd be less likely to lie that way.

"Why'd he want you to raise a ruckus in Intolerance?" Rhodes asked.

Hungerford shrugged. "I ain't real sure. Luther— Luther Cudahy—was the boss of that little deal. Best I can figure is that Logan wanted you to trail us out of Intolerance."

277

"That doesn't make any sense," Rhodes mused. "I wouldn't be too inclined to go chasing anyone out of town just for hurrahin' the town like that." He thought about it for a minute. "That's why you boys came back. To either kill me and get me out of the way for good, or to kill someone else to make sure I'd follow."

"I didn't have nothin' to do with that," Hungerford protested. "All I know is that Luther said let's make another run down the street, just to show you lawmen fellers that we wasn't gonna be run outta town so easy."

Rhodes nodded. His stomach roiled with hatred, and his soul cried out for revenge, but he forced himself to wait. He needed to know everything first. "Makes sense," he muttered. "Where'd you go?"

"Luther and me went to the shack behind Macmillan's place. All the others was waitin' there. Billy Beene was the other of us that was in that fracas. He headed on toward here, figurin' to ambush you, but you went the other way. Still Billy, he waited out there for the rest of us."

Hungerford paused to lick his lips. He was shivering now since the fire had burned down some. Rhodes noted that it was cold and tossed a couple more pieces of wood on the fire.

"Thanks," Hungerford said. "It'd help some though, if I was to have some of that hot coffee you got there."

Rhodes thought about it for a few moments. Then he nodded. He uncocked the scattergun and set it aside. He stood and rolled Hungerford over onto his stomach. He knelt on Hungerford's back as he untied his feet and hands. Then he retied the left foot and put the rope over Hungerford's right shoulder.

278

He did it with the other foot, again crossing the rope over the opposite shoulder.

"What the hell're you doin'?" Hungerford asked, confused.

"Just keep your mouth shut."

Rhodes maneuvered Hungerford over onto his back. Then he tied his hands to the rope coming over the shoulders. Tied that way, Hundgerford's hands touched just over the sternum fairly high up. Hungerford would be able—with a little effort—to drink some coffee, but since he had barely an inch or two of slack, he could not throw the coffee at Rhodes.

Hungerford did not look happy with the arrangement, but he said nothing, except to mumble thanks when Rhodes gave him a tin mug of coffee. He sipped, grateful for the warmth that splashed through him.

"Now, you got your coffee. Let's hear some more," Rhodes ordered.

"Almost as soon as you rode out of town—well, we gave it a little time to make sure you just didn't ride out and back in—we hitched up the mules to the two wagons and took 'em around back of the bank. That door back there ain't used for much except movin' the gold in and out. Half the boys went around front and kept folks busy while the rest of us moved the gold out. We covered it up and rode nice and easy out of town."

"That simple, eh?"

"Yep. The others inside the front of the bank stayed there a little while to let us fellers with the wagons get a ways away. Then they ran outside, jumped on their horses, and skedaddled."

Rhodes sat mulling it all over. It was a simple

plan, which made it workable. It would take Logan Macmillan a little while longer to gather a posse and give a halfhearted chase. A couple of the outlaws could lie in wait and shoot down a couple of townsfolk which would send the rest of the posse scurrying home. Then they could leisurely ride here to the hideout and wait out the winter. How and when they divvied up the gold remained to be seen, but he didn't expect Hungerford to know much about that.

Rhodes could find no real flaw in the explanation; nothing that would make him think Hungerford was lying. It was too simple, too clean. His only problem, Rhodes figured, would be in convincing the people of Intolerance that Logan Macmillan was behind it all.

"What were you doing out here?" Rhodes suddenly asked. He realized he had never gotten an answer to it, and changing the subject slightly might give him a little more time to decide what to do about Hungerford—and the others.

"Rode to Intolerance for some supplies."

"Couldn't have been many supplies, if all you had was that horse."

"Didn't need much," Hungerford said with a small shrug, one that was constrained by the ropes.

Rhodes rose. "Reckon I can see what was so important. You won't make any noise now, will you?" The threat was ill-disguised by the calm words and even tone.

Rhodes went to Hungerford's horse and opened one of the saddlebags and looked inside. Several boxes of metallic cartridges were wrapped in an old shirt. Rhodes pulled everything out and looked through it carefully. Most of the shells were .44s though he did find one box of .36s. Rhodes tossed that one aside to keep.

He went through the other saddlebag, and found more boxes of ammunition wrapped in another dirty shirt. But this bag also included a letter. Rhodes opened the letter. It was to "Dalton," and outlined the dividing of the loot. It had a few other things of little import to Rhodes, and was signed "Logan M."

Rhodes quietly folded the paper again and slipped it into an inside pocket of his coat, where it would be safe. The rest of the cartridges, he left in a pile. He had no use for them, but the others down in the cabin would not get any use out of them either.

He walked back to Hungerford and squatted in his old spot. "How many boys're down in the cabin?"

"There was eighteen of us. I ain't sure that one or two've gone elsewhere while I was on the trail, but maybe some did." He hoped to scare Rhodes into letting him go. Only a madman would try to take on eighteen hardcases by himself. Travis Rhodes did not strike Hungerford as a fool.

When Rhodes did not say anything after a few moments, Hungerford said hopefully, "How's about you let me go now, huh? I'll give you fifteen minutes or so to get on down the trail before I even start to the cabin. Hell," he added magnanimously, "make it a half-hour." He paused, waiting, but still no response. "You can't take on all of us by yourself. Use your head, man."

Rhodes nodded slowly. "Reckon you might be right." He pushed up and pulled out his big knife. He advanced slowly on Hungerford. The captive, now excited at the prospect of freedom, eagerly held out his hands as far as he could. He looked very

281

shocked when Rhodes jammed the knife to the hilt into his chest.

Hungerford gasped, looking at Rhodes with wide eyes. "Why?" he whispered.

"That's for an old man you left lyin' in the street in Intolerance, boy."

Chapter Thirty-four

Rhodes stood watching the cabin from his spot in the rocks. He had untied the ropes from Hungerford's body, placed one around Hungerford's chest, hauled him away, and then hung him from a tree limb to keep him away from scavengers. He intended to bring the cadaver back to Intolerance and see if there was a reward on him. He also wanted Logan Macmillan to see the body.

Now he stood near the rocks wondering just how he was going to take seventeen or eighteen men who were all armed and ensconced in a cabin. He could think of only one way, and that would take some doing. He would wait for a while yet, though. It would not do to get done too early. In the meantime, he would eat, and then prepare.

He estimated that there were two hours until daylight, such as it would be. Snow was falling again, though not heavily, and the quiet whoosh of the snow was almost comforting. He had filled himself up good on hot coffee and fatty, rich bacon and beans.

He saddled the palomino. He had considered using Hungerford's horse, but he did not know the animal, nor the animal him. He would need a horse he could trust. He climbed on, the two kegs of powder dangling by ropes from the saddle horn. He moved the horse out into the flat, snowy darkness.

He went down the hill and turned right at the base of the mountain. He followed the same course as he had the first time. He walked quietly behind the house and brought the palomino into the barn. None of the other mules or horses seemed upset at this, which suited Rhodes just fine.

Rhodes dismounted, found a nose bag, filled it with grain and put it on his horse. Then he grabbed a large armful of hay. He slipped out with it, went to the far end of the cabin at the back, and started laying the straw down as thickly as he could. He kept repeating the procedure until there was a path of straw along the back and near side of the cabin.

He was heading back to the barn when the sounds from the house grew louder for a few moments and then faded. He froze and then sprinted for the barn, figured that someone had just come out of the house. He might be headed to the barn.

Rhodes slipped inside and grabbed the pitchfork that he had moved earlier to get at the pile of hay. Then he waited, trying not to breathe too loudly. He was beginning to think that whoever had come out of the house was just going out to relieve himself or something, when the barn door creaked open.

The man headed toward what had been a fair-size pile of hay. He stopped, head cocked, knowing something was wrong, but not sure what. "Damn Dalton anyway," he muttered, angry at having to come out here to feed the horses and mules in the cold, dark time just before dawn.

Rhodes stepped out of the shadows. "Looking for this?" he asked as he skewered the man with the pitchfork. The man gasped and wilted. Rhodes pulled the pitchfork out and tossed it aside. He dragged the body outside, since the animals were uncomfortable with the smell of fresh blood.

Rhodes took a few minutes of a breather and then grabbed more hay, glad that the light snowfall had stopped as he walked back to the cabin. He left a two-foot-wide trail of the hay at an angle between the shed and the house and leading out into the snowy meadow.

Finally Rhodes went back to the barn and picked up one keg of powder and opened it. He headed toward the far end of the barn. Carefully he laid a trail of powder on top of the still dry hay, all the way to the end of the hay. He walked back and put the keg at the near back corner of the cabin. It was still about a quarter full. He tossed in several boxes of the cartridges Hungerford had been carrying.

Then Rhodes got the other keg, opened it, and walked to the far end of the cabin again. He poured a small mound of the powder and then placed the keg on it. He placed two boxes of cartridges on top and three sort of stuck into the mound of powder.

At last, he went back to the barn, took the feedbag off the palomino, and climbed aboard. He walked the horse outside to the end of the hay and gunpowder. He dismounted, pulled off his gloves, and shoved them in his saddlebags. He opened his coat so the pistols were easily accessible. Then he pulled out a match. He scraped it into flaming life, knelt, and set it to the powder-covered hay.

The hay sputtered and caught, then sizzled hotly as it latched on to the gunpowder. Once it was going sufficiently well, Rhodes leisurely pulled himself into the saddle and rode a little to his left, so that he would be straight ahead from the front door of the cabin. He pulled his scattergun and Hungerford's .44-caliber pistol. The revolver he stuck in a side pocket of his coat. Then he waited. It was almost dawn, though it looked like it would be another gray day.

He watched as the snaking sputter of sparkles moved along, until it went around the corner of the cabin. It seemed interminable, and Rhodes began to have doubts that his plan would work.

Suddenly there was a grudging roar, and Rhodes could have sworn the side of the cabin lifted up some. Gunshots rang out as the cartridges went off. The cabin door burst open and two men charged out. Rhodes let go both barrels of the shotgun, not really expecting to hit anyone at this range, which he estimated at thirty yards or so.

One man went down. The other skidded in the snow as he tried to stop. Then he spun and dove back toward the doorway of the house. There were no windows in the cabin, so Rhodes had little to fear from them shooting at him from inside. Of course, some of the chinks in the wood were big enough to get a rifle barrel through. Still, the men had almost certainly been asleep when the small blast came.

Less than two minutes later, the full keg of powder caught. It seemed this time to Rhodes that the explosion punched the building rather than just lifting it. Bullets from the other boxes of cartridges went flying about, and flames licked at the cabin's rotting wood walls.

Men scrambled for the door, and Rhodes began picking them off. Since there was only one door, the outlaws were having trouble escaping. And when they got out, they were more interested in fleeing than in shooting back at whatever army was attacking them.

Rhodes even had a little time to reload Hungerford's .44 Colt and empty it at the outlaws again. Then he tossed it away and pulled the two new .36-caliber Colts. It was, he knew somewhere down in his mind, just like being at Spotsylvania or Chickamauga or Gettysburg or any of those outdoor charnel houses where bodies were piled shoulder deep to horse. He refused, though, to allow the thought of what he was doing to affect him. He was doing what needed to be done in the best way he could figure to do it. He would feel no sympathy for these men in any case. They were thieves and murderers all and as such deserved no concern.

The palomino was a horse accustomed to moving in the face of fire, and with this short, stocky man on his back, Rhodes needed to do little to control his horse as he rode back and forth in front of the cabin, with the outlaws still trying to find freedom and safety.

Flames built up, goaded on by coal oil, whiskey, ammunition, and gunpowder inside the house. One outlaw raced, screaming, from the house, clothes ablaze. He threw himself into the snow, rolling frantically to extinguish the flames.

It was almost too easy for Rhodes as he rode back and forth, moving a little closer every now and then, plinking outlaws. Despite the fury of the battle, though, he was aware of each and every man there. He checked each one in his mental file, wanting to find Turlow and the two other men who were responsible for Joe Bonner's death.

Several men dashed toward the barn, figuring to grab horses and get the hell out of this valley.

Rhodes, though, reloading the Colts on the run, cut them off. One ripped out his own revolver, but Rhodes drilled him through the side of the head. Astride the palomino Rhodes ran the other man down. The man fell, knocked unconscious by the horse's broad chest.

Rhodes quickly found out that Turlow was a sneaky fellow. He slipped out of the cabin early on, using two of his men for cover. Rhodes had shot the two, but Turlow had slipped around the far end of the cabin. By the time Rhodes got there, Turlow was gone. Rhodes raced back the other way, figuring to head Turlow off before he could get to the barn.

Three men, at least two of them wounded, suddenly popped up in front of Rhodes. The palomino reared, almost throwing him, but it probably saved his life, since the wildly pawing horse threw off the three men's gunfire.

The palomino came down with steel-shod hooves hitting one man in the head. The animal's big chest hit another man, whose gun went off, winging the horse a little. As soon as the horse was on all four hooves, Rhodes fired once from each pistol. He hit both men, but he was not sure he had killed them.

Turlow burst from the barn, riding bareback. He held on to the horse's mane with one hand, in which he also held a pistol. His other hand held another pistol, which he was firing wildly at Rhodes.

Rhodes pulled the palomino to a stop and waited as Turlow rushed closer. Rhodes thought many times during the war that he was somehow special. More than once he had stood fast in the face of overwhelming odds and had come out mostly unscathed. Like now. He just waited as Turlow emptied one pistol at him, and then switched to the other.

Then Rhodes fired twice. Both balls struck the racing horse in the chest. The animal's front legs buckled and he skidded along on his chest and jaw in the snow. Turlow was thrown over the horse's head, and lay sprawled and motionless on the ground.

Rhodes pulled to a stop and reloaded his pistols. The scene was grotesque and eerily silent. But Rhodes had not seen the two men who had killed Bonner. He wondered if perhaps they had not been here. With fresh loads in his pistols, Rhodes dismounted and walked through the open-air slaughterhouse. Not counting Turlow, Rhodes found thirteen men, all but three of them dead. Those three would not last long, he figured, not with the bitter cold and the extent of their wounds. With Turlow and the man Rhodes had killed in the barn, the total was fifteen. That left three men unaccounted for, based on what he had seen earlier and what Hungerford had told him.

The cabin was still burning well, throwing heat over a considerable distance. Occasional bullets were fired as the flames found cartridges. But mostly it was over.

Holding the palomino's reins, Rhodes walked slowly toward Turlow. He stopped and looked down. Turlow was alive, though unconscious. Rhodes didn't know how badly the man was hurt, but he hoped it wasn't much, since he wanted to take Turlow back to Intolerance alive and healthy enough to be able to testify against Logan Macmillan.

He tied Turlow up and dragged him into the barn. When Rhodes came back out, he looked around. He sensed that there were others around, but he could see nor hear nothing out of the usual.

He mounted the palomino and rode behind the cabin. He found nothing there. Suddenly, on a hunch, he headed to where the road went out of the valley—the opposite side from where he had come into it.

A quarter of a mile away, he spotted three men lurching along. None had a coat, and all three were shivering with the bitter cold. They heard Rhodes approaching and they turned. One raised a pistol, and Rhodes snapped off a shot. The man dropped his revolver, as he spun toward the ground.

"You other two boys got a choice," Rhodes said mildly. "You either haul yourselves back up the hill nice and peaceable, or I'll put a bullet through each of you here and now. You have three seconds to decide."

One of the men held his hands up. "I ain't lookin' for no bullet, mister." He slowly lowered his left hand, eased out his Colt, and tossed it away.

"You?" Rhodes asked, looking at the other one still standing. He was one of Bonner's killers, and Rhodes more than half-hoped the man would try something. But he followed the same path as his companion.

"Your friend still alive?" he asked.

"Yes, goddammit, I'm alive," the fallen man said. He got up, having some trouble. He was the last of the men who had killed Bonner.

"Since y'all're so agreeable, now you can march nice and easy back up the hill."

"Dalton's gonna have your ass for this, you son of a bitch," the wounded man snarled.

"Turlow's trussed up like a Christmas turkey," Rhodes said pleasantly. "He ain't going to do a damn thing."

290

"Then Mac—"

"Shut up," one of the others hissed.

Rhodes smiled, but there was precious little humor in it. "I know all about Macmillan," he said quietly. "And he ain't going to do anything either." He paused to let that sink in. "Now, move on up the hill or I'll leave you here for the wolves."

The three began moving, walking slowly up the hill. Rhodes followed on his horse.

Chapter Thirty-five

Rhodes went straight into the barn, where he tied the three men up after checking to see they had no weapons hidden on them. Then he gave the palomino another nose bag full of grain.

Turlow had regained consciousness, and was cursing a blue streak. Rhodes put up with it for a few moments, before he whirled, pistol in hand. He fired and then jammed the pistol back into his pocket. "Next one'll be two inches lower," he said quietly. "Now shut your yap."

Since Turlow had felt the bullet cut through the small cowlick he had mornings when he woke up, he did not need any more encouragement.

Rhodes pulled the wanted posters out of his pocket. Turlow he knew, and the one who had not been among Bonner's killers was named Mark Chesterfield. The two who had killed Bonner did not have wanted posters—not in this batch anyway. He walked to an unwounded one and squatted in front of him. "What's your name, boy?" he asked.

"Go to hell, Marshal," he sneered. "We killed that badge-totin' old fart back in Intolerance, and we'll do the same to you, you son of a bitch."

"That's no way to talk," Rhodes said, keeping a li

on his simmering anger. Then he smashed the man in the face with a rock-hard fist. The blow mashed the man's nose and made his eyes cross. "Now," Rhodes said quietly. "What's your name, boy?"

"Bobby Hood," the man mumbled.

Rhodes looked at the wounded man. "And you?"

"Jordan Porter."

Rhodes went back outside and made another tour of the battlefield. Two of the three wounded men had died. The third was still clinging to life, but Rhodes figured he had only minutes left. As he walked around, he picked up every weapon he found and tossed it into a feed sack he had brought from the barn. When he was done, he took the sack down to the stream and pitched it in. Then he went back to the barn.

He paused, looking around. His next problem — and it was a major one — was getting the gold back to Intolerance. It would not be easy alone. He checked the four men's bonds and then strolled to the shed to look at the wagons. Then he had an idea.

He harnessed the wagons, eight mules to each. Then he tied the lead mules for one wagon to the back of the first wagon. He had no idea if this would work, but it would be the only way he could manage it that he could see.

He wheeled the elongated wagon out into the meadow. Then he got Chesterfield and Hood from the barn. He hobbled them with ropes around the ankles. They could move, but not fast. Then he took them outside. "Start loading, boys."

"Loading what?" Chesterfield asked.

"Your pals. Put some on each wagon and either tie 'em down or put another tarp over 'em. We don't want 'em bouncin' all over now, do we?"

293

The two men shrugged, but Chesterfield's eyes lit up a little. He was sure he could grab a weapon from one of the dead and blast this son of a bitch to hell and gone.

Rhodes had seen the look and smiled. He said nothing. Let them find out for themselves. A few minutes later, he could see the budding frustration on Chesterfield's face. "You didn't think I'd leave pistols lying all over for you to pick up, did you?" he asked innocently.

"Bastard."

While the two men worked, Rhodes got some jerky from one of his saddlebags and gnawed on it. He would prefer a nice piece of beefsteak, but he'd prefer some hot coffee even more. He had neither, though, and he was not about to go through the charred cabin, which might collapse at any moment, for it. He could have sent one of the outlaws into the cabin to check, but there might be some weapons left in there that were usable. Better to stay hungry, he thought.

Finally the men finished. "Nice work," Rhodes commented. He felt sick at all the death he had brought to this picturesque little canyon, but there was nothing could be done about it. All these men would have hanged anyway, had they been captured by vigilance committees or other marshals.

Rhodes hastily tied Chesterfield and Hood to one of the wagons and then brought Turlow and Porter outside. He tied Turlow to the right side of the first wagon, and Chesterfield to the left side of it.

"What the hell's this?" Turlow asked.

"We're heading back to Intolerance. You two boys are going to walk." He untied Hood and pushed him toward Porter. "You two ain't," he said flatly.

"What?" Hood asked, surprised.

"I reckon he means we're gonna ride," Porter said with a sneer. "Ain't that right, Marshal?"

Rhodes nodded slowly. "You scum remember an old man with a gold badge on his chest?"

"Sure," Porter said nervously.

Rhodes smiled, and it chilled Porter and Hood more than the bitter weather did. "There ain't anything I could do to you two that'd be equal to what you did to ol' Joe Bonner. Still, you've got to pay for it, and now's as good a time as any."

"Hey, now wait a minute," Hood said, fear cracking his voice. "There's no call to—"

"Shut your yap, you lily-livered little bastard," Porter snapped. "Don't give him the satisfaction of hearin' you beg." He looked at Rhodes and sneered again. "Go on and do your worst, Marshal. I ain't afraid of no goddamn carpetbaggin' damn Yankee."

"Us damn Yankees did all right in the war, boy," Rhodes said even more quietly than usual. "Whipped your asses good we did, and none of your whining about the glory of the Old South ain't going to change that fact one teeny little bit."

"You gonna talk all goddamn day?" Porter asked.

Rhodes shook his head and shot Porter in the other shoulder. Being so close, the blast knocked Porter down. As Rhodes bent over him to haul him back up, Hood slammed into him, knocking Rhodes off to Porter's side.

Rhodes rolled and came up with pistol cocked and ready. Hood was looming over him. Rhodes shoved the pistol up and fired. The bullet tore through the underside of Hood's jaw and blasted out the top of his head. He slumped.

"Maybe he wasn't so damn dumb after all," Rhodes said as he stood and brushed snow off him. He hobbled Porter's feet and then hauled him up.

He tied him to the left side of the first wagon. Then he smashed Porter's nose and mouth with a leather-glove-clad fist.

Porter sagged but remained upright.

Rhodes tied his palomino to the back of the second wagon. Then he let all the rest of the horses out of the barn. Sensing freedom, the animals trotted off. Finally Rhodes climbed onto the seat of the first wagon. He released the brake and moved out, silently praying that this would work.

The hardest part, he knew, would be the climb up out of the canyon. It was fairly steep, and coated with snow and rock. Even worse, he wasn't sure if the second team of mules would follow along, hooked as they were to the first wagon. Rhodes's only other choice, though, would be to let Chesterfield drive the first wagon, while he drove the second. That might be better, but it could also have some serious consequences.

He got to the trail and started up it. He realized right off that he wasn't going to be able to get the wagons up there this way. He eased backward until he was on the flat again. It took a considerable effort to keep his temper when Turlow began ridiculing him for having failed.

Rhodes climbed down from the wagon seat walked past Turlow, and kicked the outlaw leader in the knee.

"Shit," Turlow hissed.

"You still might make it through this trip if you watch your mouth." Rhodes said. He unhooked the second wagon from the first. Then he untied Chesterfield from the wagon, though he left his hands bound together. "Get on up there on the first wagon."

When Chesterfield was seated, Rhodes climbed

into the back of the wagon, wrapped a slip knot around Chesterfield's neck and tied the other end of the short piece of rope to the back of the wagon seat. He had enough room—barely—to drive the wagon, but not enough slack in his hands to allow him to do anything, and any attempt to move too much would strangle him. The only other thing he might possibly do would be to race off in the wagon. But two things made that an unlikely possibility. For one, Turlow and Porter were tied to the sides of the first wagon and would be walking. Of course, Chesterfield might not care that he dragged his two old comrades along as he made a bid for escape, but it was a factor. The other was that Rhodes would be fifty feet or less behind him, and Rhodes was not going to miss him with five or six shots.

"Move out," Rhodes said as he settled into the seat of the second wagon.

It was still difficult going up the slope, but they made it halfway without trouble. At that point, Rhodes called for a stop at the flat spot where he had entered the forest when he arrived here—was it only yesterday?

He got down and gagged Porter. Then he unhooked Chesterfield and Turlow from the wagon and directed them toward his camp. Hungerford was still swinging from the tree, frozen stiff. Rhodes cut the rope and the body fell like a lead weight.

Rhodes let Hungerford's horse go and untied his mule. "Grab your pal."

With their hands still bound, Chesterfield and Turlow had a tough time carrying the stiff corpse. They finally made it back to the wagons and put Hungerford with all his dead comrades. Rhodes tied Turlow back to the side of the wagon and then rebound Chesterfield on the wagon seat. With a check to make sure Porter had made no success at trying to free himself, Rhodes tied his mule to the back of the wagon next to the palomino.

They moved on again, up the hillside, the mules sometimes having a little trouble with their footing. Then they were on the mostly flat road toward Intolerance.

Rhodes's little caravan drew quite a crowd of gaping people as it wheeled down the wide main street. It was late afternoon and for some reason, it had warmed up some, inching past freezing. The caravan stopped in front of the First Mining and Mercantile Bank of Intolerance. Frederick Wormsley, the bank's president, came outside to stare in wide-eyed wonder along with everyone else.

"Somebody best get Dexter out here," Rhodes said as he climbed down off the wagon. "He's going to be one busy fellah."

A woman gasped after having looked under one of the tarps, and word spread — as it always does in such situations — that there were dozens of bodies in the two wagons.

Phineas Hickman shoved his way forward. "Welcome back, Marshal," he said loudly.

Rhodes nodded. "Fin," he acknowledged. "It's good to be back." He pointed to Turlow, who could barely stand. "That there's Dalton Turlow. Take him over to the jail and lock him up till we can set a trial for him."

"Be glad to. Who's the other?"

"One of Turlow's men. Name's Mark Chesterfield. He can join Turlow at the jail." Jordan Porter had not finished the trip, having succumbed to loss of blood.

298

Fairchild strutted up. "Someone call for me?" he asked officiously.

"You ought to be able to retire after this batch, Dex," Rhodes said with less humor than he had planned.

Fairchild looked under both tarps. "I should make you a partner," he said with a laugh.

"Well, now that all this is taken care of," Wormsley said, "We must get the gold back into the bank where it'll be safe."

"Hope it'll be safer than it was last time," someone shouted. Wormsley looked offended.

"Only two problems with that," Rhodes said. "One is I get ten thousand bucks in gold." He paused, but no one argued about that. "Second is that this ain't all over yet."

"Didn't you catch all the outlaws?" Wormsley asked, worried.

"All but one." He spotted Hallie St. John standing with her brother. She looked happy but shy. Rhodes nodded and smiled at her.

Hallie moved tentatively forward, until she was in the warm, protective cover of Travis Rhodes's big left arm.

"I said, do you know where the other one is?" Wormsley asked for the fourth time. His exasperation was showing.

Rhodes nodded. He pointed to Logan Macmillan, who was standing near the back of the second wagon. A gasp went up from the crowd.

"You've been riding too long, Marshal," Logan said easily, but with a touch of wariness and concern.

"No, sir," Rhodes said wearily. "You were behind this robbery, and you were behind the killing of Joe Bonner. And for that, you son of a bitch, I'm going to see you hang."

"Surely you're joking, Marshal," Logan said. His voiced quavered a little bit. "Who made these ridiculous allegations? I must say, sir, that I find them most offensive."

"Simon Hungerford told me first. Turlow and Chesterfield acknowledged it. And, I have a letter you wrote to Turlow about divvying up the gold." Rhodes tapped the breast of his old black frock coat, with the gold badge shining brightly on the lapel.

"You've gone mad."

"Have I?" Rhodes was weary; tired of deadly games, of blood and death, of intrigue. He wanted it all to end. Still, this had to be played out. With his left arm still around Hallie's shoulders, he eased out one of his trusty old Whitneys. He held it straight down alongside his leg.

"Yes," Logan hissed. His hand started edging toward the pocket Colt he wore at his waist.

"You bastard," Hamilton Macmillan screamed. The young man charged at his uncle.

Logan snapped out his pocket Colt and shot his nephew three times. The young man staggered on a few more steps, and then collapsed almost at his uncle's feet.

As Logan started to turn back toward him, Rhodes snapped his arm up, pistol cocked and ready. He said nothing.

Logan sweated despite the chill air. He dropped the pistol. "I had to defend myself," he said, a note of whining evident.

Rhodes waited three heartbeats, and then shot Logan Macmillan clean through the forehead.

Another gasp went up from the crowd, and Rhodes could feel the hostility. He shrugged. Dr. Henry Fermin hurried to the fallen Logan Macmillan and knelt there a minute. Then the doctor stood. "He's dead, all right," Fermin pronounced. "He also had this up his sleeve." Fermin held up a .44-caliber, two-shot derringer.

"I'm going home," Rhodes said. He turned, arm still protectively around Hallie's shoulders, and began trudging through the crowd toward his house.

THE SURVIVALIST SERIES
by Jerry Ahern

THE ONLY ALTERNATIVE IS ANNIHILATION . . .
RICHARD P. HENRICK

BENEATH THE SILENT SEA (3167, $4.50)
The Red Dragon, Communist China's advanced ballistic missile-carrying submarine embarks on the most sinister mission in human history: to attack the U.S. and Soviet Union simultaneously. Soon, the Russian *Barkal,* with its planned attack on a single U.S. submarine is about unwittingly to aid in the destruction of all mankind!

COUNTERFORCE (3025, $4.50)
In the silent deep, the chase is on to save a world from destruction. A single Russian submarine moves on a silent and sinister course for American shores. The men aboard the U.S.S. *Triton* must search for and destroy the Soviet killer submarine as an unsuspecting world races for the apocalypse.

THE GOLDEN U-BOAT (3386, $4.95)
In the closing hours of World War II, a German U-boat sank below the North Sea carrying the Nazis' last hope to win the war. Now, a fugitive SS officer has salvaged the deadly cargo in an attempt to resurrect the Third Reich. As the USS *Cheyenne* passed through, its sonar picked up the hostile presence and another threat in the form of a Russian sub!

THE PHOENIX ODYSSEY (2858, $4.50)
All communications to the USS *Phoenix* suddenly and mysteriously vanish. Even the urgent message from the president canceling the War Alert is not received and in six short hours the *Phoenix* will unleash its nuclear arsenal against the Russian mainland. . . .

SILENT WARRIORS (3026, $4.50)
The Red Star, Russia's newest, most technologically advanced submarine, outclasses anything in the U.S. fleet. But when the captain opens his sealed orders 24 hours early, he's staggered to read that he's to spearhead a massive nuclear first strike against the Americans!